The Protectors Series

SLADE

BY

Teresa Gabelman

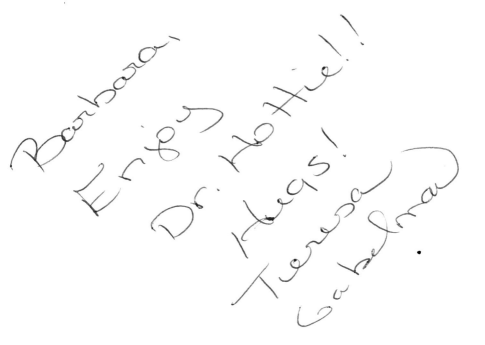

Barbara,
Enjoy Dr. Hottie!!
Hugs!
Teresa Gabelman

THE PROTECTORS

SLADE

Gabelman, Teresa (2014-30-12). SLADE (THE PROTECTORS SERIES).

Kindle Edition.

Editor: Hot Tree Editing

Photo: www.bigstockphoto.com

Cover Art: Indie Digital Publishing

ACKNOWLEDGEMENT

As I've said many times, an author never writes a story alone.

I would like to thank all the readers for their loyalty, understanding and patience. I wish I could thank each one of you personally, but know that you are all in my heart.

There are so many I would like to thank, but I'm always afraid of leaving someone out. To everyone who has read, blogged, shared or just friended me in the book world, I thank you. I do have to thank two people who during this book helped me tremendously. Donna Bossert, your honesty and friendship means so much to me. Thank you for your endless hours of looking for the perfect alpha hottie to go on the cover of this book. I know it was much to ask from you and the work was tiresome looking through countless pictures of sexy men. I would also like to thank Becky Johnson, who I know screams, and not in a good way, when she begins her edits on my books. You were the first to actually believe in me, other than my friend, Kelly Perkins, and my family. Thank you for that, Becky. It will never be forgotten and I promise to ease up on my comma killing ways, and I really mean it this time.

Chapter 1

Slade Buchanan shuffled through his small office doing his best not to trip over boxes scattered across the floor. Finally making it to his desk, he stood glaring at more boxes piled on top of it. It took every ounce of will power he had not to swipe his large hand across, knocking the clutter from his desk. Inside any one of these boxes could lay the key to halt the turning of humans into half-breeds; that in itself stopped him from knocking stuff out of his way in an attempt to find his damn desk.

Things were getting more complicated by the day and the heavy burden weighed on his shoulders. He knew everyone was looking to him for answers, answers he didn't have and that pissed him off. He never failed; he refused to fail at anything.

Grabbing his keys that lay among the mess, he made one giant leap to the door instead of carefully maneuvering his way around the boxes. Once out of the room, he slammed the door, locking it behind him. He had to get the hell out of here. The death of the male half-breed who had attacked Jill had him stumped, as did everything else since he had come to Cincinnati.

Once outside, he headed toward his bike, but the sound of a female cursing caught his attention. Making his way past Adam's car, he was not surprised to see Jill's jean-clad legs sticking out of the driver's side door as she lay half in and half out under Adam's dashboard.

Slade stared for a few seconds then looked toward his bike. Rubbing his large hand down his face, he sighed, wondering if he really wanted to know what she was doing. Since meeting this fascinating woman, he knew the answer to that. He did want to know, and wasn't that just a bitch. With one last longing glance at his bike, he shook his head.

"Dammit!" Jill's voice, low and muffled, made it to his ears clear as if she was standing right in front of him.

He watched as she scooted further under the dashboard of Adam's car, her shoes digging into the gravel to give her leverage as her shirt rose, showing more of her stomach than he wanted to see. Okay, that was a fucking lie. He'd give his left nut to see her before him completely naked. He'd seen that body once and once was definitely not enough.

"Come on, you piece of crap...start!" she cursed again, bringing him out of his hot fantasy of unsnapping those tight jeans and taking her right there, which sent urgent warnings to his brain to walk the fuck away.

"What the hell are you doing?" There it was. He couldn't pull the words back into his mouth. His mouth and brain were on totally different levels.

Her whole body went still as a few seconds of silence passed. "Nothing," she finally replied, her tone clearly indicating she knew she was busted.

Slade walked closer, putting his forearm on the roof of the car and leaning down slightly so their eyes could meet. "Looks to me like you're trying to hot-wire Adam's car, again." When she sucked her bottom lip between her teeth, he knew she knew he had her. He watched as she wiggled her way from under the dashboard. He tried to keep his eyes on her face, but his eyes said 'fuck you' as they traveled the length of her slender, toned body, which was wrapped in a pair of old faded blue jeans and a black sleeveless tee that fit snugly against her.

"Okay, you caught me." She stood, brushing her jeans off before slamming the car door. "Stupid piece of junk."

A small grin tipped his lips. "He probably disabled the ignition coil boot to keep you from stealing his car."

Jill glanced toward the hood of the car with a frown. "That

2

asshole," she mumbled before looking back at Slade. "And I wasn't stealing it. I was borrowing it."

"It's easier to ask for the keys when borrowing someone's car." Slade didn't know what it was, but goading her seemed to be something he couldn't stop himself from doing and goading women wasn't something he normally did.

Jill glared up at him with a frown. "Yeah, well, he wouldn't give me his keys if I begged him." Sticking her hands in her back pockets, she glanced down at the ground. "He doesn't think I'm a good driver, which he's totally wrong about. I'm a good driver, but he's so anal about his *precious* piece of junk."

"Most guys are," Slade replied, then grinned when she made a snorting noise. He turned to walk toward his bike. "Stop hot-wiring cars, Jill. Sid never should have shown you how to do that."

"Yeah, whatever."

Slade's steps slowed at the defeated tone in her reply. "Just keep walking, Buchanan," he mumbled to himself, but his legs stopped and his body turned toward her as his mind laughed...*dumbass.* He watched as she stood, staring at the car as if still trying to figure out how to get it to start. She wasn't going to give up getting to where she needed to go.

"What's an ignition coil boot?" She turned toward him, surprise shining from her eyes when she realized he had stopped and was staring at her.

Slade cursed at the question. If anything, she was damn persistent and he wouldn't put it past her to steal it off someone else's car to put on Adam's just to spite Adam. "Where do you need to go?"

Before she could answer, Adam burst out the door heading toward his car. "Oh, hell no! Get away from my car!" He stopped in front of Jill, hands on his hips.

"I'm not touching your piece of junk," Jill hissed, throwing her hands on her hips, mocking him, before she looked down at his hand. "Is that the ignition coil....thing?"

"Ah ha!" Adam shouted, pointing the ignition coil in her face. "I knew it. I told you to stay away from my car. You don't have a license, which is a favor to mankind since you can't drive worth a damn."

"You don't have a license?" Slade walked closer, watching the exchange, his eyes focusing intently on Jill.

"No, she doesn't," Adam answered for her. "And that is one of the big reasons she is to stay away from my car."

Slade watched embarrassment color her cheeks and he knew exactly the reason why she didn't have her driver's license. She couldn't pass the test because of her dyslexia. "Come on." Their eyes met before he turned to walk away.

"Where we going?" Jill caught up to him, stopping when they reached his bike.

Swinging his leg over his bike, he sat staring straight ahead with a fierce scowl, wondering when the hell he became so fucking nice. "To get a study book for your driving test and then wherever you needed to go in a stolen car."

"I've got one." She looked away, shifting uncomfortably. "And I can do what I needed to do another day. It's no big deal."

Slade knew she was lying. She was determined to go somewhere. He was the biggest dumbass in the history of dumbasses to want to know where she was going. Jesus, he needed to fuck someone and soon because this little slip of a girl was going to drive him insane. For a split second his mind played out him fucking Jill, and he almost ripped the handlebars clean off his bike.

"Get on the damn bike." His demand was sneered with clenched teeth, his eyes narrowed.

Looking as if she wanted to argue, Jill did the safe thing and climbed on the back of the bike. "Since you asked so nicely," she responded sarcastically as she shifted herself behind him.

Her body wiggling against him caused a growl low in his throat. His eyes closed tightly in an attempt to control himself. "Where?" When she didn't answer, Slade opened his eyes, tilting his head toward her. "Jill," he warned, his voice indicating he was not in the mood.

"My dad had a heart attack. I need to see him." She didn't say anything more, but without looking at her, he knew the conflict she was feeling. He could actually feel it radiating off her.

"Why didn't you tell me?" He started the bike, waiting for her answer.

"I just found out," she finally replied and he felt her shrug. "Even though I know I won't be welcomed there, I need to make sure he's okay. I haven't seen him since…"

She didn't finished. She didn't have to. He knew. She hadn't seen her family since she'd been turned and kicked out of her home. He was the one who sat in the hospital when she had been shot, filling out her paperwork because her family refused to have anything to do with her. And for her to want to see a father, who pretty much wrote her off, told him more than anything could about who Jillian Robin Nichols really was.

Instead of finishing her sentence, she directed him which way to drive from the compound. He tried not to respond as her hands grasped him tighter to keep herself steady behind him. Trying to block her out, he let loose and pushed his bike. With the added speed, he felt her excitement behind him as if it was his own. Jesus, he was in trouble. Pulling to a stop at a red light, he felt her shift behind him as a car pulled up beside them.

"Hey, good-looking," a woman's voice flirted over the rumble of his bike. Slade tilted his head slightly looking at the blonde through his dark sunglasses. She was pretty, but he knew her type and didn't have time, plus blondes suddenly didn't appeal to him as much. With a short nod, he turned to look straight ahead.

"Why don't you let your little brother off at the next light so you and me can grab a drink." She smiled innocently, her friend in the driver's seat laughing loudly.

Slade didn't have to turn to look at Jill to feel the anger and tension trembling through her body. He continued to ignore the woman and wondered if the damn light was stuck on red. Before he could do anything, he caught a glimpse of Jill's hand raise in his side mirror. Just as the light turned green, the woman's head smashed into the dashboard. Jill's snort reached his ears.

The woman's hand flew up to her forehead, then away checking for blood. Jill laughed louder. "Seatbelts save lives, Blondie."

Slade had slipped his sunglasses up and was glaring at Jill in the side mirror, yet he couldn't help the curve of his lips at how quick her triumphant face turned innocent. "Been practicing?" He cocked one eyebrow.

She shrugged, trying to hide her grin. "A little." She glanced away, then back. "The light's green."

With one last long look at Jill, he slipped his sunglasses back into position and took off. As they passed the blonde woman, he glimpsed at her looking in the mirror at her forehead, an expression of horror and embarrassment coloring her face. His deep laugh was drowned out by the roar of his bike speeding onto the interstate.

Within minutes, Slade was pulling behind an old blue Chevy truck. Turning off the bike, he sat waiting for Jill to make a move. When she continued to sit still as stone behind him, he removed his sunglasses, hanging them on the handlebars. His eyes met hers in the side mirror, and at that moment, he wanted nothing more than to turn and comfort her. She looked terrified of what he figured was the rejection she may suffer again at the hands of her family. Jesus, these feelings were not good. Not good for him and definitely not good for her.

"We going to get off the bike or sit here all day?" His question was harsh even to his own ears.

Jill swallowed nervously, looking away from his reflection. "Sorry, just been a while since I've been here." She slipped off the back of the bike, looking around. "Not much has changed. I mean, I know it hasn't been *that* long, but it seems like it."

"We can leave now, Jill." Slade stayed on the bike, watching her closely. He felt like an ass for snapping at her because he knew damn good and well she was nervous. It wasn't her fault; well, it was mostly her fault that he had these fucked-up feelings. It *had* to be her fault because no other woman had affected him so strongly, strong enough for him to want to throw her sweet body down in the driveway and….*shit*! "I can check on your dad later," he snapped at her again.

"No," she snapped back with a glare. "I just want to see him for a second, then I'm gone."

A deep bark grabbed their attention. "Sable!" Jill turned toward the sound. A large black German Shepherd stood just around the corner of the house. "Sable, it's me." The excitement in her voice echoed across the yard.

Slade dismounted his bike, his eyes never leaving the huge animal. "Jill, hold on," Slade warned, his grip tight on her arm stopping her.

Another bark sounded, this one not as deep or aggressive, but excited. A smaller dog, which looked like a mini-me of the German Shepherd ran past Sable. Jill knelt in time to catch the smaller dog in her arms, receiving excited licks and nips. "You remember me, don't you, Bebe?" Jill laughed, rubbing the dog's head roughly before putting her forehead against Bebe's. "I've missed you so much, girl," Jill whispered, grabbing her by the neck and hugging her closely.

Slade watched the reunion with a better understanding of this woman who had his mind in shambles. She had been dealt a hard blow in life, a life she had abruptly been pushed away from by no fault of her own. Even with his eyes on the black German Shepherd, who was edging closer to Jill, Slade couldn't help shifting his eyes back to watch Jill savor the moment with her missed pet. He tensed as her attention went back to the large black dog.

Jill raised her hand slowly. "It's me, Sable," she repeated in a whisper. "Please remember me."

Her words hit Slade like a sledgehammer. The love she wanted so badly, even from an animal, was clear in the tone of her words. The dog sniffed her hand, its eyes never leaving hers before a large tongue snaked out, licking Jill. Slade couldn't help the smile that slid across his face in relief when both dogs overwhelmed Jill, fighting for her attention. He was glad because he really didn't want to have to kill her pet to protect her. As he watched, he wondered briefly if it was normal to feel jealousy toward a dog. He also couldn't help thinking how fucked-up that was.

Chapter 2

Jill laughed, trying to get up off the ground. Once Sable warmed up to her again, she couldn't get the large dog off her. Slade's hand appeared and she grabbed it while he grabbed Sable's collar, gently pulling the dog back.

"Thanks." Jill brushed off her jeans, then touched her cheek with the back of her hand, surprised to feel wetness. She wondered if it was tears or dog kisses that made it wet.

"Jilly!" A young voice froze her hand, the wetness forgotten. Turning, she saw her six-year-old brother on the porch. "Jilly!" His excitement had him jumping two steps at a time, tumbling to his knees before scrambling back up and running at breakneck speed, skidding to a stop right before her, his eyes wide.

"Whoa, Seth." Jill put her hands out to steady him, but frowned and pulled away when he jumped back.

"You look different." His young eyes stared curiously at her mismatched eyes. "Your eye is bleeding."

With both hands she wiped the wetness away, cursing when she looked down at her hand, seeing red smeared with the wetness. Looking back at her younger brother, whom she loved more than anything in the world, made her want to scream at the unfairness. Her mother wouldn't let her see Seth the day they kicked her out. She had begged, but her mother refused and her father had stood by and let it happen. Clearing the large lump in her throat, she knelt down to Seth's level, but didn't move closer, not wanting to scare him.

"I'm the same Jilly, Seth," Jill smiled, then remembered her fangs and closed her mouth quickly before covering it with her hand.

Seth stood still, his face expressionless as his eyes searched hers. Finally, he reached up to move her hand away from her mouth. His small hand touched her lip, pushing it up to reveal one fang. Jill allowed him to do it, his eyes darting back and forth between her eyes and fang.

"Are you going to eat me?" he whispered as he pulled his hand back, his tone serious for a six-year-old.

"Are you a chocolate candy bar?" Jill whispered back, mocking his serious tone.

"Nooo," he giggled, rolling his eyes.

"Then I'm not going to eat you, silly," Jill chuckled, a large grin spreading across her face. "Why would you think I'd eat you?"

"Seth, get away from her!" A shout and sounds of running came from the front door.

Jill stood and felt Slade step up beside her. Her older sister, Janie, came running almost as quickly as Seth had. "Did you tell him I would eat him?" Jill growled at her sister, who picked Seth up, turning him in a protective manner.

"What are you doing here?" Janie ignored Jill's question, looking nervously between Jill and Slade. "You need to leave, Jill. You're not welcome here."

Jill looked up at the house and saw her mother looking out the living room window. Her hand automatically went up to wave, but the curtains shut and her mother disappeared. Anger and hurt made her want to strike out, but when her eyes went back to her sister, all she could see was Seth looking at her confused.

"Where's Dad?" Jill tried to keep her voice void of any emotion, but she wasn't successful with keeping the anger out of her gaze.

"Why?" Janie took a step back. "He's in no shape to see you. You'll only upset him and his heart can't handle that."

"He's cutting firewood," Seth spoke with the innocence of a child.

"He just had a heart attack and he's out cutting wood?" Jill's eyes popped open. "Where in the hell is Trevor?"

"Oh, Jilly, you said a bad word." Seth covered his eyes, instead of his ears.

"Sorry, buddy," Jill replied, but her eyes never left Janie. "I asked you a question. Actually, I've asked you several which you haven't answered. As soon as I'm finished with Dad, you and I are going to have a long conversation." Jill turned to head in the opposite direction of the house toward the woods.

"My fiancé is going to be here any minute," Janie warned, her voice shaking. "You better leave. He's very protective of us. He doesn't like your kind."

Jill stopped suddenly, but didn't turn around. "Then he'll get along fine with this family, won't he," Jill hissed. Seth called out to her, but she kept going because she didn't trust herself not to plaster her sister against a wall.

"You okay?" Slade's deep voice in the quiet woods just beyond her house startled her.

"No, not really," she replied. Her head down, she let her feet carry her to where her dad was. She had played in these woods as soon as she could walk. It had been her escape. She knew every tree, rock and trail for miles. "Just doing everything in my power not to kill my sister and…eat her," she spat in disgust. She still couldn't believe her sister, who she had been pretty close to, could tell their little brother she would eat him. Feeling anger burning up through her body from her toes to the top of her head, she lifted her hand, aiming it toward a small tree without stopping. The tree uprooted in one fluid motion, and as she flicked her hand, it flew a few feet before smashing into another one, then to the ground with a large crash.

"Nice." Slade raised his eyebrows impressed.

She didn't answer as they broke into a clearing. Her father sat a few yards away on a fallen tree, sipping water from a bottle. Hearing their approach, he dropped the water and stood in surprise. "Jill?"

Jill didn't stop, just kept going. "What are you doing cutting firewood?" Jill frowned as she marched toward him, her arms whipping around at all the cut wood laying on the ground. "Are you crazy?"

Her father, looking pale, sat back down heavily. "Jill?" he said again, his eyes glancing toward Slade, then back to Jill. "What are you doing here?"

Stopping in front of him, she placed her hands on her hips. "I've come to see you." Her voice had calmed, somewhat. "I heard you had a heart attack and wanted to see if you were okay."

He looked away, shaking his head slowly. "Why?"

Jill dropped her hands from her hips, her arms falling to her sides. His frailness scared her. Her father, who could do anything in her eyes, her hero still, even after everything, looked older than his forty-so years.

"Because you're my dad," she whispered past the lump in her throat, praying he would reach for her and hug her like he used to do when she felt lost. She was a daddy's girl and losing him had devastated her; seeing him like this, knowing she could lose him forever would destroy her. "And I love you."

His eyes shot to hers in shock. "How can you love me after what I've done?" He stood as he spoke, his pale face flushing red with anger. "I never gave you a chance. I kicked my baby girl out when she needed me most, but your mother…"

"I know." Jill took a step closer, still hoping for that hug, praying for it with everything she had. Any kind of affection, she didn't care; she'd take it. Yeah, she was that desperate. Like an abandoned dog begging for scraps, she was begging deep down inside for a scrap from the man who had been her life. "She was afraid of me, still is. But I would never hurt my family. Well, I might bite Janie, but other than that everyone else is safe."

Her father's head snapped back, but a small smile tipped his quivering lip and then the moment she prayed for happened. He reached for her and she flew into his arms, careful not to crush him with her strength. "I'm so sorry, Jelly Bean." He pulled her away to get a good look at her and gave her arms a squeeze. "I should have come looking for you. It's been eating me alive knowing what I did to you."

"I'm fine now, Dad." Jill pulled him back into the hug, not ready to let go just yet. She felt him wobble. "Dad?"

Slade was there in a flash helping her ease her father down to the tree. "Mr. Nichols, are you having any pain?"

"No." Her father looked up at Slade surprised. "Who are you?"

"This is Dr. Slade Buchanan," Jill introduced them, her worried eyes never leaving her father. "Slade, this is my dad, Chuck Nichols."

"You're a doctor?" Chuck looked at his golden eyes in surprise.

"Yes, sir." Slade glanced at Jill, then back at her father. "Do you mind if I take your pulse?"

"No, not at all." He held out his hand, still looking shocked as Slade took his wrist. "They let vampires be doctors?"

"How long ago was your heart attack?" Slade frowned, ignoring his question.

"Over a month ago. Triple bypass. They said I was lucky." Her father wiped sweat off his brow.

13

Slade nodded. "Very lucky, but your luck is going to run out if you don't follow your doctor's orders."

"Which are?" Jill demanded of her father, but didn't let him answer. "I'm sure those orders didn't include cutting firewood."

"No, they didn't." Her father frowned, then stood with the help of Slade. "But somebody has to do it. Winter's coming and I need to get it done."

"Then let Trevor do it." Jill grabbed the chainsaw before her dad could. "Where is he anyway? Why isn't he doing this?"

"He moved out," he answered with a long sigh. "After you came home that night and then left, Trevor came home and found out. He was angry and stormed out. He has been coming home more since my heart attack."

"He left because of me?" She stared at her father. Trevor was a year younger than her, with Janie being a year older. She had always been the middle child until little Seth, who had been a surprise blessing. Their mother, Julianne, had been told her childbearing days were over. Seth proved them wrong when he came screaming into the world. "She pulled her phone out. "What's his number?"

"Jill, I'm the man here and I will take care of my..." He frowned, using his 'father' tone with her, but Jill wasn't having it.

"Health?" Jill finished for him with a snort. "If you don't, then you won't be here for long to take care of anything. Now, what's his number?"

Waiting for the number, she looked at her phone in surprise, not expecting there to be a signal deep in the woods. She gave a light scoff, constantly amazed by the VC Warriors' ability to have the best technology of everything. She beat the number into the phone, then put it to her ear, waiting, her eyes going back and forth between the watchful eyes of her dad and Slade.

"Has she always been like this?" Slade nodded toward Jill.

"You mean bossy?" Her dad nodded, "Yes."

Jill rolled her eyes, but then turned serious. "Trevor?" She paused, then frowned. "No, this isn't busty Barb. What the hell is wrong with you? Yeah, it's Jill, your sister, you jerk."

"They close?" Slade asked, his eyebrows raised in question as he watched Jill talk to her brother.

"Thick as thieves," her dad answered with pride.

"Don't worry about that, I'm here now. Here, at the house with Dad who is recovering from a heart attack and is cutting firewood. You should be ashamed of yourself." Jill looked at her dad, then pointed a finger at him. "Well, he didn't wait. I found him down here in the grove cutting firewood. No, he didn't tell me you told him that."

"Tell you what? What's he saying?" Her dad asked, an unhappy frown curving his lips, but didn't wait for her to tell him. He already knew what his son was saying. "I can't wait for him to get free from busty Barb or whoever in the hell he's dating this week. Winter is coming and we need wood. I'm fine and will finish this. You kids are more stressful to me than this damn wood."

A sadness filled her soul at his words. "Hurry up," she said into the phone before she clicked it shut. "I'm sorry, Dad. I never meant for any of this to happen to me, but it did and I'm dealing with it. Actually, I'm doing fine and would do better just knowing I can come and visit you sometimes."

"I didn't mean…" Her father sighed again. "I didn't mean it that way, Jill. I really didn't. And I would love to see you."

Jill nodded, then grabbed his arm, squeezing tightly, letting him know how much his words meant to her. "Now, come on. Trevor is on his way. Let's go up to the house so you can drink something cold and rest."

"I'm fine, dammit," her dad responded, but let Jill and Slade lead him out of the grove. "I'm not an old man."

"I know, but honestly, I want to get back up there before Janie tells Trevor I ate Seth," Jill growled, still totally pissed about that.

"She's just afraid, Jill." Her father tried to do the fatherly thing and play referee.

"She's an idiot," Jill mumbled under the breath, not wanting to upset her father more.

Once they made it into the clearing and were close to the yard, Janie followed a large man holding a shotgun. "I got a gun full of silver here, vamps. I suggest you get on that fancy motorcycle and ride on out of here before things get nasty."

Slade pushed Jill and her father behind him. "I suggest you aim that gun somewhere else." Slade's words were harsh enough to show he meant business, but his calmness effectively made one wonder. Jill knew, however; she'd had seen Slade in action. It wasn't pretty and it would get ugly…fast. Not a good thing with her father in the line of fire.

Jill stepped around Slade, heading toward the man who she figured was her sister's unfortunate fiancé. "Silver don't do shit to half-breeds so you best drop it and run, asshole." She jerked her arm out of Slade's grasp when he tried to stop her. "Who do you think you are, aiming a shotgun toward my dad?"

That seemed to take some of the authority out of the dumbass, but he didn't lower the gun. "Chuck, get out of the way," he ordered her father, nodding his head to the side as if that would make it right.

Jill walked right up to the barrel of the shotgun pointing at her chest and stopped. "Pull the trigger," she dared him, her head tilted in defiant anger.

Before anyone knew what was happening, the shotgun was knocked away from Jill's chest and the badass was on the ground with Slade's boot holding him down by the throat. "You have a death wish?" Slade roared the question at Jill as the man tried to remove Slade's foot from his throat. Slade unloaded the shotgun, the shells hitting the idiot as they fell toward the ground. Slade's furious gaze never once strayed from Jill. "If you ever do anything like that again, I will lock you in a room."

"Is that a threat?" Jill, who was still fired up, stupidly pushed Slade.

"It's a promise that I will prove as soon as I take care of this son of a bitch." Slade leaned over her, keeping his foot in place with no problem, even with the man using everything he had to remove it from his neck. "Keep pushing me, Jillian, but I swear if you ever pull anything like that again, you *will* regret it."

Jill opened her mouth, but Slade leaned in even closer as if daring her to say anything more. With his face so close to hers as well as being in control of the asshole on the ground, her brain went to mush so she closed her mouth. His authority over her was a total turn on. The knowledge surprised her speechless, which was shocking—she always had something smartass to say.

"Smart choice," Slade growled before finally leaning away from her space. He handed the shotgun to Chuck, who had walked up and was looking down at his future son-in-law.

"Can he breathe?" Chuck asked, looking up at Slade.

"He's fine," Slade replied, pressing down a little harder. "Just learning a hard lesson."

"Daddy!" Janie cried out. "Make him stop."

"Shut up, Janie!" Jill snapped, giving her sister a hard glare.

"I'm going to let you up, but if you make one wrong move, you are going to end up worse than this," Slade warned, but didn't move his foot. "Do you understand?"

"She's a half-breed." The man wheezed, his bulging, watery eyes looked from Slade to Jill. "It's our duty to protect our family against them. There's a standing order to have them turned over."

Jill snorted and crossed her arms. "This is my family, not yours." Her eyes roamed to the porch where her mom stood, shielding Seth behind her. Her eyes wandered to her dad whose face was lined with worry and stress. It hit her hard. She was causing this. She may not have been holding the gun, but in the end, her being there caused this to happen. Touching Slade's arm, she tugged. "Let him up."

Slowly, Slade lifted his foot, but stood over the man who had to roll away before standing.

"Janie, go call the police," he ordered, brushing himself off, but kept his eyes on Slade. "Tell them we have a half-breed here who needs to be taken in."

Watching her sister, Jill was surprised Janie hesitated. "But, she's leaving. Isn't that right, Jill?" Janie's voice shook in confusion and fear.

"Yeah, Janie," Jill nodded, knowing that was her only option at this point. If she stayed, it would only cause more stress for her dad and that was something she couldn't live with. "I'm leaving."

"What's your name?" Slade demanded of the man, his eyes as hard as his voice.

"What does my name have to do with anything?" the man stuttered. "She's the nasty half-breed. I'm just a good citizen doing my duty."

Slade took a threatening step toward the man. "You have

18

threatened not one, but two VC Warriors, and that, my *good* citizen, is against the law." He pulled out his phone. "Now, while I'm calling my superior, I suggest you apologize to Ms. Nichols."

"But…" The man's tone changed quickly.

"Now!" Slade's shout was a deadly demand that even made Jill jump.

"I'm, ah, sorry. I didn't know. I just thought she was a nas—" At Slade's growl, Janie's fiancé looked ready to faint. He was a large man with light blond hair and ruddy cheeks against pale skin. He looked tough, but next to Slade, he looked like a scared teenager who needed a change of underwear.

"Jill?" Her father grasped her arm. "Is it true?"

Glancing from Slade, she turned to her dad. "Yeah, it is," she replied, then lifted her head proudly. "I'm in training now, but yes, I will be a VC Warrior."

"How can a half-breed be a VC Warrior?" Janie's fiancé's voice was filled with disdain.

"She is *my* daughter and her name is Jill, not half-breed," her father shouted, then went deathly pale, staggering sideways.

"Chuck!" her mother cried out, running from the porch to her husband's side.

Slade was there at his side steadying him. "You need to calm down, Mr. Nichols."

"Get off him," Jill's mom tried to push Slade's hands away.

"He's a doctor." Jill stepped between her mom and Slade. "Is he okay?" Her eyes searched Slade's concerned face.

"He needs to sit down, calm down and have some water," Slade ordered.

"I'm fine," her father repeated.

"No, you're not." Slade led him toward the lawn furniture near the house. "And if you don't listen to me, I will call an ambulance and your cardiologist."

"You wouldn't." Chuck Nichols, who Jill knew hated being sick, period, looked panicked.

"I would," Slade countered. "You have just had major heart surgery. Even though it's good you are active, cutting wood and getting overly excited is not what your doctor would be happy with. So if you don't want to find yourself back in the hospital, I suggest you do as I say."

Before anyone could say anything else, a beat-up Mustang came flying up the gravel drive. A tall, well-built male version of Jill hopped out of the car and took off toward Jill in a dead run, but stopped when Slade stepped in front of her, blocking his path.

"You her brother?" Slade's deep voice echoed across the yard.

"Yeah, who the hell are you?" Trevor looked up at the large vampire.

Slade stepped aside letting him pass. Trevor gave Slade one last long look before picking up Jill in a tight hug. "Where the hell have you been?" He set her back down looking her over, then pulled her blue tipped hair. "I've looked everywhere for you."

"I stayed with Tessa and Adam Pride for a while," Jill replied, leaving out she had lived out in the woods by their house, scared and alone, before meeting up with Adam.

"I didn't know what happened until it was too late and you were gone, Jill." Trevor frowned at his mom and sister. "It wouldn't have happened if I had been here."

"It's okay." Jill glanced at her dad, whose color was coming back.

20

He was sipping on water with Seth sitting on his lap. "Now's not the time to talk about it."

Trevor's eyes followed hers and he nodded. "He hasn't been the same since that night."

"Neither have I," Jill smiled sadly, as her eyes met Slade's. "Slade, this is my brother, Trevor."

Slade reached out his hand. "Slade Buchanan."

They shook hands both eyeing each other, sizing each other up. "You were just protecting her when you stepped in front of her."

"Just making sure you were who I thought you were." Slade nodded. "We had a little excitement with a shotgun just before you got here, so I'm a little on edge."

"What?" Trevor's eyes widened. "Who in the hell had a shotgun?"

"Janie's fiancé." Jill frowned, looking toward her sister and, hell, she still didn't know his name. "Who is he?"

"Anthony Bonner." Rolling his eyes, he snorted. "He's a douche who is anti-vampire; he came around right after I left. I don't even know how they met, but he has Mom and Janie all stressed out about half-breeds and vampires."

Wanting to change the subject so not to upset her dad again, Jill glanced toward the house. "Hey, can you run up and get a couple of things from my room?"

Trevor looked away from her, scratching his head. "Well, yeah I could, but…"

"But, what?" Jill asked, not really wanting to know the answer. When he still didn't answer, only shuffled his feet nervously, looking anywhere but at her, she sighed, "They got rid of my stuff." It wasn't a question.

Always one to fidget when nervous, Trevor rubbed his eyes, then forehead. "Not exactly." He finally looked at her, lowering his voice, "Dad found Mom and Janie going through your stuff, boxing it up and throwing stuff away. He *literally* had a heart attack."

Jill looked over at her dad who was playing with Seth, her mom close at his side and her eyes glaring right at her. "Why does she hate me so much?" Jill turned back to her brother, confusion and sadness on her face.

"She doesn't hate you, Sis." Trevor clasped her shoulder. "She fears you."

"No, she hates me," she pushed his arm away. "Do you fear me?" Her voice held a hint of challenge, but her gaze held a trace of plea hoping his answer would be no. That he still saw her the same way, his annoying older sister who he liked to mess with.

Trevor snorted, rolling his eyes. "Fear you?" He pushed her, making her stumble into Slade who had been standing silently by her side. "That's a joke, right?"

"Careful, bro." Jill crossed her arms, tilting her chin up. "I've got skills now."

"Skills?" Trevor's laugh boomed across the yard, gaining everyone's attention. He looked up at Slade. "You better watch out, big man. And just so you know, I won't hurt her...too bad. Just don't want you killing me or anything, but I need to make sure my sis remembers who's the bigger badass."

"You mean the bigger ass," Jill smirked. "Which would be....you."

Slade's grin slowly spread across his face as he stepped back. "Go for it," he nodded at Trevor.

Trevor rubbed his hands together as he took two steps toward Jill. Just as he reached for her, she moved out of his way so fast his human eyes couldn't track her. He frowned as his eyes found her. "Damn. Okay, I see. Not bad." He nodded impressed, then frowned at something behind her. "Seth, don't sneak up."

Turning, Jill cursed, realizing she fell for the oldest damn trick in the book and in front of Slade, her trainer. As soon as her brother's arms made contact, she grabbed one arm, flipping him over her shoulder to the ground. With lightning speed, she straddled him, pinning him to the ground where he struggled to get the breath that was knocked out of him.

Snapping her fangs playfully at him, she grinned, "You give?"

"I give." Her brother wheezed out a laugh even as he struggled once again to break away from her. "Damn, for a little thing, you weigh a ton."

"Hey! I do not!" Jill snapped at him again, feeling better than she had since becoming a half-breed. She never realized how much she missed her family, especially Trevor who she had always been close to. "Don't make me bite you."

"Get off him!" Her mother's shrill scream broke their play.

Jill turned just in time to see Slade grab the stick that was coming toward her face. Jill jumped up just as Slade threw it with a fierce scowl. "She was not hurting him, Mrs. Nichols." Slade glared down at her, a tick in his jaw plainly visible. "You need to calm down. You're scaring your son." Slade nodded toward Seth, who stood just behind her with fear on his face.

"Don't you dare tell me what to do on my own property, you filthy…thing," Jill's mom spat in anger and fear. She didn't even try to hide the disgust shining brightly from her eyes.

Jill stepped between Slade and her mom. "Don't you talk to him like that!" Jill hissed. She had never talked to her parents with disrespect, but she'd be damned if her mom would treat Slade like this. Not happening. "He, along with the other VC Warriors, have done nothing but help me, *your* daughter. A daughter you discarded when I needed you most and why? Because of fear? Do you realize how afraid *I* have been going through this alone, without my family? Why? Why do you hate me so much?"

Her mother didn't say anything, didn't even look a tiny bit remorseful.

Looking around at everyone staring at her, she purposely avoided Slade's eyes. "You have always been embarrassed of me." Jill felt her emotions bubbling up and knew she had to get the hell out of there, but the words just kept flowing out of her mouth. Things she had wanted to say for years clogged her throat with a bitter taste. "God forbid, anyone find out not only is your youngest daughter illiterate, but she's a half-breed vampire. I was never good enough." She had always thought her mother was beautiful, but at that moment, she was seeing a totally different person in her mother and there was nothing beautiful about either.

Her mom's face showed she didn't like being called out; a sneer thinned her lips. "You're the reason he had his heart attack." Her mother's voice grew low enough that only Jill, Trevor and Slade could hear her. "So, if you love him, stay away."

"Mom!" Trevor stared at his mom with shock, and then went to grab Jill's arm as she turned to walk away. "Jill, stop!"

"Don't!" she warned, not trusting herself. But she stopped suddenly, not knowing when she would see her brother again. Turning, she hugged him tightly without saying a word.

"She needed to hear the truth." Jill heard her mom saying as she headed toward her dad, totally ignoring Janie and her fiancé.

The sadness in her dad's eyes almost did her in, but she had to hold it back. Hell would fly if she started crying blood; her mom would probably want to stake her. Reaching down, she slowly wrapped her arms around her dad, praying he didn't flinch away. He didn't. "I love you, Dad, and I will be back to see you if that's okay?" Her heart flipped when he hugged her back just as tightly. "I don't want to cause problems for you with Mom."

"You let me take care of your mother, Jelly Bean." He kissed her cheek. "I'm sorry. I should have—"

Jill shook her head, smiling sadly as she pulled away, newly loving the nickname she had hated in the past. "No, things are the way they should be. All you need to do is take care of yourself." She straightened and forced a smile on her face. Her gaze found Seth. "That little guy over there needs you. We all need you."

Clearing her throat when he squeezed her hand, she reluctantly pulled away and went toward Seth, but stopped when her mom grabbed his little arm, pulling him behind her. His face peeked around her leg, his eyes sad and confused. Jill smiled, hiding her fangs the best she could and waved. His lips curved into a small smile as he gave a little wave with his free hand.

Sable and Bebe followed her and Slade to the bike. Without a word to them, she hugged both dogs tightly before hopping on the back of the bike behind Slade, wishing with everything she had she could wrap *him* in her arms and disappear, but she couldn't. She was alone. Looking back at what used to be her family, she realized she would probably be alone for the rest of her life. If her family didn't love her, what made her think anyone else would? Taking a deep breath, she looked away. Never one to throw a pity party for herself, she lifted her chin, straightened her spine and looked straight ahead.

Chapter 3

Slade could feel Jill's anxiety radiate into his body as they hit the road. What he witnessed didn't surprise him. He'd seen it before. Families torn apart from fear of the unknown, fear of a loved one who had been turned. Though, he felt Jill's mother was taking it to extremes. He felt bad for her dad who was caught in the middle of his love for his daughter and wife, not a good place for a man to be, especially as his health had suffered for it. Slade knew better than to show any pity toward Jill. She would, without a doubt, throw the pity back in his face, which set her apart from most women he'd known. She wasn't dependent on anyone, yet he knew she desperately wanted to be loved and cared for. He also knew she would cut out her tongue before saying so.

Glancing down at his watch, he knew they were late. Duncan had rented out the large shooting range a few blocks down from the compound. They didn't have much time to get the half-breeds trained, so it was pretty much around-the-clock work and training, which didn't bother him at all. He needed to stay busy, busy keeping his mind and hands off the woman whose hot little body fit perfectly around him as she sat on the back of his bike.

Parking next to Adam's car, Slade turned off the bike, waiting for Jill to hop off first. Sliding off in one fluid motion, Slade turned, only to see Jill already heading toward the building. Her spine straight, head tilted in her own arrogant way. Cursing himself for being ready to ask her if she was okay, Slade followed her, keeping his eyes up and not on the sexy sway of her hips, a natural sway not intended to attract male attention, and that turned him on more than anything. She had no clue how much her innocent sex appeal attracted him and that made her even more dangerous.

"Fuck!" Slade mumbled loud enough for her to stop and look back at him. At her questioning stare, he shook his head, motioning with his hand for her to continue. Once she turned, he adjusted his jeans; his dick didn't get the memo from his brain about not being interested. He stood outside the closed door Jill had walked

26

through and cursed. Feeling more in control after a deep breath, Slade grabbed the door handle, swinging the door open so hard the top door hinge broke away from the frame. "Son of a bitch!"

"Having a little trouble?" Jax walked around the corner, eyeing the door without stopping.

Slade cursed again, wedging the door so it stayed upright. "If you only knew," Slade mumbled, not really caring if Jax heard him or not.

"You're late." Jax pushed open a door to one of the rooms with ten shooting lanes.

Walking in behind Jax, Slade kept his mouth shut. He took in everyone, finding Jill standing back with her arms crossed, her stare blank. He knew she was reliving what happened with her family.

"I said you're late." Jax stood in his line of vision. "If we are going to get these guys ready, you need to get your ass and that sweet little ass of our only female—"

Slade took one step in Jax's personal space; his eye narrowed. "I know my fucking job." Slade stood slightly taller than Jax, but Jax didn't step back; instead, they leaned in toward each other.

"Then get your head straight and start doing it," Jax warned before turning away.

Fists clenching tightly, Slade wanted nothing more than to knock Jax through the wall, but glancing at everyone looking at them, he knew his need at the moment wasn't the issue. These guys were counting on him. Jax was right. He needed to get his shit straight; something he usually prided himself on. His shit was always straight.

Everyone had picked a gun except Jill, who still stood back. Before Slade could make it to her, Jax stepped in.

"Get your ass in gear, Jill." Jax picked up a small gun with a pink handle. "I got this just for you."

"Awww...how cute is that," Steve snickered, holding his gun, attempting to look like a badass.

Jill ignored the gun Jax held out, grabbing a different one. "I prefer the GLOCK-21 because of its accuracy and stopping power, which would probably even put a full-blooded vamp on his ass." Jill snapped the already loaded clip into the gun, grabbed a target, and then headed to the lane ignoring the open mouths gaping after her.

Slade's grin spread as he watched the scene. Not many people could put Jax in his place, but Jill just did and he fucking loved it.

"What the hell you smiling at?" Jax walked up, grabbing a pair of earmuffs and safety glasses. Without waiting for Slade to answer, Jax turned away and headed toward Jill. "Here! Don't shoot that gun until you have these on."

After setting her target, she put the safety glasses on and placed the earmuffs around her neck waiting for instructions, as did Steve and Adam.

Stepping away from the table he had been leaning on, Slade looked at each of them. "Set your targets at a comfortable level. We aren't looking for distance shooting yet. We just want to see how accurate you are with a firearm." He nodded toward the lanes. "As soon as you unload the clip, bring in your target."

Jax and Slade watched closely to see how comfortable they were. Soon the sounds of firing filled the room. Slade's eyes kept returning to Jill, who looked the most comfortable in her stance and hold. He stepped sideways to get a full visual and realized how attractive he found a woman who was comfortable with a firearm. Feeling Jax staring at him, he turned his attention back to Steve and Adam.

"Looks like she's shot before," Jax commented, nodding toward

Jill.

"Yeah," Slade remarked, trying not to show too much interest in anything Jill did.

"Steve looks like he's having a damn seizure every time the gun recoils." Jax frowned, then rolled his eyes when Steve turned the gun sideways like a gangster. "What the fuck is he doing?"

As Jax left to chew Steve's ass out, Slade glanced back at Jill, who was already bringing her target in. She had pulled her empty clip out of the gun. When she glanced back, he waved her over. Adam had also finished and was bringing his target to the table. Slade took both targets, laying them side by side. Steve quickly brought his over.

"Damn, Adam." Steve stared at one of the targets that had every shot straight to the heart, each bullet hole easily spaced so you could count them. "You're freaking Rambo."

"That's not my target." Adam glanced at Jill, surprised.

Jax picked up the target, staring at it, then looked at Jill. "Where'd you learn to shoot like that?"

"My dad made sure his kids knew how to protect themselves," Jill replied with a proud tilt of her head.

"Yeah, well, let's see how well you do this next go around." Jax shoved a new target at her, and then picked up Adam's target. "Good job, Adam, but you need to relax your stance more. All of your shots are left of center. Adjust your stance. Keep it at the same distance."

"Yes, sir," Adam replied, taking the new target.

Slade kept his mouth shut as he watched Jill frown at Jax's treatment of Adam compared to her. Grabbing Steve's target before Jax could, Slade looked at it. Only three of Steve's shots hit a vital part in the target. "You need to control the recoil of the gun, Steve, and definitely stop the gangster hold shit you have going on. Keep it at the same distance."

Steve nodded, grabbing his new target, but kept looking at Jill's. "Didn't know girls could shoot like that," he said low to Adam as they headed toward their lane. "Remind me not to piss her off when she's got a loaded gun anywhere near her."

"How far do you want my target?" Jill asked Slade, but Jax stepped in and went toward her.

Nudging her out of the way, he pushed the button sending her target down the lane; he kept going and going. Finally, he stopped the target. "Let's see how good a shot you are at a distance."

Jill stared at him for a second with her brows furrowed in confusion before slipping her earmuffs on. Snapping in a loaded clip, she positioned her body, her head turned slightly to glance over her shoulder at Jax. Slade was surprised at the hurt look in her eyes. He was even more surprised that Jax's treatment of her pissed him off more than anything had in a long time.

Once again, the room erupted in gunfire. Jax turned, catching Slade glaring at him. "What's your problem?"

Before Slade could answer, Jill stopped shooting, brought her target in, popped out her empty clip and calmly walked over, putting her target on the table. Each shot placed with strategic accuracy, but this time to the head.

Neither Jax nor Slade said a word as they stared at the target. Adam followed, laying his target down as did Steve.

"What the hell?" Steve reached over, putting his finger in one of the eye holes made by Jill's bullet.

"I'm better with a shotgun," Jill shrugged, staring at her target. "We did turkey shoots all the time. We never had to buy a turkey because one of us always won."

"She's better with a shotgun," Steve snorted, rolling his eyes.

"Can shoot the balls off an ant at one-hundred paces." Jill grinned at Steve's expression.

"Wait a minute." Steve's eyes went from impressed to narrowed. "An ant doesn't have balls."

Jill cocked her eyebrow at him before grabbing a clean target. "Really?"

Steve took a target. "No, I mean I've never seen an ant with balls."

"And you've looked?" Adam frowned at Steve, following him to the lane.

"No, I haven't looked for ant balls, but I'm sure if an ant had balls, you'd see them hanging and I've never seen hanging balls from an ant."

"If you guys are done talking about fucking ant balls…" Jax started, but stopped when Jill laughed then shut up real quick at his glare. "I want you to set your targets a few yards further than the last time. Slade is going to call out what shot to make. You will have only four shots this round."

"After I call out the area to shoot, you will have seven seconds to take your aim and fire," Slade instructed, watching as they all set their targets. "This is an accuracy test and will be counted as a score."

"But we didn't get to practice much and we all can't be like Annie Oakley over there who can shoot the balls off an ant. Can't we get a little more practice?" Steve looked worried.

"We don't have time to stay on one thing too long," Slade responded, looking at each of them. "We have too much to cover.

It will be up to you to practice in your own time as we move ahead. If you need help with anything, help each other or grab a Warrior who is free and can help you."

"I'll help you, Steve," Jill called down from her lane.

"Oh, thanks, Jill," Steve called back. "Having a girl teach me how to shoot shouldn't make me look like a loser."

Jill rolled her eyes with a snort. "Having a girl run around telling everyone she's a better shot than you with proof would take care of that problem."

"Shit," Steve mumbled, putting his earmuffs on before yelling, "In that case…sure, Jill, I would love for you to help me."

"That's what I thought," Jill smirked.

"There goes my man card," Steve cursed as he stood in his lane waiting for instructions.

"Didn't know you could lose something you didn't have," Jill shot back.

"Funny stuff, Jill," Steve yelled over the lanes. "If you fail at this protector stuff, you should do stand-up."

"We are seriously fucked," Jax grumbled to Slade as they stood watching the bantering back and forth.

Slade ignored him, stepping behind the three, stopwatch in hand. "Bring your weapons into position." He waited, but when Jill kept hers down, he walked toward her. "Aim up, Jill."

"If it's okay, I'm more comfortable with my weapon down until I know where I'm to aim." Jill peeked at him over her shoulder.

"That's fine, but remember this is going to count," Slade replied, giving her one more chance to change her position.

"Let her fuck up," Jax nodded toward Jill. "She'll learn to listen before it's too late. Or maybe she won't."

Slade's hold on the stopwatch tightened. As soon as this was finished, he was going to find out what the fuck Jax's issue was with Jill. "Ready?" he called out, waiting for each to nod. "Heart." He clicked the stopwatch as soon as he yelled the word.

Three consecutive shots rang out, only five seconds of silence followed before Slade's voice boomed another body part and shots fired. Once the exercise was finished, they brought in the targets, each staring at their work.

Slade looked at each nodding his approval. "Not bad."

"Looks like sure shot there should have listened and brought up her aim." Jax picked up Jill's target, looking at it closely.

Slade knew shit was about to hit the fan when Jill's face scrunched up in anger. It seemed Adam and Steve also knew Jill's facial expressions because they took a step back.

"I was only off on the groin shot," Jill confirmed, her voice low and even. "The others are dead on."

"Not good enough." Jax laid it down before looking at her, daring her with his glare to say another word.

Slade slammed his hand on the table. "Leave." When no one moved, he looked at Jill, Adam and Steve. "I said leave!"

Steve ran into Adam trying to get out of the room, but Jill remained for a second longer, her eyes not leaving Jax. When Slade growled low in his throat, she turned and walked out of the range, slamming the door behind her.

"What is your fucking problem?" Slade turned on Jax. "We are supposed to be building them up, not tearing them down."

"She needs to go." Jax didn't back down. "She is, and I repeat once again, a liability."

"She deserves to go through the program like anyone else," Slade countered, his temper on the edge of exploding.

"Why don't you just fuck her and get it over with." Jax sneered then looked away, which was a mistake; he should have been looking for the punch that landed him across the room.

"Whether I fuck her or not is not and never will be your business, motherfucker." Slade reached down to pick him up, but Jax moved faster, swinging out, but missed when Slade moved out of the way. "You better rethink fighting me because I guarantee, you will lose."

Jax worked his jaw back and forth as he glared at Slade. "This is exactly my point. Would you have reacted this way if I had said Steve was a liability, which looking at his targets isn't far off the mark."

"No, because you wouldn't be telling me to fuck him," Slade countered, still itching to hit Jax again.

Thinking about that for a minute, Jax nodded with raised eyebrows. "True."

"She deserves to be here as much as anyone else," Slade countered. "And I'm in charge of this program. If you can't handle it, you need to remove yourself. She will be just as ready as any of the men."

Jax glared for a second longer before sighing, still moving his jaw. "Did you have to hit me so fucking hard?"

"I don't disrespect women and neither will anyone else in my presence," Slade warned, grabbing up the targets.

Once again, Jax cocked an eyebrow. "Didn't you just respond with and I quote… '*Whether I fuck her or not is not and never will be your business, motherfucker'?*'"

"That was a warning, nothing more," Slade cursed under his breath, wondering where those words *had* come from. They just popped out in a fit of anger.

Jax snorted. "Ah, yeah…okay, but I'm telling you, she is going to get one of those boys out there killed and you released from the Vampire Council. I've seen it happen before, and Goddammit, she's a liability."

Unfortunately, Slade couldn't argue with that point because he knew it was true, and there wasn't a damn thing he could do about it.

Chapter 4

Jill walked out of the shooting range behind Adam and Steve.

"You did good, Jill." Adam looked down at her. "Jax is just an asshole trying to—"

"Do ants have balls?" Steve spoke into his phone.

"What the hell are you doing?" Adam looked back at Steve as if he'd lost his mind.

"Asking Siri," Steve replied, looking at his phone.

"If ants have balls?" Adam's voice was a mix between exasperation and disbelief. "How in the hell is your phone going to know if ants have fucking balls?"

"It's not my phone; it's Siri." Steve rolled his eyes. "Come on, dude. Don't tell me you've never used Siri."

A female-like robotic voice sounded from Steve's phone. "This is what I found on the web for 'Do ants have balls'."

"Ha!" Steve pointed at Adam, then to his phone looking surprised. "Well, I'll be damned. Ants do have balls, but—"

"Steve, shut the fuck up." Adam smacked Steve's phone, almost knocking it out of his hand. "I don't care if ants have balls or not."

Jill barely heard their conversation. Her focus was on the conversation she heard going on behind closed doors and it was pissing her off. Adam and Steve stopped talking and listened to the angry Warrior voices also. Their pitiful glances toward her did her in. God, she was getting tired of fighting for every damn thing she wanted.

"Whether I fuck her or not is not and never will be your business, motherfucker." Slade's voice boomed from the other room as if he weren't standing behind closed doors. Even without their superb hearing, that statement was hard to miss as it rattled out into the hallway they stood in.

Glancing at Steve and Adam, Jill's face burned. How freaking humiliating to be standing there while being discussed loudly in the next room.

"Ah, yeah…okay, but I'm telling you, she is going to get one of those boys out there killed and you released from the Vampire Council. I've seen it happen before, and Goddammit, she's a liability." This time it was Jax's voice that reached them.

"Jill, that's bullshit," Adam said, shaking his head. "You know it and we know it."

"Yeah, it is." Jill glared at the door and before anyone could stop her, she headed that way and burst into the room they had been told to leave.

"Jill, don't!" Adam called out, but it was too late.

"Transfer me!" Jill walked into the room, her glare going from Slade who looked pissed and Jax who didn't look any happier. "If it's such an issue me being here, just transfer me."

"No one will take you," Jax stated, not in a mean taunt, but as a fact.

Jill opened up her mouth to respond, but the realness of those words hit her pretty hard. Shutting her mouth, she looked away from her peers, swallowing hard before nodding. She felt Adam and Steve walk up behind her. "If it came down to anyone on my team dying or having to make a decision against the Council because of me, I would take myself out." Jill jerked her chin up, praying she could do just that if the time came.

"And that will not make any of us feel any better." Jax tilted his head, staring hard at her. "Whether you like it or not, you are a woman and a woman is a man's downfall on the battlefield. It's a proven fact from the beginning of time and war."

Jill felt a frantic laugh bubble in her throat. She felt everything slipping away and had no clue how to turn it back around. "It doesn't matter what I do, does it?" Jill looked from Jax to Slade and then back to Jax again. "When I don't do something right, I'm a liability. And when I do something I'm good at, it's not good enough."

He shook his head. "Either way, you're a liability. It doesn't matter how good or bad you do anything."

The room was deadly silent. Jax finally looked away, but Slade's eyes never left her. Adam and Steve looked everywhere else. She had never felt so alone as she did at that moment.

"If she goes, I go," Adam's voice rose from the silence.

"Adam, don't." Jill shook her head.

"No, this is bullshit." Adam pointed at Jax. "You don't talk for me. If I had to choose from anyone to stand by me, it would be Jill."

"Easy to say…now," Jax sighed.

"No, easy to say, period." Adam took a step forward, but Jill stopped him. "And I will say it again, if she goes, I go."

"Same goes for me." Steve stepped forward. "Not having a sharp shooter who can shoot the balls off an ant is a bad move in my book." Steve winked at Jill, giving her his goofy smile.

Emotion gripped Jill's throat in a choke hold making her unable to speak at all, but her eyes thanked Adam and Steve more than her words ever could.

"Jill is an asset to the VC Warriors," Slade's voice rolled over her emotions, almost doing her in. "And if you don't like it, I release you from assisting me in their preparations for their initiation. I'm sure Sloan has other duties you can do. Either drop it or get out."

Jax leaned back, looking at each of them, and then shrugged. "It's your funeral." He looked at Steve and Adam before turning his attention to Slade. "And your early retirement."

"I said to fucking drop it," Slade growled, taking a step toward Jax. Jax held up his hands as if surrendering. Slade glared at him for a second longer before grabbing the clipboard. "You guys go ahead and wait outside. We'll get your scores and then head back to the compound. Sloan texted me earlier and has a job that needs doing."

Jill nodded before looking at Jax, who was leaning against the wall, staring at her. "What?" Her tone wasn't pleasant.

"Nothing really." Jax's half-grin didn't fool her.

Before anyone else could say a word, a woman's robotic voice came from Steve's phone, "This is what I found on the web for 'Do ants have balls'."

"Ah shit." Steve looked down at his phone. "I must have hit something to make it go off again."

Jax's mocking laugh grated on Jill's last nerve. Without thinking, she flung her hand toward Steve and to everyone's astonishment, his phone was pulled away from his hand and flung into Jill's hand. Hitting the button for Siri, she brought the phone to her mouth. "Male chauvinistic pig."

"What the hell?" Steve stared at his hand to Jill holding his phone. "How the hell did you do that?"

As soon as Siri answered, Jill looked down at the phone with a smirk, and then tossed Steve's phone to Jax before walking out of the room, slamming the door behind her. She knew she would pay for that little stunt, but she didn't care. What she really wanted to do was tell him to fuck off, but Jax was a scary guy and she wasn't quite that brave or stupid.

Heading out of the shooting range, she walked back to the compound, which was only a few blocks away. She didn't want to answer questions about what she had just done with Steve's phone, because she really didn't know how she did it, just knew she could. She had been practicing a lot, and one night in her room, she managed to move a cup across her small desk to her open hand. With more practice, she discovered not only could she move things with her hands, but pull objects toward her. It was pretty cool. She was sure Jax found it lame, but she didn't really care. Okay, that was a lie. She did care what the asshole thought. She had always been a pleaser and hated, absolutely hated when someone was upset with her or didn't like her. It sucked, but it was what it was.

Checking her pockets as she ran up the compound steps, she frowned. Dammit, she forgot her keys again. She was hoping to go to her room without being seen so she could get her mind right before seeing Sloan and the rest of the Warriors. Hitting the buzzer, she looked around, wondering what Slade had thought about her taking Steve's phone like that. She released a frustrated breath; there she went again, wondering what others thought. She needed to get over that and not care. It was a cool power to have and she was perfecting it; that was all that should matter. Not what the hot doc thought.

"Jill?" Tessa's voice came over the intercom.

Stepping fully into view of the camera, Jill smiled and waved. "It's me. Forgot my keys again."

The door opened and Jill walked in to see Tessa heading back to the game room in a hurry, motioning for her to come. "Hurry up," Tessa called out over her shoulder.

"What's going on?" Jill hurried across the entryway then stopped at the doorway. Sitting in front of the big screen television were Nicole, Lana, Pam, Angelina and Tessa plopping down on the couch.

"Okay, Lana, hit it." Tessa settled in with a big smile.

Jill looked at the television as Russell Crowe's face and buff bod dressed as a gladiator entered an arena. "You have got to be kidding me."

"Angela and Lana have never seen it," Tessa grinned.

"Do the guys know you're watching it?" Jill walked further into the room, leaning against the couch, her eyes glued to the television, putting the Warriors in place of the actors. It was kind of surreal.

"Hell, no," Nicole grinned with a snort. "I could hear them now…"

"Yeah," Tessa laughed. "Russell Crowe's a pussy," she deepened her voice to mock Jared.

Jill felt the presence of the Warriors as soon as they walked into the room. Glancing over her shoulder, Damon, Jared, Duncan and Sid wore matching frowns.

"He *is* a pussy," Jared's deep voice boomed throughout the room.

Tessa screamed, trying to control the remote she bobbled as she attempted to turn the television off. All the women had turned with the 'oh, shit, busted' look on their faces. Jill sidestepped, making room as the Warriors headed toward the women. As shitty as her day had been, it might as well end on a bad note, even though she really wasn't part of the *Gladiator* party the women were throwing.

"What the hell are you watching?" Sid frowned at the still image of Russell Crowe dressed in gladiator garb in the middle of an arena.

"Ah, well, we…." Tessa began until Sid's eyes flashed to her.

Nicole stood in front of the television as if trying to hide the frozen screen. "We are watching a movie," Nicole finished for Tessa before moving toward Damon. "Same thing we usually do when you guys go out on a job. Calms our nerves." She reached Damon, putting her arms around his neck.

Damon smiled down at her, placing a kiss on her lips. "What movie are we watching?" His deep voice was low, but radiated throughout the room.

"Oh, that doesn't matter now." Nicole winked up at him. "Now that you are home, I'm not in the mood to watch a movie."

Jill watched Nicole flirt with Damon in awe. It actually looked like it was working. His attention had turned fully to her. Damn, she was good. Tessa, Lana and Pam all stood, heading toward their men in hopes of turning their attention away. It seemed to work until Steve and Adam walked into the room.

"*Gladiators!*" Steve grinned with a nod. "That's a kickass movie."

"Steve!" Every woman except Jill yelled, making Steve jump.

"What?" He actually looked nervous under their angry glares.

"*Gladiators?*" Sid frowned at the frozen television screen, then turned to Lana. "Are you kidding me? What the hell are you watching that for?"

Jared grasped Tessa's hand, taking the remote she still had in her death grip. Re-clicking the pause button, the movie began to play. A lot of grumbling came from the Warriors as they watched the gladiators in the arena.

"Look how he's holding that sword," Duncan snorted, shaking his head, his arms tight around Pam as she stood in front of him.

"Those guys would be pissing themselves if they ever found themselves in a real arena." Jared's voice was full of disgust, but his golden eyes stayed on the screen watching the scene unfold.

Jill glanced around at each Warrior who somehow had their hands on their mates. Even Adam had Angelina wrapped up in his embrace. She and Steve were the only ones without any physical contact. Steve wasn't a bad guy, goofy, but not a bad guy. He was nice looking, in a 'boy next door' kind of way. Frowning, Jill wondered where in the hell those thoughts came from. Loneliness? Yeah, definitely loneliness because Steve was so not her type. It was pretty bad if she was even looking toward Steve as a…mate. Holy shit, she was losing it. She had to get the hell out of there before she grabbed Steve like the lonely loser she was.

Turning quickly, she took one step, running into a brick wall named Slade. Her face actually smashed against his chest. "Ouch!" Looking up at him, she lifted her hand to her nose. "Sorry, didn't know you were there."

"I know." His deep gravelly voice did that thing to her where she felt hot all over, like a fire from the inside out heating her skin. His golden eyes searched hers before looking over her head then back to her with his eyebrow cocked. "*Gladiators?*"

"Hey, for once I'm innocent," Jill grinned, hearing the Warriors moan and groan at the acting in the movie. "I just got here. They did this all on their own."

"Got the popcorn!" Caroline walked into the room with a large bowl, then frowned. "Hey! You started the movie without me."

"Not a huge loss." Sid rolled his eyes at the television, and then grabbed toward the popcorn, but Caroline pulled it away.

"Go make your own," Caroline growled at him. "This is for my girls."

Jared grabbed from the other side of the bowl getting a handful. "Yeah, Sid, go make your own."

Jill watched the play between the Warriors and the women, the loneliness seeping more deeply into her gut. Her eyes caught Jax who leaned against the wall, his eyes were on Caroline, doing the elevator routine, moving up and down her body, and by the look on his face, he really liked what he saw. Slowly, his eyes moved toward her as they narrowed and his lip turned up in a sneer. That look would scare most people and should scare the shit out of her, but she had just witnessed a more human side to Jax when he watched Caroline and was in awe. A small grin played on her lips, her eyes meeting his in a knowing stare.

Chapter 5

"Please tell me my Warriors are not watching what I think you're watching," Sloan's voice boomed over the talk and loud television set. He walked closer and the closer he got, the more disbelief came over his face. "What in the fuck is wrong with you?" His eyes glared at each of them.

"You want an individual list or will just one generalized…" When Sloan's eyes shot to Sid, Sid nodded. "Shutting the fuck up."

"Shush!" Caroline turned toward the television with a frown.

"Did that woman just shush me?" Sloan's eyes turned black.

"What's up, boss?" Damon as well as the other Warriors blocked Sloan's view of the television and the women.

Jill glanced over at the women, happy to see they were involved in the movie once again. Talk about balls… Caroline shushing Sloan demonstrated either a large set or just plain stupidity. After looking at each Warrior with his pissed-off glare, his eyes focused on her and she had a feeling things were about to get real.

"One of our informants contacted me last night." Sloan glanced around to make sure the women were still occupied with the movie. "We may have just hit the jackpot on gaining valuable information from the Mayor's right-hand man."

"Let's go." Sid rubbed his hands together. "The quicker we stop the roundup of half-breeds, the quicker Duncan can relax."

"I'm relaxed," Duncan replied. "No one will touch her." He looked toward Pam and the power of possessiveness in his stare let everyone know he meant exactly what he said. No one would touch Pam or their child.

"This is where it gets tricky." Sloan's eyes found Jill again. "This is going to fall on you, Jill. Are you up to it?"

"If she's not, I'll do it," Steve jumped in, his eyes and tone eager. "I'm ready to go with this stuff."

Sloan cocked an eyebrow at him. "You ready to strip in front of horny men?"

"What?" Steve's eyes popped open, his excitement dimming.

"What?" Slade growled, eyes narrowed, his attitude turning dangerous.

"Excuse me?" Jill's eyes found everyone looking at her; her dreams of becoming a Warrior vanished in front of her eyes.

Sloan ignored Steve and Slade, looking directly at Jill with no humor whatsoever in his gaze. "It seems the Mayor's right-hand man has a thing for the ladies at the Master's Gentlemen's Club."

"What does that have to do with me?" Jill frowned, breaking out in a cold sweat; she knew she had just asked a very stupid question, one she already knew the answer to.

"We need you on the inside," Sloan replied, ignoring Slade shaking his head. "The informant has overheard this man on several occasions bragging to the women about things I'm sure the piece-of-shit Mayor would not be happy about. I want to know everything, and you're the one who can find out."

"What exactly will I be doing?" Jill asked after taking a deep, calming breath.

Sloan was quiet for a second before answering, never once breaking eye contact with her. "This is a gentlemen's club, Jill." He seemed to sense Slade's barging in and pointed straight at him. "It is her choice," he warned.

"She's not even close to being ready for something like this," Slade's voice was loud and angry.

"Then she doesn't belong here," said Jax, who along with the rest of the Warriors, had been silent up until that point.

"You, shut the fuck up before I shut you up." Slade pointed at Jax, taking one step toward him.

"Both of you shut the fuck up," Sloan warned before pulling out his phone. "I have video of the club. You won't be alone. A Warrior will have you in sight at all times." He messed with his phone before handing it to her.

Well, there it was: her first big test. Holding the phone, she did everything in her power to stop her hands from shaking. She watched the video that was poorly done, but she could see enough to know she was in big trouble. The video scanned the club clumsily as if the person taking it was trying his best to hide the fact. Women were stationed throughout the dark club on round tables with stripper poles. Men sat around each pole staring up at the women, who surprisingly were in different modes of dress. Jill didn't realize the breath she held until it eased out in a relieved hiss at seeing none of the women were completely naked. The video cut off abruptly. Raising her eyes from the phone, she noticed everyone was staring at her. Handing the phone back to Sloan, she could only nod.

"So does that mean yes?" Sloan took the phone, maintaining eye contact.

Before she could answer, she noticed Tessa had come up to their circle. "Have you ever used a stripper pole?"

Jill shook her head. "No."

"As much as I hate to admit that Slade is right, but *he* is right." Jax crossed his arms. "She's not ready for this. I say find another way."

"How do you know they have stripper poles?" Jared frowned at Tessa, everything else forgotten in his mind.

"Everybody knows about the Master's Club." Tessa frowned back.

Jill's gaze shot to Jax, who stood staring at her with a cocky smirk. He expected her to back away from this mission and she'd be damned if she'd prove the asshole right. She looked back at Sloan. "When do I go?"

Slade hissed behind her, not happy with her choice. "Jill, these are professionals. You can't just go in there and wing it."

"I'll help her," Tessa replied, keeping her eyes averted from Jared.

Jared stepped into the middle of the group. "Excuse me." He held out his hand before anyone else could speak. "What the fuck do you know about strippers and poles?"

"We have a pole at the bar," Tessa said without thinking; even Jill's eyes popped open. Tessa laughed at all the shocked looks on everyone's face. "What?"

"*What?*" Jared growled, stalking toward her. "I hope for everyone's safety in that bar, you have not used that pole."

"Of course I have." Tessa tilted her head staring at him.

Before Jared could explode, Nicole walked up to stand next to Tessa. "So have I. What's the big deal?"

"What's the big deal?" Jared's laugh was not humorous at all. He looked toward Damon. "You going to help me out here, bro, or just glare them to death."

Jill watched the scene and smiled when Nicole winked at her. Her smile faded when she glanced up at Slade who frowned down at her with a sneer. Actually, all the Warriors were frowning and growling, even Sloan.

"Nicole, you better make that statement a little clearer before I go to that bar and beat the hell out of every male there," Damon's deep voice boomed throughout the room.

"What's the big deal?" Pam joined the group.

Duncan, who rarely said anything, snapped his head toward his mate. "Don't even say it."

"Say what?" Pam's head snapped toward him. "That I've used the stripper pole? Well, I hate to disappoint ya, but I've used a stripper pole, but not the one at Tessa's work."

A deafening roar erupted in the room making Jill jump closer to Slade. Sloan actually stepped in front of Duncan. "Step down, Duncan."

"If shit gets real and Warriors go wild, my ass is out the door," Steve whispered to Adam, who was looking at Angelina with a questioning look. When Angelina smiled and nodded, Steve took a step back from Adam. "Ah, shit."

Caroline laughed loudly along with Lana. Sid, who was grinning at what was going on concerning his brothers now dropped his grin, his fangs growing as he stared at Lana. "There's going to be a lot of dead men in the Cincinnati area." Sid's tone was deadly.

"Oh, my God, this is classic," Caroline laughed. "Tame down that testosterone, boys, before you blow the place up."

"Caroline," Sloan warned, shaking his head at her, but his eyes were on his Warriors who were about to go berserk with dominant force.

When the growls grew even louder, Caroline stepped into the middle of the angry crowd of Warriors. "Guys, seriously, get a grip. Do none of you remember the stripper pole craze?" When none of them answered, she sighed with a roll of her eyes. "It's a great way to get in shape. Women everywhere were learning the art of pole dancing to either get in shape or to seduce their man."

Jill grinned when Caroline looked at her then winked with a smug look.

"You know, if I was one of these women, I'd be pissed," Caroline continued, then glared at Sid. "Actually, I am pissed because you, the person who is supposed to keep my sister happy in all things, just accused her of being a stripper."

Sid's head snapped back, a comical look of shock crossed his face. "No, I didn't."

"Yes, you did." Caroline nodded along with all the other women, including Lana.

"You kind of did, bro," Steve spoke up then jumped behind Sloan when Sid snapped at him with his large fangs. "But I don't know shit so just don't listen to me."

"There is nothing wrong with strippers or stripper poles." Caroline ignored Steve, turning her attention to Jared, then the rest of the Warriors.

"We didn't say there was." Jared's face grew even angrier with frustration. "But if it's my woman up there on a stripper pole, then I have a big fucking problem with it."

"Even if she had to support herself," Caroline kept going, liking the fact she could shake these Warriors up a little. "Most of these women are hardworking and just trying to get by."

"She doesn't have to support herself." Jared pulled Tessa next to him, his arms wrapping around her. "At least not in that way because I will kill any son of a bitch who was dumb enough to even watch her."

"Jared, I'm not a stripper." Tessa laid her hand on his chest looking up at him. "And I haven't used the stripper pole since you. It's just a way the bar brings in money with contests and stuff. No one strips. Everyone has their clothes on."

50

Caroline's grin grew as she looked at Jill. "So, Jill, I think you have plenty of us here willing to help you on this mission."

Jill never wanted to hug anyone more in her life than she did these women who were all grinning at her. Glancing at Sloan, who was still on edge but looking at her and not the Warriors, she knew this mission would either prove to them how serious she was about becoming a Warrior, or be the biggest fail in her life to this point. "When do we do this?"

"Three days." Sloan nodded at her. "I will have everything in place by then."

"Won't she need to drive there?" Jax asked, staring at Jill, yet asking Sloan the question.

Jill looked up at Slade in horror. How did Jax know? Her gaze narrowed as she pinned first Adam then Steve with an 'I will kill you' look.

"Ah, yeah," Sloan replied, frustration blazing from his eyes. "I guess there's a reason behind your question, Jax."

"Well, yes, sir, there is." Jax looked away from Jill to Sloan. "She doesn't have a driver's license."

Sloan stared at Jax for a few seconds before running his hand down his face. "Did you know this, Buchanan?"

"Yes, I did and it's being taken care of," Slade replied in his deep voice, which sounded confident as if it was already taken care of.

"It fucking better be," Sloan growled, pointing at Jill then Slade.

Jax's sly grin spread across his face when he looked at Jill, pissing her off. He was trying to get her in trouble as well as Slade, and she wanted to know why. "What is your problem?" She took two steps toward him before Slade stopped her.

"Just stating facts," Jax replied, still grinning.

"Yeah, well, with all due respect, screw you and your facts." Jill pointed at him. "I'm going to make it whether you like it or not, and the more you push me, the more I'm going to sacrifice to make it."

Something flashed across Jax's face, but then it was gone. "Yeah, good luck with that."

"She's not your sister," Caroline, who had been watching closely, replied.

Jax's whole body stiffened, his eyes turned dark as if a shutter slammed across them. "What did you just say?"

"You heard me." Caroline didn't back down when he took a step closer to her. "And I'm not afraid of you because your sister said you'd never hurt me."

Jill witnessed for the first time since meeting the Warrior, who hated her for whatever reason, look unsure of himself. Slade positioned himself closer to Jax.

"Get out of my head," he hissed at Caroline, his eyes narrowed.

"I'm not in your head," Caroline countered. "She's in mine. Well, actually, she's not in my head, but standing right there." She nodded to a place between them.

Jill almost felt sorry for Jax as pain and uncertainty flashed across his face when he looked at the spot Caroline indicated, but it was gone just as quickly as it came, anger replacing it. "You are a liar!" He pointed in Caroline's face.

"Caroline," Sloan warned her with a shake of his head. "That's enough."

Jill wondered if Caroline would continue and wasn't surprised when she did.

"Alisha Wheeler is your sister's name, is it not?" Caroline didn't back down. She stood her ground staring directly at Jax who had finally dropped the finger he had pointed at her. When he didn't answer, she sighed. "I'm not a liar, Jax Wheeler, but your sister wants you to help Jill."

Jax stared at Caroline for what seemed like forever. Finally, he looked away to focus on Jill then back to Caroline. "Don't ever mention her name to me again." With that, he walked out, slamming the door so hard it broke off the hinges and would have hit Caroline if Sloan hadn't pulled her out of the way.

Chapter 6

Slade smiled as he left Duncan and Pam's room after giving little Daniel his check-up. Seeing the badass Warrior, Duncan, pacing nervously was definitely a sight to see. Daniel was doing fine and growing normally, as any other eight-month-old child would grow. Slade had been worried at first that Daniel would have an accelerated growth, but that wasn't the case. It puzzled him a great deal, but it was something he hadn't been able to figure out yet, just as he hadn't been able to figure out a lot of issues lately, namely Jill and his feelings toward her. Passing her room, he stopped, knowing she was in there, and the urge to knock on her door was overwhelming to the point he had to force himself to leave. It was a fight he was having with himself constantly. Hearing a loud bang come from her room, he turned around taking two steps back to her door, knocking loudly. He was ready to knock again after a few seconds before it opened.

"You okay?" he asked, looking over her head into her room.

"Yeah," she replied with a small nod.

Slade spotted the *Driver's Handbook* laying on the floor next to the door and immediately knew what the bang was he heard. Picking it up, he opened it to the question and answer page. "Unless posted, what is the speed limit in a residential area?" When Jill remained silent, Slade turned to look at her. "Jill?"

She stared at the book as if it was the devil himself. "Slow?" she replied, then frowned when he grinned. "I'm not stupid," she hissed.

"I didn't say you were," he shot back, feeling bad for grinning, but her answer was cute. "Slow is good, but would it be 35, 25..."

"I don't know." Jill walked to her bed, plopping down with a sigh. "This is such a waste of time. Even if I somehow pass, there is no way they are going to give a license to someone who is dyslexic. I can't even read the signs right."

54

Slade sat down in a roll away chair next to a small desk. Putting both elbows on his knees, he leaned toward her. "So the woman who is going to go into a Gentlemen's Club to dance is giving up on something as simple as this?" He held up the book.

"Simple for you." Jill's eyes were almost pleading with him to help her. "Impossible for me. Why can't I just drive? I mean, if I practice driving, I'll be fine."

"Because it's against the law." Slade cocked his eyebrow at her, and then sighed at her defeated look. "Listen, I don't know a lot about dyslexia, but I've done some research and I'm going to help you. You *will* pass the test."

"Why?" Jill's voice held the same shock her eyes relayed.

"Because I'm going to help you pass," Slade replied, not exactly understanding what she was asking. He stretched his legs out trying to get comfortable in the little chair, but it was no use. The chair wasn't made for his large frame. Standing up, he walked toward the bed. "Scoot over."

Jill did, still looking at him as he sat on her bed, leaning against the bedframe. "No, I meant why did you research dyslexia?"

Slade was looking through the book to see where to start when she questioned him. Looking up, his eyes met hers and he felt a protective need to grab her, just to let her know she wasn't alone. If he didn't know anything at all about her and her past with her family, he could still read the loneliness in her eyes and it hit him hard. He was attracted to her in ways that he had never been attracted to another woman, but he wasn't ready to admit that to anyone, even to himself.

"I was bored," his reply was serious, but his wink told another story. When she smiled, he felt as if he could conquer anything. Her smile was womanly with a mix of innocence and the innocence was what scared the hell out of him. He was way too jaded to do innocent. Shaking his head, he picked up the book.

"Time's running out. If we get this tonight, you can do your written test tomorrow."

"Tomorrow?" Jill moved and sat cross-legged on the end of the bed, facing Slade.

"Yeah, tomorrow." Slade started to say more, but Jill's door flew open and had him on alert.

"Hey you don't have to take that test." Steve burst into her room then stopped, his eyes widening at seeing Slade on her bed. "Ah, damn, my bad. I didn't know you guys were…well, you know." He turned around quickly.

"Slade is helping me study for the driving test." Jill rolled her eyes at Steve, who turned to peek over his shoulder.

"Oh, well ah…" Steve turned back around, his eyes going back and forth between the two.

"Steve, what the hell do you want?" Slade glared at him, not moving an inch from his position on the bed.

Snapping his head back to Slade, he raised his index finger before reaching into his back pocket. Pulling out a driver's license, he handed it to Jill. "Problem solved."

Jill stared at the driver's license then back to Steve. "Ah, this isn't me." Jill looked back at the license. "Who is this, Steve?"

"Maria Hernandez," Steve replied, looking proud of himself. "I got a deal on it."

Slade waved his hand, wanting to see the license. Jill handed it over and Slade stared down at a Mexican woman who was at least ten years older than Jill and looked nothing like her. "Jill isn't Mexican."

"No." Steve frowned, then gave a nod as if he just solved the world's problems. "But she's got dark hair."

Slade flicked the license back at Steve. "No."

"Ah, man." Steve caught the license, looking down at it. "I mean, it looks something like her. In a dark nightclub, no one would know the difference. Those guys don't check that close." He held the license up, looking from it to Jill.

"And if she gets pulled over by the cops?" Slade questioned, wanting to smack the kid upside the head, but in a weird way, he was trying to help Jill and that showed he cared.

Steve thought for a minute, then put the fake license back in his pocket. "Guess I wasn't thinking about that since I had mine to get into bars," Steve sighed. "I just know you have a hard time reading and wanted to help."

"Who told you that?" Jill frowned, shifting nervously on the bed.

"Adam." Steve walked over to sit next to Slade on the bed, but stopped half bent when Slade growled. Giving a nervous smile, Steve walked back over to where he had been. "He said you have Dys…ah…"

"Dyslexia," Jill finished for him, her voice tinged with a nervous edge. "And does anyone else know?"

"No, I mean I haven't said anything to anyone," Steve replied, shaking his head. "And I won't and I know Adam won't either."

"Sloan can't know." Jill bit her lower lip. "Or Jax. None of them can know."

"Chill, Jill." Steve snorted at his rhyme. "Your secret is safe with me."

"It better be or I'll kick your ass," Jill warned, giving him a glare.

"Hey! Trust me…babe." Steve pointed at himself, then grinned at the look Jill threw his way at being called babe. "So you guys need help? I'm an excellent driver."

"No." Slade stared at Steve, a small tick in his jaw. Steve calling Jill babe made him want to kick the shithead through a wall so it was best he leave and soon.

At first, Steve looked confused at the refusal of his help, but then a slow knowing grin spread across his face. "Ah, okay. I get it." He winked at Slade. "You don't have to tell me twice."

"Obviously, I do," Slade murmured, wondering if Steve would walk out of the room in one piece. The kid's mouth just kept going and going.

"You kids have fun." He winked again at Slade.

"Why do you keep winking?" Jill frowned. "You got a problem or something?"

Steve laughed. "Slade knows, don't ya, bro?" He winked again.

Yeah, he was going to have to kick the kid's ass. "Get the fuck out of here before I throw your ass out." Slade started to stand.

A comical look of horror flashed across Steve's face as he turned to head out the door; instead, he ran into it since it was still halfway open from when he flew into the room. "Ahhh…dammit." Steve grabbed his forehead. "Son of a bitch." He continued his cursing, holding his forehead while stumbling out the door.

"Shut the door!" Slade ordered loudly as Steve disappeared.

Steve reappeared, not looking at either of them, but moved his hand to close the door and a large red bump stood out on his forehead.

Once the door closed, Slade glanced at Jill who had her hand across her mouth, her eyes squinting in laughter. Slade's deep laughter filled the room and Jill's soon followed.

"He means well," Jill smiled.

"He's a pain in the ass." Slade growled, but with a grin as he opened the book once again.

"So am I," Jill countered, eyeing Slade under lowered lashes.

Slade looked up from the book, his eyes meeting hers. "Yes, you are."

******

Jill did her best to concentrate, but how in the hell was that possible with Slade lounging on her bed as if he belonged there. She had worked up enough nerve to lie across the end of the bed, her head resting on her hand as her eyes feasted on the large Warrior who read the questions and answers to the test she had to take tomorrow.

"What's the answer?" Slade looked at her from over the book, his golden eyes intense, yet they held a lazy appeal that was sexy as hell.

Shit, what's the question? Jill had no clue; she was too busy staring at him. "Ah, I don't know."

"Yes, you do," he answered, dropping the book to his lap, her eyes followed and she wished they hadn't. Damn, he was one hell of a man.

She had to get her mind back on track and off Slade. "No, I really don't."

"Did you even hear the question?" Slade frowned. "Because you have answered this question correctly every time I've asked."

Shaking her head, she frowned back. "Sorry, I didn't hear it."

"Then why didn't you say that?" Slade studied her hard, too hard.

What was she to say to that? 'I was too busy looking at your sexy eyes and listening to your voice', or maybe, 'the bulge in your pants is just too distracting'.' Yeah, she was screwed. "I don't know." She finally came out with that intelligent response.

"Jill, you have to pass this test tomorrow or Sloan is going to have my ass." Slade leaned away from the headboard to stare down at her. "What's the problem?"

Sitting up quickly, Jill tucked her legs up underneath her and looked him square in the eyes. "Maybe Jax is right. Maybe I'm not cut out to be a Warrior."

"Jax is a dumbass," Slade hissed, then reached out, cupping her chin to lift her face to his. "And you really don't mean that, do you?"

Searching his eyes, she shook her head. "No, but—"

"Listen, Jill."

The way he said her name made her sigh and when she did, she saw understanding cross his face. Dammit, what the hell was wrong with her? She might as well slobber all over him, that would be less evident.

"If I didn't have confidence that you could do this, I wouldn't be wasting my time. I know you have confidence that you can do it so I know that's not the problem. You had a rough-ass day and then everything that piled up on you after that is more than a lot of people can take, but I still don't think that's the problem." He let go of her chin, but didn't lean back. "So I suggest you come clean with what's going on."

She sat looking at him, wondering what Nicole, Tessa, Pam or Lana would do. Did they come right out and tell their Warrior they had the hots for them. This was new territory for her. Her eyes roamed from his golden stare to his neck with the large vein pulsing...bite me...to his wide shoulders, chest and even down...

"If you don't stop looking at me like that..." Slade's voice had grown harsh and deep. When her eyes shot to his, they had grown darker.

"Like what?" Jill asked innocently, even though she knew exactly how she had been looking at him. She couldn't help it. He was too handsome for his own good, and dammit, it wasn't fair. How was she supposed to look at him? Hell, she had even caught the other women glancing his way when they already have handsome Warriors who adore them.

He cocked his eyebrow at her, his grin curved his full lips. "Probably the same way I'm looking at you."

Okay, that confused her. He had made it clear to her and everyone else, there was and would never be anything between them, yet he was flirting with her. She was going to go insane soon and it was going to be all his fault. Not being able to sit still, Jill rolled off her knees and stood up, and then pointed at him. "You're driving me crazy."

"Good, because fair is fair." Slade kept his relaxed position on the bed, which only irritated her more.

"What does that mean? Fair is fair?" Jill threw her hands up, and then dropped them to the top of her head. "There is nothing fair about any of this. Okay?"

When he didn't say anything to that, but sat staring at her with that grin still in place, she dropped her hands to her sides, clenching her fists.

"What do you find amusing, Slade?" Jill's voice remained mostly calm, but her insides were going crazy, making her want to jump out of her own skin. "That the poor little half-breed wannabe Warrior can't even remember a question you asked because she was too busy staring at you wondering what it would be like to be kissed, and not just a little kiss, but *kissed* by you? Is that amusing to you? I'm screwed, so I'm not amused. You can have any woman out there, but for me there is not a man compared to you anywhere in this fucked-up world; so yeah, I'm screwed because I don't want any other man. I want you. Have wanted you since that first day you pulled Jeff off me and I turned to see you. Do you know how hard it is to be around someone you want so badly when all they do daily is remind me and everyone else there will never be anything between us? Well, it's harder than anything any one of the Warriors could throw at me during this damn initiation."

Jill stood in the middle of the room after her little rant, wondering where in the hell that came from and why the hell she let it spew from her mouth. Her gaze met Slade's and she wished she could suck every word right back into her stupid mouth. She had never seen him look more intense than he did at the moment, and his grin was absolutely gone.

"There. It's out in the open and nothing is left unsaid. Now you can go spread the word to the other Warriors and laugh at my expense, but no one can say I'm a coward for not saying what I feel." Jill tilted her head and when he still didn't say anything, just stared at her with that intense glare, she turned toward the door. "I'll leave you to stew on that...while I go kill myself," she whispered the last part, not really caring if he heard her or not.

Before she could open the door, his large hand appeared above her head keeping the door closed with his strength. Jill kept her face toward the door. She may not be a coward for saying what she said—stupid maybe, not a coward. No, the coward part came when it was time to face him.

"Turn around." It was a harsh demand that sent shivers down her spine in an erotic way. "Now!" he growled.

Jill did, but kept her eyes closed. She felt him all around her, his energy and power suffocating. Taking a deep breath, his unique smell hit her senses, making her shiver.

"Open your eyes and look at me, Jill." Slade's demand sounded far away. Slowly, she opened her eyes, bringing them up at a leisurely pace devouring his hard chest, thick corded neck, strong square jawline, full kissable lips, perfect nose and finally to his sexy eyes that were dark and searching.

"I didn't—" she whispered, but his words stopped her.

"Shut up." His demand cleared her foggy mind.

"Don't tell me to shut—" Her words were cut short as he slammed his mouth down on hers. Jill had been kissed, but never like this. Slade took total control with his mouth, tongue and body. He took her breath as he ravaged her with his lips. Suddenly afraid this would be the only kiss she would get from this Warrior, she sprang into action, kissing him back with the force of a woman starved for attention, his attention…only his.

Slade grabbed her jaw in a tight grip, pulling away, his breathing harsh. "I've wanted you, against my will, from the first moment I saw you. You have haunted me, but I'm warning you, Jillian, once you are mine, it will be body and soul. Do you understand me?"

Did she? Did she understand? Her nod said one thing, but her eyes reflected the uncertainty of his words.

"Fuck!" Slade pulled away, but didn't let her go. He looked above her head, taking deep breaths. "I don't think you are ready for a man like me." He laid his chin on top of her head. "I may ask too much of you, need too much from you."

Wishing she could see his face, Jill pulled back. "No one has ever needed anything from me, Slade. I need to be needed." She drew in a shaky breath. "I need you."

"Do you know what dominance is, Jill?" His glanced down at her, his eyes still searching for something Jill prayed she could give him.

Understanding finally evaded her brain. "Yes, I do..." She looked into his eyes, then with a small smile added, "Sir." She may not be able to read, but she loved books and listened to audios anytime she could find the time and thank God, for that and Cherise Sinclair.

His growl at her response sent sensations through her body almost scaring her with the intensity. "I'm very demanding behind closed doors," Slade warned, his breath hot against her face.

"Are you trying to scare me off?" Jill asked, her hand grasping his shirt in an attempt to show him it wasn't working.

"Yes, I am." Slade cursed again managing to pull out of her grip, but kept his eyes on her, looking torn.

"You either want me or you don't, Slade." Jill stood there, terrified of what he was going to see if he looked too hard.

"Oh, there is no doubt I want you, Jill." He grabbed her hand placing it on his hard cock that was pressing to be free. He bent down, tilting his head to see her better. "Does that scare you?"

"No, it doesn't." She pressed her hand harder against him as she tilted her head mocking him. "Does that scare *you*?"

Slade totally pulled away as if her touch burned him. "You're playing with things you don't understand."

"No, actually, you're the one playing, Warrior." Jill knew without a doubt he could walk out that door right now, but her mind and body couldn't take much more. She was either going to go insane or up in flames; hell, she might do both. "I said what I had to say, even as embarrassing as it was, but I fucking said it. Now, it's your turn."

When he remained silent, the tick in his jaw beat a frantic pulse as he glared at her.

Taking off her shirt, she threw it at him. He just stood as it hit his chest and fell to the floor. The only thing that moved was his eyes as they caressed her body. "And I repeat...you either want me or you don't." Inside, she prayed he wanted her. If not, she was pretty confident she would die. His silence might kill her anyway. "Say something, dammit!"

Her words seemed to snap him out of it. "Fuck!" With a curse, he made his way past her toward the door. Jill watched, her heart sinking to her stomach as angry tears threatened to explode from her eyes.

"You bastard," Jill's words quivered as she turned her back on him. She couldn't stand seeing him walk out the door. She grabbed the nearest object ready to throw it at the closed door, but stopped when she heard the loud sound of the lock clicking.

"Let's get one thing straight, Jillian." Slade's deep voice washed over her like a caress. Whenever he used her full name, her insides shook. "If you ever threaten to kill yourself, even in a teasing manner or call me names again, I will blister your ass."

Only turning her head, she peeked over her shoulder. Her eyes going from the lock to him, something inside her that she didn't know existed came to the surface, a sexy half-grin formed on her lips. "Promise?" Even her voice sounded different to her own ears. She knew without a doubt she was playing with fire. As he grabbed her pulling her to him, her body became supersensitive, her skin and insides felt electrified. This had to be what heaven felt like.

Chapter 7

When Lana and Sid started whispering to each other, Caroline knew it was time to go. After a great night of hanging with her sister and the other girls watching *Gladiators* on television and in real life, so to speak, it was time for her to go. Smiling, she watched the way her sister reacted to Sid. She had never seen Lana so happy with a man, and Sid, what could she say about him other than he openly adored her twin sister and the family loved him, as did she.

Envy heated her chest, but Caroline pushed it away. She was happy like that once, but that had all changed in the face of Rod's lies. Her family was everything to her, but Rod never took to her sister or their gift. It scared him, so Caroline had pushed it down, telling everyone that her gift frightened her. In truth, it did frighten her, but she had learned to deal with it. Her phone went off, making her jump. Glancing at it quickly, she frowned, clicking the ignore button. She had blocked Rod's number, but he would borrow someone's phone and call from a different number. She knew it was him because she never received unknown numbers on her cell phone before.

"Hey!" Lana walked up behind her. "Was that Mom?"

Startled, she dropped her bag. "Ah, no." Caroline hoped to get out of there before her sister could interrogate her further, knowing Lana she would go hunting for her ex. "Why? You need to me to tell her anything?"

"Yeah." Lana stared at her for a few seconds. "Tell her we can do dinner Wednesday."

"Will do." Caroline smiled, giving Lana a quick kiss on the cheek before rushing toward the door. "Thanks for the movie."

"Caroline," Lana stopped her, "is Rod bothering you?"

"I've got it under control, Lana." Caroline finger-waved to Sid who gave her a wink from across the room where he was talking to Damon and Nicole. Ignoring Lana's frown, she didn't even look her way as she headed out of the room calling out over her shoulder, "Now, I gotta go. See ya Wednesday."

Once out of the room, Caroline let out a long breath. Almost making it to the door, she heard the beautiful, soothing, but faint sound of a guitar. Tilting her head, she looked up the steps that led to the living quarters. Taking a glance around, she looked back up the steps to see Jax's sister on the stairs looking down at her. Knowing now who was playing, she made her way to the steps and began to climb. His sister faded from sight as Caroline made it down a few mazes of hallways and doors before the music became louder. Standing outside the door, Caroline leaned quietly against the wall, listening to the beautiful strumming, wondering how in the world she had heard it from downstairs, but she was glad she did. She could actually feel her nerves ease, making her feel light and slightly sleepy, almost to the point she jumped a mile high when a deep male voice boomed from behind the door, "Are you going to stand outside my door all night or knock?"

Caroline glared at the door before rolling her eyes. She didn't really want to knock, but if it would get him to play again, she would do it. Raising her hand, she started to knock, but the door flew open before her hand made contact.

"What?" Jax's tone was not pleasant as he looked down at her. He stuck his head out the door, looking up and down the hallway.

She didn't expect a shirtless Jax to open his door, but there he was. Beautiful tattoos covered his upper body. Her eyes followed the patterns. Holy wow, he was a sexy specimen. She wondered briefly what each tattoo meant, because, knowing the intense Warrior, he didn't do things without a lot of deep thought.

"More messages from my dead sister?" he asked, his tone taunting as he looked down at her. "Or are you just going to stare?"

Color bloomed across her cheeks as a lie built inside her head and almost made it out of her mouth, but she pulled it back. She had to understand that most people were not going to be so accepting of her gifts, especially if it was painful. As she looked into his golden eyes, she saw a glimpse of pain brought on by the words he spoke of his sister. "Listen, I'm sorry about that," Caroline, who rarely apologized, apologized. "I shouldn't have blurted out in front of everyone about your sister. I should have warned you first."

"Yes, you should have," Jax agreed. "Not that I believe in all that bullshit."

Caroline glared at him before turning away from his door. "Whatever." She headed down the hall. "I apologized and I couldn't care less if you believe it or not."

"Wait a minute," Jax called out. "Is that the only reason you came up here?" There was suspicion in his tone.

Being a teacher who faced a room full of kids ready to call you out on anything and everything, nothing much fazed Caroline, but this man's attitude did, and not in a good way. "You know what," Caroline turned around and walked back toward him, "actually, that wasn't the reason I came up here at all. I heard the guitar and thought it was beautiful."

A small grin played at the corner of Jax's full mouth. "So your apology meant…?"

"Absolutely nothing." Caroline tilted her chin. "It's what I do. It's what my sister and I do. I fought it for a while and that got me into a world of trouble, changing my life. So yeah, I'm not sorry."

Jax leaned against the doorframe, crossing his arms. "School teachers shouldn't lie."

Now that surprised her. "How did you know I was a school teacher?"

"Not the fancy way you find out things about people like talking to the dead." He cocked his eyebrow at her. "I asked Sid."

"Actually, you did do exactly what I do," Caroline replied in her best teacher tone. "Sid is technically dead."

Jax's laugh boomed through the hallway. "Not only beautiful and smart, but quick with humorous comebacks."

Caroline felt herself blushing, and then cursed at herself. She couldn't afford being attracted to anyone right now, especially a gorgeous jackass like Jax Wheeler. "Just stating a fact."

Nodding, Jax stared at her with his intense golden gaze. "So was bringing my sister up just stating facts also?"

Not really knowing what he meant by that, Caroline frowned. "No, actually, it was because you were being so hard on Jill." Caroline leaned up against the wall across from him. "Whether you like it or not, Jill is not going to stop. Lana has told me a lot about the girl and it takes a lot to impress my sister, but Jill has. I know what happened with your sister, Jax, and it wasn't your fault, but if you continue your campaign against Jill, which I think even you know is bullshit, it will be your fault if something happens to her. She needs your support."

Jax straightened away from the wall during her little speech and was leaning over her. He didn't look happy. "First of all, *teach*, you don't know shit about what happened in my past." He slammed one hand on the wall next to her head, leaning in. "And Jill has plenty of support."

Not one to be intimidated, Caroline slammed her hand on his chest and pushed. When he stepped back, she knew it was his decision to do so because he was nothing but solid muscle and her small push wouldn't have budged him unless he wanted to be budged. "Your sister was killed during initiation into the VC Warriors over 200 years ago. You also had a younger brother, but he didn't go through with the initiation." Caroline didn't stop at the shocked look on his face. "There was nothing you could do. She made her choice to follow her big brother into the program. You did everything you could to help her."

"And it still wasn't enough." Jax frowned, and then glared at her. "Women do not belong in this program. They are liabilities."

Caroline really looked at Jax, seeing the man behind the anger. His dark Native American looks and badass attitude almost had her fooled, but she saw a glimpse into his past through his sister and this was a good man, whether he wanted to admit it or not. "No." She took a step toward him. "The person, whether male or female, who doesn't believe in someone is the liability, because that small feeling of doubt a person gets in themselves during a time of the tests comes not from themselves, but the doubts someone put in their mind."

Jax shook his head. "What in the hell are you talking about?"

Tilting her head, she looked up at him, wondering which Indian tribe he came from. He was a damn handsome man and smart, so she knew he knew exactly what she was talking about. "The more you put Jill down, give her a hard time, the more you put doubts in her head. When it comes down to it, you are her liability. She is no one's liability."

Surprise flashed across his face, but soon disappeared. "What do you teach?"

"History. And I sure would like to talk to you about your past." Caroline smiled at deepening frown on his full lips. She decided since he was changing the subject, she would too. "Why didn't your brother go through with the initiation? Alisha doesn't talk about him much, but—"

"My brother is dead to me." Jax's eyes turned dark with something Caroline figured was a deep anger. "Seems you know more than you should about my past as it is," Jax grumbled.

"Not even close." Caroline's smile turned into a full-blown grin.

"Don't worry. I won't ask your sister anything and I haven't. She has given me all this information voluntarily."

Her phone rang at that moment and the ring tone was unfamiliar, so she knew who it was. She did her best to ignore it.

"You going to answer that?" Jax frowned down at her bag where the ringing was coming from.

"No," Caroline replied, hefting the bag further on her shoulder. The ringing stopped, only to start again. Rolling her eyes, she dug into her purse pulling out her phone. "It's just my ex."

"He giving you a hard time?" Jax eyed the phone, which she turned to silent.

"Nothing I can't handle." She tossed it back into her purse, dismissing the phone and Rod without a second thought. "So are you going to stop giving Jill a hard time and start helping her?"

"You're pushy." Jax glared down at her, leaning back against the doorframe.

"Very," she nodded in agreement, her eyes not leaving his. "She needs all of you behind her, Jax. And your sister is not going to leave me alone until you do."

Jax looked away from her, and then a small grin tipped his lips. "If you have dinner with me, I'll think about it."

Caroline snorted, but her stomach dipped at the thought of having dinner with this man. "And you really think I would agree to have dinner with you for you just to think about it?"

"Yes." The tilted smirk Jax gave her was full of confidence that she would agree.

"Well, obviously, you don't know me very well," Caroline countered back. Her phone, which she turned silent, started to buzz and vibrate. She watched his eyes move to her purse then back up to her.

"You want me to answer that for you?" he asked, a look of irritation narrowed his eyes. "I'm sure I could help you with *that* problem."

"No, it's fine," Caroline lied, but there was no sense getting everyone involved in her issues with Rod. It was over and he would soon get tired of being ignored and go away. "But I do have a deal for you. If you stop harassing Jill—"

"I am not harassing Jill," Jax corrected her.

Caroline rolled her eyes at him. "Oh, okay then. When you stop *provoking* Jill and start helping her, teach me how to play guitar and, then I will have dinner with you." Biting her lip, she wondered what he thought about her second stipulation. She had always wanted to learn to play guitar. She actually had an old acoustic guitar in the back of her closet. Jax laughed. The deep timbre of his voice washed over her and she suddenly found herself wanting to see him laugh more often. She surprised herself when she realized she wanted it to be her who made him laugh.

"I'm not provoking either," Jax laughed again. "I'm being realistic."

"In your own mind maybe." Caroline cocked her eyebrow at him. "You like her."

"And you know me so well that you know that as a fact," Jax sparred with her some more, seeming to enjoy matching wits with her.

"I do," Caroline nodded, also liking their banter. "If you didn't, you wouldn't care whether she was a liability or not, which she's not."

"No, I'm the liability." His tone was disbelieving.

"Yes, now you're getting it," Caroline grinned, and then frowned when her phone buzzed again. In one long stretch, Jax reached into her purse expertly locating her phone. Flipping it open, his eyes met hers.

"Hello!" Jax's tone was tolerant, not nasty, but definitely not nice. "You called this phone so why don't we start out by you telling me who you are and why you are constantly ringing this phone."

Caroline threw her hands up in the air, looking at Jax in disbelief. She was actually amazed he found it so quickly when it usually took her minutes of searching through all her crap to find it. When he continued to stare at her while listening to the other end, her stomach knotted up. This wasn't going to be good.

"Rod? Did you say your name was Rod?" Jax made a face at Caroline as if saying 'you dated a guy named Rod'. Then he snorted. "I bet you're a muscle head. You go to the gym? Ah, that's what I thought." Jax looked proud of himself for calling that one.

She could hear Rod's voice through the phone and he didn't sound happy. Damn, this probably just complicated her plan of ignoring him. Now, he was going to be more persistent. Shaking her head at Jax and reaching for the phone only caused Jax to turn slightly so she couldn't reach it, unless she went into his room since that's where he stuck his head. "Dammit."

"Well, listen, Rod. I don't give two shits you and Caroline were engaged. She obviously doesn't want to talk to you and I've taken it upon myself to warn you to stop calling her. If she wants to talk to you, she will call you." Jax's smile turned sinister. "Yes, I can back that warning up. Have no doubts about that."

Taking her phone back that Jax handed her, she put it in her purse then looked up at him. She cleared her throat, trying to think of what to say.

"So you can dish out advice, but dated a guy named Rod." Jax saved her from saying anything at all.

"He was my fiancé." Caroline didn't know why she threw that bit of information out there, but the way he was looking at her made her feel like one of her school kids.

Raising both eyebrows, he nodded. "Well, it sounds like it's not a big loss on your part."

"Yeah, he treated my sister pretty bad." Caroline frowned, not proud of the fact she had no clue how much Rod had tried to run her life and separate her from her twin until it was almost too late. "It took me a while, but I figured it out, and well, just dealing with the end results of a failed relationship."

"It happens," he replied, still staring at her with those intense eyes.

"Yeah, it does," she nodded with a frown. "And I have no idea why I'm talking to you about this."

Jax didn't say a word, just stood in the same pose against the door looking relaxed, yet she had no doubt he was ready to take anything head-on in a minute flat. It was pretty intimidating, especially as he continued to stare at her.

"Okay, well, I need to be going." Caroline gave him a short smile before turning.

"Dinner. Wednesday." It wasn't a question. "I'll pick you up at seven."

"You're going to be nice to Jill?" Caroline looked back at him, wanting to see his face when he answered.

"A saint." His grin was far from saintly.

Caroline snorted. "Let's not overdo it. I don't think you've done saintly…ever and I'm warning you I will ask Jill, so you better be nice or the deal is off." Caroline pointed at him like she would a student in trouble. She eyed him a few more minutes before adding, "My address is—"

"I don't need it." Jax smiled at her shocked look.

"Okay, that's creepy." She bit her lip in thought. She didn't need another Rod.

"I'm a Warrior, nothing creepy about it. I just have access to a lot of stuff, your address being one of them." Jax grinned when she looked relieved. "You need to watch your back with him," Jax warned, turning more serious.

"He's just annoying," Caroline replied, heading down the hallway. "He'll stop when I don't respond and find someone else."

"Definitely his loss." Jax's words hit her as she made her way to the end of the hallway.

Caroline stopped and turned, but Jax was gone. Okay, maybe she hadn't really heard that last part or maybe she just wished he felt that way and she heard the words in her subconscious mind. He was one hell of a man who she wouldn't mind forgetting about Rod with. Taking off down the steps, she smiled then wiggled her eyebrows. Hell, men did it all the time, so what was wrong with her doing it with Jax Wheeler. Damn, she had to go shopping. One did not dress like a school teacher when going out with a man like him.

Chapter 8

Jill didn't want to breathe as Slade enveloped her with his body. Her back to his front, he snaked his arm around her bare waist, pulling her tightly against him. His head bent as his other hand reached up to the side of her face, tilting her head so he could bring his lips against her temple, down her cheek to her jawline and finally to her neck where he nipped, then licked. Her body exploded with feelings of intense pleasure making her toes curl into the carpet. The deep moan coming from within her throat sounded foreign to her own ears. "Slade," she whispered.

His fingers brushed underneath her bra line, teasing her mercilessly. "What does a flashing yellow light mean?" he whispered in her ear before taking her lobe into his mouth.

Jill tilted her head, giving him easier access. "What?" she replied in a breathless whisper, but then his words hit her, making her eyes pop open wide. "What?!" She tried to turn toward him, but he stopped her.

"Stay where you are," he demanded in a tone that meant business. His hand moved from under her breast, running slowly yet with pressured heat down her stomach, over the snap of her jeans and closer to the spot on her body that wanted this man most, and stopped. "What does a flashing yellow light mean?"

"Are you kidding me?" Jill moaned, almost in tears. Dammit, he was so close, so damn close. When he didn't answer, she started to panic. Oh, God, what did a flashing…what color did he say…ah, shit this was not happening. She finally had Slade where she wanted him, with his hands all over her, and he's wanting to quiz her on driving. "Can we please finish that after?"

"After what, Jill?" Slade didn't move his hand, but added pressure, making her moan. "After I make you scream with passion you never knew existed?"

Jill wanted to laugh and cry at the same time. "Oh, God, yes." She tried to slowly raise on her toes so his hand would move down closer to the throbbing nub that needed his attention so badly.

Slade did move his hand lower, but only to smack her lightly, making her cry out, but not in pain. "Do not move." His demand was spoken in clipped tones. "Answer the question or I'm going to tie you to your bed and leave until you remember the answer."

She could feel his hard cock against her back. She had to make herself stay still so not to rub up against him. Okay, that was stupid as hell. If she moved against him, he would smack her through her jeans again, because fuck that felt so damn good. She ground against his hardness waiting for ecstasy to follow, but his hand remained still as his lower body moved away.

"I know what you're doing, Jillian," he bent, whispering in her ear. "I may not be able to read your mind, but I sure as hell can read your sweet body. Now answer the question." After a second, he pulled her back into him again; this time he ground against her ass, his hand staying still as if super glued to the damn spot. He kept grinding in perfect timing, knowing when she was about to go over the edge and then stopped, moving away.

Not knowing whether to use her strength to pull away from him and attack—meaning rip his clothes off and go for it—or just get her mind straight and answer the damn question. Jill struggled against his hold because she couldn't remember the damn color he said. His grip was too tight. Slade was way too strong for her to break free. Her eyes slit open in frustration and when she was ready to scream, her eyes landed on the fabric of a yellow shirt that stuck out of her drawer. "Slow down," she screamed in excitement. "Yellow flashing lights means slow down."

His deep chuckle reached her foggy mind as her body waited impatiently for his touch. Her body wasn't disappointed. His hand moved, cupping her as his fingers worked magic against her jeans. Her head fell back against his chest, using him as leverage to stay upright. Her own hand reached down to unsnap her jeans, but his free hand grasped it, keeping it prisoner against her stomach. Her moan of frustration and pure pleasure seemed to please him. Damn him.

"Good girl." His voice broke through her thoughts that were rushing ahead thinking of him inside her. "Who has the right of way at a crosswalk? The driver or the pedestrian."

Jill growled her displeasure at being asked a question during the most erotic experience she had ever had. "Slade, please."

"Hmmm, I like when you say please," Slade growled back. "Now answer the question." His hand kept moving against her with expert ease.

"Pedestrian," Jill breathed out. Then her body jolted when his hand stopped and moved up to her breasts. Within seconds, he had the bra off her, his hand cupping her breast, but nothing more. "Dammit, you're killing me."

Slade bit the side of her neck and when she turned her head toward him, he took her mouth with a hot, overbearing kiss. "This is nothing, Jillian," he warned against her mouth. "We can stop anytime."

"If you stop, I'll die," Jill answered, and then took his mouth back, kissing him deep and hard.

"So if I keep going, I'm killing you, and if I stop, you will die." Slade's mouth turned up in an arrogant grin.

"You don't have to be so smug," Jill frowned, trying to move her body so his hand would move and not just cup her breast. "But yes, either way, I'm going to die, but it will be an awesome death."

He reached up to pinch her nipple with enough pressure to send pings of pleasure throughout her body, which stopped at her pulsing pussy. "I told you not to move."

"Sorry." Her moan indicated she was anything but sorry.

Slade continued with his questions with Jill answering right every time, when she could remember the question. By the time he was done, she was completely naked and plastered against his clothed body. He had finally let her turn around to face him. Jill watched as Slade took his shirt off, tossing it to the side. Her hands went to reach up to touch his hard, ripped stomach, but stopped, her eyes meeting his, asking permission.

"You don't need permission to touch me, Jillian." His voice wrapped around her.

"Thank God." She smiled at his masculine chuckle, her hands moving to his hard ripped stomach, up his chest and back down. She could spend hours touching him, feeling his rippling muscles beneath her hands, something she never thought she would experience. She could hardly believe she was standing in front of Slade Buchanan, Dr. Slade Buchanan, naked and enjoying his body. Her own body quivered at the thought of what else was to come. Glancing up, she caught his dark gaze. "Is my eye as black as yours?"

He growled with a nod, staring into her mismatched half-breed eyes. "And I've never seen anything sexier."

Her hands continued to explore and took a chance as they headed toward his jeans. She hoped with everything that he wouldn't stop her, and that he was commando. Luck was on her side. He didn't stop her, and as she unzipped his tight jeans, her wish of commando came true. Her eyes widened as more of him was revealed. Pulling her eyes away from his large cock, she swallowed hard looking up at him. "Holy shit."

Slade growled and laughed at the same time. "Music to a man's ears." He pulled her up as he kicked his jeans the rest of the way off. Pulling her toward him, he kissed her hard, his tongue working in and out of her mouth in a show of what was to come. He walked her backward to the bed where he laid her down. He stood above her, his eyes searching hers before roaming her body. "Open for me."

Not wasting any time, Jill slowly opened her legs, raising her arms up above her head giving Slade absolute power over her.

******

Slade had to clench his fists to keep from grabbing Jill and pounding into her soft flesh. Son of a bitch, she was so ready for him. She was shaking with need, as was he. Calling upon every single bit of self-control he had, Slade reached out, grabbing both of her legs, and pulling her closer to the end of the bed. His mind and body called for full domination over her and he would dominant her, but carefully. She was like no other woman he had ever had and he'd do well to remember that. He wasn't a true Dom and didn't want a slave, but he was very demanding in the bedroom and wanted his orders obeyed during sex. Only certain women could handle that and he hoped Jill was one of them. So far, she seemed more than up for the challenge, and in some crazy way, that scared the hell out of him.

Running his hands up her soft thighs, his fingers hit her core. She was more than ready for him, dripping ready. Always being in control, Slade felt that control slip at the feel of her wetness. His eyes shot to hers and that's all it took for his control to slip totally away. Her eyes, half opened, begged him for everything that he could give her. He wanted to shout out a warning to her, that she didn't know what she was asking. His selfish side took over, as he—without thought other than being deep inside her—pulled her to him, his rock hard cock sliding into her tightness with mind-blowing resistance.

"Fuck!" he growled in pleasure, his fangs growing as he pushed past her sweet tightness. She wasn't a virgin, but son of a bitch, she was as tight as one.

"Music to a woman's ears," she purred, throwing his words back at him.

Slade hovered over her, placing one hand on the bed as the other went under her ass. His plunging didn't start out slow and sweet, but hard and thrusting. To his surprise, he didn't have to bring her up to meet his demanding thrusts; she kept up on her own, thrusting right back at him with more passion than he'd ever experienced. Taking his hand off her sweet ass, he placed his hands on each side of her head, and spread his legs apart more so he could thrust with everything he had.

The sounds coming from her turned him on as no other woman ever had. Her body moved against his, her hands touching him everywhere and something snapped inside him, his control totally vanished. Leaning his head back, he continued to pound into her soft, hot body; nothing else mattered, but finding release. His fangs fully exposed, the thirst hit him hard as his black eyes snapped to her breast. Without thinking, his head swooped down. His mouth opened, clasping across the fullness of her left breast. As his fangs sank into her tender flesh and a scream left her lips, he didn't stop…couldn't stop. He continued pounding, and sucked her warm blood down his throat, the erotic flavor going straight to his cock, stretching her wider. Suddenly, he let go of her breast as his spine stiffened and his cock emptied into her hot, sweet tightness.

That's when the door went flying off its hinges. "What the fuck?!"

Slade shielded Jill as he grabbed for his gun he had within reach. Turning, he aimed it right between Sid's eyes. "Get the fuck out of here." Slade roared his rage at being interrupted.

Sid looked him over, his frown growing. "Jill!"

"I'm fine, Sid." Jill rolled her eyes as she tried to pull the sheet over her body, but Slade's knees were on it.

When Lana walked up behind Sid, Slade lifted the barrel of the gun toward the ceiling. "Jesus." Lana looked shocked staring at Slade's black eyes and bloodied mouth. "Where in the hell did that blood come from?"

"I'm going to give you one second to get the fuck out of this room before I start shooting." Slade's tone was beyond pissed, his eyes narrowing in on Sid.

"Don't threaten me while my mate is in the room." Sid took an angry step toward Slade.

"Lana, please get him out of here," Jill's voice called out from behind Slade's body. "I'm perfectly fine, embarrassed as hell, but fine."

"Come on." Lana pulled at Sid.

Sid pointed at Slade. "You better not have hurt her."

"Fuck you!" Slade sneered.

"Me and you are going to have a talk." Sid pointed back at himself and then back at Slade.

"You got that right, motherfucker," Slade growled, his body still protecting Jill.

"Get out!!" Jill yelled as she eased herself off Slade's softening cock, which wasn't really soft at all and that in itself gave her pause, but then she remembered what was going on. "I'm a grown ass woman, Sid Sinclair, and don't need you running into my room without knocking."

"Well, excuse the fuck out of me! I hear banging and screaming coming from your room and thought maybe, just maybe you might need help." Sid tried to peek around Slade to look at Jill. Slade clicked the trigger in warning, the gun lowering to Sid.

"For shit's sake, Sid." Lana pushed him out the door, and then turned to try to close the door, but it wouldn't close. "Ah, I'll stand out here to make sure no one comes in until you're ready." Lana's eyes went to Slade's ass.

"Lana!" Sid growled. "I'm close to killing the son of a bitch. Do not push me over the edge."

"Oh, calm down." Lana's voice faded as they moved further down the hallway. "You know I only have eyes for your ass."

Slade's chest heaved with effort as he tried to control himself. Turning, he looked at Jill who had distanced herself from him and covered up with the sheet. His eyes searched her before seeing the blood seeping through the whiteness of the sheets. Grabbing it, he yanked it down to see two puncture wounds bleeding freely. "Dammit." Slade reached for her, lifting her so he could lick the wounds closed.

Jill smiled up at him, wrapping her arms around his neck. When he reached around unclasping her arms, she shook her head. "Don't do this." Jill's voice shook.

"Do what?" Slade tossed the sheet over her, and then got off the bed, grabbing his pants.

"Push me away." Jill sat back on her knees letting the sheet fall away unashamed. "That was…"

"Something that shouldn't have happened," Slade finished for her as he jerked his pants on, careful not to rip his manhood off. Picking up his gun, he tucked it in the back of his waistband before grabbing his shirt and putting it on. "Did I hurt you?"

"When? Now or before?" Jill asked, shooting him a nasty glare.

"You know exactly what I'm talking about," Slade hissed, tossing her bra and shirt at her.

"No, you didn't hurt me." Jill sat, holding her things.

"Put your clothes on before someone else comes barging in your room," Slade growled, tossing her underwear and jeans at her.

"What do you care?" Jill angrily snapped on her bra and pulled her shirt on, her underwear was next. "You got what you wanted, right?"

"And what the fuck is that supposed to mean?" This time he did look at her. Slade knew without a doubt, he needed to go cool off and think before he did or said something he would regret.

"Good thing Sid did bust ass into my room, huh?" Jill kept going, wiggling into her pants. "Gave you an excuse to push me aside with your pissed-off attitude."

"Dammit, Jill," Slade warned, watching as she buttoned her pants.

"Go on." Jill tossed him his boots. "Get out. Go like you want to. High five Sid on the way out, you asshole. You're just like everyone else in my life."

That did it. That pissed him off more than Sid breaking into her room. Grabbing her, he snapped her around, his face inches from hers. "I never promised you anything."

"I didn't say you did," Jill shot back, trying to pull away from him. "But you're ready to hightail it out of here, aren't you? At least fake it and stay for two seconds."

"I'm not like them, Jillian," Slade growled, wanting to kiss her, but knew it would be a mistake. He had to think, get his shit straight and beat the fuck out of Sid. He gave her one last look. "I'm nothing like them."

"Then prove it and stay." Jill's eyes begged him, but her body language said she didn't give a shit whether he stayed or went.

With a sigh, Slade picked up his boots and put them on. "I have to take care of some things."

"Yeah, you do that, Warrior," Jill called out as he left the room, trying to sound tough, but Slade heard every hurt she'd ever suffered in each word.

With each step, he moved faster. Seeing Sid standing at the end of the hallway with a nasty expression aimed his way, Slade found his outlet. Passing Lana, the Slade Train tackled Sid with force, sending them down a flight of steps.

Slade knew his control was gone, but he didn't care. Sid was right to be concerned about Jill, but he also knew Sid could take his anger, and honestly, he was afraid not to unleash it. Jax was the first to get to Sid and Slade, passing Lana down the steps. Sloan met him, grabbing Sid as Jax grabbed Slade.

"What in the hell is going on now?" Sloan bellowed, pushing Sid back when he went toward Slade again. "Sid, I swear if you don't calm the fuck down I'm going to knock you out."

Slade snapped out of Jax's hold, swiping his hair out of his face. "Nothing is going on." Slade glared at Sid, giving him a warning look. He knew if Jill's name was brought up then it would be bad for her. Relief rushed over him when Sid caught on.

"Yeah, nothing." Sid wiped the blood from his mouth, his gaze never leaving Slade. "Just a misunderstanding."

Sloan looked at each of them. "This is it!" he demanded. "I don't want any more of this shit happening between my Warriors. Is that understood?"

"Yeah, understood." Slade nodded, turning to walk away.

"Got it," Sid replied when Sloan looked at him with his 'you better give the right answer' look.

"Hold up, Buchanan," Sloan yelled out, and then looked at Jax. "I got the paintball arena to agree to let you guys go in during business hours today. Be there by eleven this morning and make damn sure no citizen gets hurt or it's your ass."

Slade looked down at his watch and cursed. That was only two hours away. "Shit."

"Is that a problem?" Sloan asked, his tone clearly indicating he didn't give a shit if it was.

"Yeah, is that a problem?" Sid growled, being a total asshole.

"No problem." Slade walked out of the room without turning around. If he had, he would have killed Sid, and no one would be able to stop him.

Chapter 9

Jill rode in the back of Adam's car, her mood at a dangerous level. She was hurt, pissed and tired. Not a great combination for her at all. Someone had called a contractor and a new door was in the process of being put up in her room. Damn Sid, she could kill him, but then again, what happened with her and Slade afterwards may have happened anyway. Sid just gave Slade an excuse.

"What the hell is going on?" Adam slowed down.

Not having paid much attention, Jill looked out the window, anger churning her stomach to the point she felt nauseous. The building where they were holding half-breeds loomed ahead, the tall wrought iron fence making the place look more menacing. Cop cars with their blues flashing lined the street. People were outside the fence holding signs and screaming toward the building in protest.

"Sunglasses on!" Adam slipped his on as Steve and Jill followed. "Son of a bitch."

Jill watched as everyday people stood outside the fence yelling for their loved ones. Police patrolled with a nervous hand on their guns. Adam stopped at a red light and all three of them stared, watching the chaos outside their car. Her eyes searched beyond the fence looking for the bitch, Alice, and the Mayor, but all she saw were guards or what she thought were guards looking alert.

The light turned green and Adam started to pull away. Jill's eyes caught on an older lady falling to her knees in front of a police officer, her hands together as if she was begging for something. The cop just shook his head and walked away. The woman's head dropped in defeat, her shoulders shaking.

"Somebody needs to get inside." Jill looked away from the woman, back to the building. It was a large block building. She noticed something new…a sign had been added since they had been there last. Vomit thick and sour rose to the back of her throat as she read.

'Eastern Halfway House'. "Halfway house? That's not a halfway house, it's a freaking prison where they do God knows what to half-breeds," Jill spat, disgusted.

"Just keep those sunglasses on." Adam pressed on the gas pedal and he took off, slowly, passing police who were looking into cars.

"You think they'll catch on since it's cloudy as hell and we all have sunglasses on?" Steve snorted, but his voice had a nervous edge.

Once they passed, each of them sighed in relief, but Jill turned, staring at the building as it faded from view. "Halfway house my ass," she muttered.

The rest of the ride was silent until they pulled into the Battlefield Paintball Compound parking lot. Jill followed Adam and Steve out of the car, and looked around. She spotted the Warriors' bikes, but Slade's was missing. Relief washed over her as did irritation. Relief that she didn't have to face him after their mind blowing sex and irritation that he was a pussy for not facing her.

"Uh, I don't think we are going to be the only ones here." Steve looked around as they headed through the parking lot. "I thought they'd shut it down for us."

Making their way through the gate after telling the guy behind the counter who they were, they spotted Damon, Duncan, Sid, Jax, Jared and Sloan waiting impatiently.

"Glad to see you decided to show the fuck up." Sloan frowned at them.

"Yeah, well we got caught up in traffic in front of the Halfway House," Adam replied.

"How can they get away with calling it a halfway house?" Jill asked, still cranky about the fact. "It's not like half-breeds are walking up to the doors for help. I saw a woman on her knees begging a cop. Doesn't look like any halfway house I've ever seen. Cops were everywhere."

"You don't like the name, I take it?" Jared eyed her. "It's just a way for them to calm panic among the community. We know what it really is and will shut them down."

Sloan nodded, but didn't add anything to what Jared said. Instead he looked around. "Where's Buchanan?"

Jill looked anywhere but at Sloan. When her eyes met Sid's, he was staring at her; she looked away, but not before shooting him a glare.

"Don't know, but let's get this going." Jax stepped up, glancing at Jill before grabbing paintball guns and handing them to Adam, Steve and then Jill. "You four…"

"Four?" Steve frowned, pointing at Jill, Adam and then himself. "Three."

"Sorry I'm late." Dillon stepped up, surprising Jill and Adam.

"Dillon?" Jill's shocked expression made him grin.

"In the flesh.' Dillon opened his arms.

Jill rushed him and had to stretch to give him a hug. Dillon had been the smallest of any of them. "You grew!" she laughed, hugging him tightly. At that moment, her eyes met Slade's, who stood just behind Dillon. Looking away from Slade, she screamed at herself to chill out and be cool as she looked up at Dillon.

"And I haven't stopped," Dillon laughed, looking at Jared with a grin. "I think that's why the Warrior branch in Kentucky sent me back here. They can't afford buying me new clothes."

"Well, I'm glad, no matter what the reason is." Jill smiled, and then watched as Adam and Dillon did a bro hug. He looked so different. His blond hair had darkened and was longer, instead of the summer buzz cut he always wore. His body and face had filled out, forming a damn good-looking man. Adam introduced Dillon to Steve and Jax, and then Slade who took Dillon's hand in a shake. Jill watched as their handshake lasted a little longer than the others, and the confused look on Dillon's face when he turned from Slade made her frown, but before she could think any more on it, Jax explained their training for the day.

"We are breaking up into teams." Jax handed them each safety glasses. "Us against you."

"Well, that seems a little unfair." Steve removed his sunglasses to put the safety glasses on.

"Tough shit." Jax picked up a paintball gun that looked like a damn Uzi. "You are only out on a kill shot. For you guys, a kill shot is the heart or head and for us, it's the head. There's five acres of land, woods and buildings. You have an hour to survive without having been hit with a kill shot. Within the hour, a horn will blow indicating the exercise is over and you have passed this portion of your testing. We will give you fifteen minutes to set a plan and get a head start."

"But what about all of these other people here?" Adam looked around at groups of people heading out with paintball guns.

"They are off-limits to you, but you are not off-limits to them," Jax replied.

"Are you serious?" Steve looked around. "Not only do we have you badasses hunting us down, we can be taken out by a mom out on a family outing?"

"Yeah, awesome, isn't it?" Jared grinned.

Jill was still looking at all the Warriors' guns with a frown. "Can't we at least choose our own weapons?"

Jax cocked an eyebrow at her, and then waved his hand. "Be my guest."

Looking at the guns displayed behind the counter, Jill instantly found the one she wanted. "Give me the sniper rifle." She told the guy behind the counter.

"Ah, you sure?" The guy looked at the gun then at her. "That's a pretty…"

"Give me the fucking gun," Jill growled, not in the mood for male bullshit. Once she was handed the gun, she opened the hopper of the gun she discarded to remove the paintballs. "Pink? Really?" She glared up at Jax, doing her best to ignore Slade who she knew was watching her every move.

"We have black." Jax didn't even hide his smile. "Those three have different colors than you or anyone else out here today so we can tell who gets the kill shot, and you got pink. Deal with it."

"Yeah, you're going to look pretty in pink, asshole," Jill whispered to herself as she loaded her hopper, and then slammed it shut. When she straightened up, she noticed everyone staring at her with large grins, except for Steve who looked ready to bolt. "Said that out loud, didn't I?"

"Pretty much a butt-pucker moment." Steve nodded, looking at Jill like she'd lost her mind.

Jill glanced at Jax, who didn't even look pissed, which surprised her. "Sorry, just have a competitive mentality going on right now. No disrespect."

"Good. I'm glad you have that because you are all going to need it." Jax nodded at her. "You got fifteen minutes before we hunt."

"Say hello to my little friend." Jared re-enacted the scene from *Scarface*.

"We're fucked." Steve turned, walking away, his head already dropped in defeat.

"Stop talking about your dick, Jared." Sid loaded his hopper with a grin.

"If I whipped that out, we'd all be dead," Jared shot back.

Jill rolled her eyes, their gross manly banter not even getting to her as she followed Steve and Adam, totally ignoring Slade as she passed him by inches. Dillon waited for her and she was surprised when he wrapped his arm around her shoulders, then messed her hair with his hand. "Where in the hell did little, quiet-as-a-mouse Jill go?"

Wrapping her empty arm around Dillon, she finally grinned a genuine smile. "Dead and buried."

Once they arrived at an area far enough away that the Warriors couldn't hear them, they stopped. "Okay, is it just me or is everyone freaked out about getting shot in the fucking head with a paintball?"

Dillon laughed. "Not on my top ten list of things I look forward to, but the key is not to get shot."

"We're fucked," Steve repeated again.

"Will you stop saying that?" Adam growled. "We're not fucked. We're highly outnumbered, but I have a plan."

Jill listened, but her eyes stayed on the Warriors who she could still see. Her frown deepened and her attitude became dangerous the more she watched them, one in particular.

"Awesome," Steve nodded, looking relieved. "What's the plan?"

"We need to split up," Adam instructed, but stopped when Steve snorted.

"That's a stupid-ass plan." Steve shook his head. "Haven't you watched *any* movies? When they split up, people die and *we* get shot in the freakin' head with paintballs. I vote for a new plan."

Stomach churning with anger, she watched as Slade laughed with ease with the other Warriors. She couldn't shake the hurt his carefree laughter caused her. Just hours before, they had what she felt was the most amazing sex, which she freely and with all her heart went into with eyes wide open. What she didn't expect was being treated like nothing after it was over. As if she was just another whore he had fucked and regretted. As if compelled, her arms lifted bringing the gun up, and one eye looked through the scope at her target…the Warrior who tore her heart out.

"Then what do you think we should do, Steve?" Adam shot back, no one watching Jill. "What awesome plan do you have?"

Closing her one eye, she moved the gun from his head, knowing their time hadn't started so she couldn't take him out…yet, then to his back. No, that wasn't good either. She moved the gun lower, her aim directly dead center his ass. With a large smile of a woman scorned, she pulled the trigger and a feeling of vengeful release spread throughout her body as pink exploded across his ass. Slade didn't even jump, but his head snapped around, his eyes finding her instantly as she still looked at him through the scope. "You're mine," he mouthed, his eyes promising things that didn't go in her favor.

"What the fuck did you do?" Steve shrieked, looking from Jill to the Warriors, then spotted the pink on Slade's ass. "Oh, shit!!"

"Dammit, Jill." Adam threw his head back in disbelief. "What the fuck is wrong with you? We don't have a plan."

Jill went to answer, but dropped the gun quickly. "Yeah, we do." She turned to take off. "Run!"

Okay, so now as she ran for her life, shooting Slade in the ass didn't seem like such a good idea. Oh, who was she kidding; she'd do it again in a heartbeat, she just hated that it might have hurt her team. Running into the woods, Jill zig-zagged through trees and brush. Seeing a large tree, she stopped behind it to listen. What sounded like an elephant busting through the woods was Steve tripping, falling and rolling past her. Grabbing him, she pulled him up beside her. Putting her finger to her mouth, she then peeked around the tree. Seeing nothing, she let her breath ease out.

Hearing a branch snap had them both sucking in their breath. Peeking again, she saw Jared going from tree to tree, cocking his ear to listen. Glancing at Steve, she gave him a look. "Do you trust me?"

"Why?" He looked at her without any trust at all.

"I want you to take off running and don't look back," she whispered as low as possible.

"Ah, no." Steve shook his head. "I got a better idea. You fucking take off running."

She looked again to see Jared getting closer. "Dammit, Steve, trust me." She nodded toward the woods. "I swear I won't let him shoot you."

Steve just looked at her, then gritted his teeth. "If I get shot in my fucking head, you will be my slave for life."

"Just run, Steve, and don't look back." Jill pushed him away from the tree. She watched as Steve took off in a blur of movement. Jared spotted him and with a grin lifted his gun. Jill stepped out from behind the tree raising her hand and prayed that this would work. With everything she had, she took control of Jared's gun and thankfully it was a surprise attack because his grip wasn't tight. The gun flew out of his hands heading toward Jill. Once their eyes met, Jill threw her arm back before swinging it hard, sending the gun through the woods.

Proud of herself, she smiled, but it disappeared as soon as she heard the deep growl coming from Jared. "You'll pay for that, cheater."

"Not cheating if I wasn't told I couldn't do it," she defended herself before she took a shot at Jared's head, but he was too quick, knowing the shot was coming.

"Nice try, breed." Jared smirked then gave a loud whistle before yelling, "Pinky is using her powers. Hold onto your guns."

Whistles answered him back and they were close. Jill took off as Jared laughed and then headed for his gun. Not really knowing where Steve went, Jill headed in the direction he initially ran. A noise coming from her right had her crouching down in tall brush. Her eyes focused to see two men heading her way. She lowered herself and took aim. With two clear shots, she hit them both within seconds of each other, and then realized it was two civilian men. Oh, she was going to catch crap on this one, maybe no one would notice.

"Sorry, guys." She grimaced, looking at the bright-pink paint spattered across their chest. Yeah, she was busted big time. She turned, looking around for Warriors before taking off.

"Son of a bitch," one of them cursed. "Where in the hell did she come from?"

"Hell if I know." The other one tried to wipe the paint off his chest but it just smeared.

Jill could still hear them as she found a large tree. With expert ease, she managed her way up to the top and concealed herself. It gave her a great cover, but didn't obstruct her view. She could see all around. Spotting Sid and Jared, Jill held her breath. They stopped the two men she shot.

"Where did she go?" Jared asked, pointing to the pink on the man's vest.

He pointed toward where she had hid. "That way."

"We didn't even see her before it was too late." The other one frowned. "Ain't gonna live this one down with the guys. Fucking pink." He was still trying to wipe it off.

Jill slapped her hand over her mouth with a grin, even knowing she was going to be in big trouble. Sid and Jared headed her way. Slowly and quietly she moved out of sight, holding her breath and trying to slow her heartbeat. She watched with nervous anticipation as they walked right under her tree. Slowly, she aimed her gun.

"You and Slade good?" Jared asked as they looked around on alert.

"No, not really," Sid replied, stopping also looking around for any targets running around, but then his eyes flashed to Jared's. "His ass better watch it with Jill. She's like a sister to me. I swear I'll kill him if he hurts her."

"She's a grown woman, Sid." Jared actually leaned up against the tree Jill was hiding in.

Jill's finger twitched on the trigger, but she calmed herself. She could only hit one and then the other would be on her before she could do anything. It wasn't worth it. Shooting Slade in the ass was worth it; this wasn't worth it.

"I figured it was bound to happen between them. Hell I even bet it would, but not like that," Sid growled.

"He just likes it rough," Jared shrugged. "Tessa likes it when I get a little rough."

"Too much info, bro." Sid glared at him. "So shut the fuck up."

"Ah, come on," Jared laughed. "You can't tell me you haven't given it to Lana, pushed the limits. Some women get off on it and it's our job to give our women what they want."

"Okay, first off, don't ever talk about Lana and sex," Sid warned him. "Secondly, I don't think it was Jill who wanted it rough or whatever it was I walked in on."

"Oh, and you know that because you were there," Jared snorted as they walked away. "Sid, stay out of it and let those two work it out. I'd be the first in line to kill the doc if I thought he had hurt her in any way, but honestly, this is none of our business."

After a few minutes of silence, Sid glanced at Jared. "So Tessa really likes it rough, huh?"

The smile that plastered on Jared's face was full of male pride. "She's a fucking hellcat, my brother."

Sid's grin widened. "We are lucky bastards."

"That we are," Jared laughed as they headed deeper into the woods.

Jill let out her breath and waited for a second before slipping out of the tree. Looking around, she felt confident that she was alone. Making her way behind Jared and Sid probably wasn't the smartest move she could make, but she did it anyway. Feeling a sting in her shoulder then hearing the pop of a gun, she took off running haphazardly, making her a harder target. "Shit." She ran hard and suddenly her feet hit nothing but air. Seconds later, her body hit hard ground as she rolled down a steep hill until she came to a stop against a tree, knocking the wind out of her. Scrambling, she rolled into some brush and lay still.

"She's gone." Jax's voice came from her left. "She must have gone across the creek."

She barely turned her head to watch Jax and Duncan a few yards away from her. Once they were gone far enough away, she sat up, looking around. The sound of more guns popping in the distance had her standing. The Warriors had found someone. With no more thought of herself, she took off toward the sound. In a clearing, sat a building surrounded by Warriors, except she didn't see Slade. Not knowing what to do, she glanced around frantically. Seeing another large tree, she snuck that way and climbed, finding a good area to shoot from. If they figured out where she was, she'd be screwed.

Aiming, she looked around the area with the scope and spotted Dillon on the other side of the woods hidden and waiting with his gun aimed. The Warriors dodged in and out of the woods getting closer and closer to the building. Seeing green splatter on Damon's leg, she knew Steve was in the building. Where in the hell were Adam and Slade? Jax was the first she had a clear shot of and her hands began to shake. She had him and could make the kill shot, but did she have the balls. Her father's words came back to her as if he was with her teaching her how to shoot. "It's you or them, Jilly." Her father's words repeated over and over again in her mind.

Moving her shoulder, she wiped the sweat from her temple. Taking aim again, she pulled the trigger. Pink exploded on the back of Jax's head. Jill's stomach heaved as she pulled back behind the trunk of the tree. Damn, that was going to suck for her. Now Jax would hate her even more and she actually didn't feel the satisfaction that she thought she'd feel.

"Where the fuck did that come from?" She heard Damon yell above Jax's cursing.

Jill peeked around the other side of the tree, praying Steve made a run for it out the back of the building. Seeing him take off toward the woods, she turned to aim to give him cover and freaked when every Warrior other than Jax had their guns pointed toward her tree. "Ah, shit!" She took cover again, squeezing her eyes shut as black paint splattered all around her. Keeping against the tree she climbed higher, then stopped and took aim hitting Damon and Sid, but not in the head. Another volley of paintballs rained around her, one getting her in the leg, the other in the side. "Dammit, that hurts," she hissed. God, she hated pain and those damn paintballs pinging against her body was almost unbearable. Yeah, she and pain did not mix.

Dillon started shooting from his spot, drawing their attention his way. Jill took that opportunity, climbing and jumping down, but soon the paintballs were flying hitting her everywhere, except the head. She just tucked her head and ran…smack into Slade. Falling onto her ass, her gun bouncing out of her grip, she rolled to try to grab it, but he kicked it away.

"Stand up." He aimed his gun at her, no emotion on his face.

Slowly, she stood, her brain working overtime. If he shot her in the head now, it was going to hurt like hell this close. Not liking her back exposed, she side-stepped so the tree was behind her.

He cocked his eyebrow. "Nice move."

"Thanks," she replied, and then shot her hand up quickly trying to knock the gun out of his hand, but it didn't budge. She frowned and tried again.

"Not happening." Slade shook his head at her like she was a naughty child.

"Then go ahead and shoot." Jill even plunged her head forward. "Get the kill shot."

Without moving her eyes, she could see Adam sneaking up on Slade; she didn't want to give her teammate away. Just as Adam aimed, Slade turned, shooting Adam right between the eyes, knocking him on his back before swinging the gun toward Jill whose eyes were wide with shock. "Holy hell." She looked around Slade to see Adam picking himself up, holding his head.

"Fuck, that hurt." Adam stumbled sideways before sitting down on the ground.

"You still want me to take that kill shot?" Slade asked, watching her closely, a grin playing at the corner of his mouth.

Jill gulped, deciding if acting like a badass was worth it. Looking at Adam again holding his head, she decided that no, it wasn't. She hated pain; pain sucked and getting shot in the head close range was going to hurt like hell. Suddenly, the horn echoed throughout the area ending their practice, giving new meaning to 'saved by the bell'.

Walking over, she picked up her gun. Dillon and Steve headed over, followed by the Warriors. Dillon had been hit by a kill shot, black paint splattered his face. Sloan looked Jill over.

"No kill shot?" Sloan looked at Slade.

"No," Slade replied, his eyes leaving Jill to land on Sloan. "Close range."

"Didn't seem to stop you with Adam." Sloan frowned as Adam still weaved a little.

"It was me or him, and I picked me." Slade's tone didn't change.

"She's not going to learn anything by being treated differently." Sloan frowned. "You had a shot and didn't take it, why?"

Jill watched from a distance where she picked up her gun. Slade didn't even look her way.

"She was apprehended. No threat." Slade's tone did change this time.

"And that wasn't the exercise." Sloan sighed and shook his head, then looked at Jill. He raised his gun.

Jill was looking at Slade when she heard the pop of a gun, next everything went pitch black as pain exploded in her head.

Chapter 10

Slade watched Jill go down. Every instinct he possessed urged him to go to her, but Sloan was watching his every move. His decision at that moment decided Jill's fate in the program. Sloan warned them both to keep it professional, and well, he sure as hell fucked that up, and just a few short hours ago.

"Jesus, Sloan." Sid ran over to Jill who was just now moving. "What the fuck?"

"What happened?" Jill's voice was faint and confused.

"You got shot," Sid answered her.

"But the horn blew," Jill griped. "Who the hell shot me?"

Slade heard it all, but didn't take his eyes off Sloan. "Are you done testing me?" Slade growled, wanting to rip Sloan's head off. "Can I check these guys out to make sure they're okay?"

Sloan nodded, but Slade could tell he was still being watched closely. Turning, his eyes scanned Jill quickly and he was relieved to see her sitting up. Adam was sitting down being quiet, but he was also looking at Jill.

"Hurts like a bitch, don't it," Adam called over to Jill.

"Can you stand up?" Slade asked, trying his best to keep his eyes off Jill and focus on Adam. If he went to Jill first, then Sloan would open his mouth and shit would get bad, real bad.

"Nice shot," Adam grinned, standing. "How the hell did you know I was behind you?"

"Just a feeling," Slade responded, prying Adam's human eye open. "You have a headache?"

Adam nodded. "A little."

Slade looked him over noticing the black paint all over him. He pushed on the red lump on Adam's forehead where he had shot him. Adam winched, but didn't move his head. "You'll live." Slade clapped him on the shoulder. "Good job today."

"I died." Adam looked confused and disgusted. "I failed."

"But you stayed alive until the end." Slade turned away. "And you gave up your life for a teammate. You get points for that."

Heading toward Jill, who was standing up but had her eyes closed and arms crossed, he stopped in front of her. "You okay?"

Jill slit her eyes open to squint up at him. She went to nod but stopped with a hiss. "Yeah. I'm good."

Slade snorted when she closed her eyes again. "You dizzy?" He reached up touching the large bump on her forehead.

"No." She stated her lie as she jumped at his touch, almost losing her balance. "A little."

"Headache?" Slade moved her head back and forth, working her neck.

"Yes." She kept her eyes closed. "But I'm fine. Just need a minute."

"Sit down and stay put." Slade helped her sit before turning toward Dillon, but Jax with his pink splattered hair was in his line of vision. "You good?" he asked Jax, trying to keep the grin off his face. That had been a proud moment when he saw the back of Jax's head explode in bright pink. That was a hell of a shot.

"I'm fine." Jax gave him a sideways glance. "Go doctor one of these other pussies."

Slade did grin then as he passed him and went toward Dillon who waved him away.

"I didn't get hit close up. It barely stung," Dillon told him as he felt his head, "and I don't really have a bump."

Looking toward Steve, who had the biggest grin on his face, Slade shook his head. Out of any of the half-breeds, Steve was the last one he'd pick to survive this test, though he would have never told Steve that. "Good job, Steve," Slade nodded.

The rest of the Warriors followed suit, congratulating Steve.

Steve soaked it in for a few minutes looking proud of himself, but then he looked to his teammates. "Honestly, I wouldn't have done it without my dudes and dudette." Steve smiled at each of them. "I was about to piss myself when you all had me cornered, but with their help, I was able to get out and then the horn sounded."

"We didn't do much, Steve." Jill's voice sounded tired, but happy for her friend. "You earned it."

"No, it all turned in my favor when you shot Jax in the head. Great fucking shot by the way," Steve grinned, heading toward Jill to give her a high five when he spotted the look Jax was giving him. His hand dropped to his side real quick. "Ah, I mean…well anyway, thanks, guys."

Even with Slade's dangerous mood, he couldn't help but grin at Steve. This poor kid just didn't know when to shut the fuck up.

"You guys did pretty good," Sloan said, looking at each of them. "You lasted longer than we thought you would. Jax and Slade will go over everything with you tomorrow. Go get cleaned up and get some rest."

Slade held back as everyone left the area to head out. His gaze watched Jill, making sure she was steady on her feet. He started to go to her when she stumbled, but Dillon was at her side giving her a hand, a hand Slade wanted to snap off and shove up his ass. Feeling Sloan staring at the side of his head, Slade sneered his way, "You got something to say to me?"

"Not yet," Sloan's voice was even. "You got something to say to me?"

"Yeah, I do." Slade turned to look him square in the eye. "I respect the hell out of you and always have, but if you ever hurt her again to make a point to me, I will kill you."

Slade didn't even wait for a response, he just turned and followed the rest. As he watched Jill and the little fucker, Dillon, who he honestly had nothing against except his hand on Jill, Slade knew he was in deep shit. He also knew that he and Jill would happen. They'd already happened, yet he totally fucked that up, but as soon as her initiation into the Warriors was complete, she was *his* and no one better have a problem with it.

"Maybe Jax was right," Sloan called out behind him. "She's a liability."

Slade slowed, but didn't stop. "Jax is an asshole," Slade responded. "You'd be a fool to let her go, Sloan, and you know it." Not sticking around to hear what else Sloan had to say, Slade took off. His eyes instantly going to Jill who was a few yards ahead of him, a thought hit him right in the gut. He'd be a bigger fool to let her go. Son of a bitch, this was a mess.

******

Jill was glad Dillon was back, but he was getting on her last nerve. Every few seconds, he was asking if she was okay, did she want him to carry her, on and on he went. Yeah, her head and body hurt, but she knew it would be short-lived. She was half-vampire, just like them. She would heal. She was fine and she wanted to tell him to shut the hell up.

Spotting the two men she had shot in the woods, bright pink splattered across their vests, she sidestepped and tried to avoid being seen by them as they walked by, but she wasn't that lucky. One of their buddies spotted her.

"Is that the one who got you?" he said loudly, pointing at Jill. "Hey, girl, come here. I want to get a picture."

Ignoring him, she continued to walk behind Steve and Adam.

"Jill, who is that?" Steve was looking at the guy coming up to them, then his friends. Seeing the pink splatter, his eyes shot to Jill. "Shit, did you shoot them? Sloan is gonna be pissed. Citizens were off limits."

Jill mumbled, nudging at Steve, "Just go."

"Hey! I'm talking to you." He grabbed her arm. "I want to get a picture of you with my boys."

Jerking her arm away from him, she turned to glare. "Get off." He was decked out in his paintball gear with a hunter's hat on his bushy head and a lip full of chewing tobacco.

He stumbled backward when he got a good look at her eyes. She had taken her safety glasses off after getting shot. "Holy shit, you're a breed." He looked at Steve, Adam and Dillon who were giving him a death stare. "You're all breeds."

Slade walked up, stepping between Jill and the man. "You got a problem?"

"Yeah, I do." The man spat, looking from Jill to Slade. "They're breeds."

The rest of the Warriors surrounded them as Slade lifted his sunglasses off, sizing up him and his friends. "And you're a redneck asshole, but *we're* not making a big deal out of it."

"Oh, hell, man." The man held up his hands, backpedaling after seeing Slade's golden eyes. "We don't want no trouble."

Slade dropped his sunglasses back in place giving them a nasty grin. "Good choice."

"Really, man. I just wanted to get a picture with my buddies and the pretty girl there that shot them." He smiled as if he and Slade were now buddies, but his smile disappeared when Slade took a step toward him.

"But she's a breed," Slade growled back the man's word. "Isn't that what had you all upset?"

"Ah, no…" The man laughed nervously. "It just took me by surprise is all. Didn't want that sexy thang taking out my neck or something. I've heard breeds are unpredictable….ya know?"

"No, I don't know." Slade's growl turned menacing.

Sid stepped in, waving his two fingers to the guy. "Come here." As the man took a few hesitant steps, Sid grabbed him, putting his arm around his shoulders like they were the best of friends. "Listen, Cooter."

"My name's Buck." The man gave Sid a sideways glance, not sure what was about to happen.

"You don't say," Sid grinned. "Well, listen….*Buck*. I suggest you and your boys go on about your business before you get an asswhoopin' you'll never forget."

The man nodded then hurried toward his friends when Sid let him go. Jill really didn't want to look at any of the Warriors, but her eyes went to Sloan because he was the one glaring at her. She started walking ahead knowing he was coming up beside her.

"So, Jill." Sloan moved up beside her as they headed into the parking lot. "Did you not hear the part where I said all citizens were off limits?"

Jill grimaced, trying to think up something intelligent to say, but Sloan made her nervous, really nervous. "I got excited," came out of her mouth; well, at least it was the truth. "Sorry."

"And is there a reason you shot Slade in the ass before time started?" Sloan grilled her more.

Jill's grin was filled with evil glee; now that was worth it. She glanced at Slade, who was giving her a 'payback's a bitch' look, then to Sloan, wiping the grin off her face. "I slipped."

He actually laughed at that, shaking his head, but then his face turned serious as if he had never laughed at all. "Next time you…slip, or get excited and shoot civilians, you will get written up."

Jill cleared her throat with a nod. "Yes, sir."

Sloan glanced at her sideways as he walked beside her, his silence made her nervous. "You take your driving test yet?"

"No, I was…."

Before she could finish, Sloan broke in, looking at his watch. "You have plenty of time to do it today," he ordered, heading toward his bike. "I want it done. I'll make a call so you don't have to wait the required time to do the driver's test, but I want that written test done today."

"Yes, sir." Jill frowned, and after Sloan started his bike, she cursed, "Dammit."

"Come on." Adam heard the whole conversation. "We'll stop there first."

Waiting for Adam to unlock the doors, Jill tried not to watch as Slade rode past on his bike, but her eyes, damn them, had a mind of their own and went to him like a magnet. As if that wasn't bad enough when he rode past, his head slowly turned, and even though his sunglasses hid his eyes, she felt the heat of his stare burn through her body. Quickly, she looked away, climbing into Adam's car.

The ride to the DMV was silent. All Jill could think about was taking the test she was surely going to fail because she couldn't read without it taking her hours, and remembering the questions was going to bring up memories of what Slade did to her body as he quizzed her. As Steve would say, she was screwed.

Adam pulled into a empty parking spot. Dillon followed in his car, parking beside them. Once they were all out of the cars, Adam stopped Dillon and Steve from walking. "Why don't you guys stay here? I'll go in with Jill."

As they made their way inside, Jill was relieved Adam had told Steve and Dillon to stay outside. She was a nervous wreck and really didn't need an audience for her humiliation. Having Adam there was bad enough, but out of the three, she'd rather have Adam with her. The woman behind the counter stared at them as they walked up to the counter. "I need to take the written test."

The woman continued to stare until Jill gave her a look. She fumbled with a paper, stood, did something and came back. "Take this and go to computer number four." She handed the paper to Jill, still staring. "After you finish the test, bring the paper back up."

Taking offense at the woman staring, Jill sneered, "Is it my mismatched eyes or do I have something on my face?"

The woman was taken back for a second. "Ah, actually you do."

"Do what?" Jill's tone was not polite.

"Have something on your face." The woman pointed. "It's black."

Jill's hand flew to her forehead then brought it back down, nothing was on her hand. "Do you have a bathroom?"

The woman nodded toward the right. "Over there."

Jill headed toward the bathroom, pushing the door open hard. Going directly to the mirror, she laughed. Hell, no wonder the woman was staring. She looked like total shit. The whole side of her forehead was splattered black and her hair was pushed back and standing straight up from the blast of the paintball gun. She had a large bump where she'd been hit. Specks of black was scattered all across her face. Turning on the warm water, she bent over the sink, bringing water to her face and scrubbed. After a few minutes, she looked up into the mirror. It wasn't totally gone, but at least she looked a little better.

Grabbing the paper, she looked at it and her stomach dropped. She was going to fail this test, she knew it. The words on the paper were jumbled to her eyes. She just hoped she saw some familiar words and could figure it out on the test. Slade said it was multiple choice so at least she had a slim chance of picking the right one. With one disgusted look in the mirror, she turned and walked out. Adam sat in one of the metal chairs. He gave her an encouraging smile as she headed toward the computers.

Sitting down, she saw notes posted on the computer figuring it was instructions on how to start. Hitting a button next to the note, the computer made a loud noise, which she figured indicated she had hit the wrong button. Hot embarrassment swarmed her body. Closing her eyes, she gave herself a quick pep talk. She could do this.

"Hey, you can't go over there while she's testing," the woman called out.

Jill opened her eyes to see Adam heading her way. "Just let me help her get started. She's dys—"

"Adam." Jill shook her head with warning.

Adam walked over, hit a button and a screen came up with more jumbled up words. "You can do this," he told her before walking away. "Just take your time."

While Adam knew she was dyslexic, he had no clue how bad it was. "Thanks," she managed to say with a calmness she didn't feel. She was freaking out. It was like she was back in school and being asked by the teacher to stand up and read.

Jill didn't know how long she sat in front of the computer. Some of the words made sense, but her dyslexia was severe and was going to prevent her from doing what she wanted most in the world. She heard the door buzz as someone came in, but she ignored it. She didn't want to see whoever came in because her pride really couldn't take it. Three people had come in since her, taken the test and left. She couldn't even bring herself to look at Adam. She had hit some buttons figuring she was taking the test, but she really didn't know.

A chair scraped against the floor toward her. Looking over, she saw Slade turn the chair backward to straddle it. "What are you doing?" she whispered, shocked, looking back at the woman behind the desk. "You can't be over here."

"Yes, I can." Slade was looking at the computer screen as he reached over using the mouse. Then he turned around. "Can you please start this test over?"

Watching the woman get up quickly to do what Slade asked, Jill frowned. "You know her or something?"

"Nope, but she knows Sloan." Slade scooted closer, still looking at the screen, then looked at her, his eyes going to her forehead with a frown. "How's your head?"

"Sore." Jill sighed, "Slade, what are you doing? You can't take the test for me."

His eyes searched hers before he spoke, "I'm not taking the test for you. I'm going to read the question. Give you the options for answers."

"How did you even know I was here?" Jill was actually relieved, despite her discomfort. She wasn't a dumb person, but having him read to her like she was a five-year-old made her feel less than.

"Adam," Slade replied. "Okay, you ready?"

She looked back at Adam who shrugged as if he didn't care if she was pissed he called Slade or not. She gave him a smile, letting him know she was cool with it, when in reality she didn't know what the hell she felt. Not even twelve hours ago, this handsome man was inside her and now he was sitting next to her helping her take a written driving test. Her life sure had taken a strange turn. For him to take time to turn around and come here for her almost had her tearing up, but she controlled it. She was still mad at him, so she simply nodded, afraid she would start blubbering if she opened her mouth.

Slade gave her a small encouraging smile before looking at the screen. Then he hesitated, a funny expression crossing his face. He cleared his throat, his eyes on the screen. "What does a flashing yellow light indicate?"

Jill's eyes shot to his in disbelief. They then slammed back to the computer screen. Heat that had nothing to do with embarrassment flushed her body. She looked back at Slade and the heat in his eyes melted her to the chair. "Slow down," she said quickly, her voice shaking. "Next question." She watched as he clicked something on the computer and a new, what she figured question, popped up. Holy shit, that did not just happen. Knowing her luck, it did just happen. Her stomach clenched painfully.

"Who has the right of way at a four-way stop?" Slade's voice sounded deeper as he read the question and then gave the four possible answers.

Jill answered, watching his strong hand clicking the mouse.

On and on the questions came, as did other people taking the same test that was taking her forever to complete. Jill's eyes kept closing as she listened to Slade's voice. She was so tired. Even though she was part vampire, her human part needed rest and she hadn't slept in…hell, she didn't know when she slept last. She still had to go with Tessa to learn pole dancing. The thought made her want to vomit. Would her humiliation ever end?

Slade bumped her as he moved the mouse around, startling her since she was half asleep. "Okay, that's it."

"Did I pass?" Jill yawned and then stretched.

"We'll find out." He stood, taking the chair back where he found it, and then came back, grabbing her paper. Jill still sat in the chair, her eyes staring sleepily up at him. "You need to get some rest."

"Tell me about it." Jill yawned again as she stood. "Better yet, tell Sloan."

Slade walked over, handing the paper to the woman. Jill leaned against the counter as the woman went to a computer, typing in stuff. After a few minutes, she walked to a printer.

"Congratulations." She handed Jill more papers. "Take this down the hall to get your temps. You have about a half an hour before they close."

"I passed?" That woke her up. She took the papers, looking at them, then up to Slade who was staring down at her with a pleased smile. "I passed!" Jill jumped, hugging Slade, not caring that she was still mad at him. She had passed.

"I knew you would." Slade hugged her tightly against him.

Jill backed away, instantly missing his touch. "Thank you," she said, telling herself she could be mad at him again in a few minutes. At that moment, she appreciated what he had done to help her. How he went about helping her study…well it was fucking awesome, but yeah, she was still pissed about the way it ended.

"You're welcome." His knowing eyes searched her face, looking like he wanted to say more, but didn't. "Come on, before they close."

Jill nodded then walked toward Adam. "I passed!" She couldn't keep the excitement from her voice as she shook the paper at him.

"Oh, shit," Adam teased, looking horrified. "We need to warn everyone in the Cincinnati area."

Jill punched him in the stomach, but couldn't wipe the grin off her face to give him an evil glare. "Shut up."

"Just kidding, Jill." Adam grabbed her up in a brotherly hug. "I knew you could do it, but you're still not driving my car until you have driving lessons."

Rolling her eyes, Jill headed down the hallway and into an almost empty room. Standing in line, she waited to be called. Adam had gone on out to his car while Slade stood with her. She noticed all the women sneaking looks at Slade. Jealously nipped at her, but then again, she couldn't blame them. He was one hell of a handsome man. She also couldn't blame them for looking at her as if wondering why a man like him was with someone like her.

As nonchalantly as she could, she glanced at Slade. If she really wanted to be honest with herself, she had to wonder the same thing. Why would he want to be with someone like her? He was a doctor, while she couldn't read. He was gorgeous and she was just…meh. Her mind swarmed a million miles an hour. Some of her happiness at passing her test evaporated into thin air. Had that stupid bitch, Alice, been right? Was she making a fool of herself over Slade? Was what they shared a…pity fuck? Ah, damn, there was nothing worse than a pity fuck, no matter how amazing it was.

"Hey." Slade was watching her closely. "You're up."

Jill's eyes were unfocused as she looked at him, her mind going over everything that had been happening between them. How many times had she heard him tell others that there was and never would be anything between them?

"Jill." The concern in his voice snapped her out of it. "Are you okay?"

Nodding, she looked away. "Yeah," she answered, but her mind screamed *NO* as she walked up to the counter, handing her papers to the pretty blonde with light blue eyes her papers. Jill knew the woman's smile and fluttery fake eyelashes weren't for her, but for Slade. The woman asked her a few questions, her voice low and sexy. Jill wanted nothing more than to reach over and smack the woman, but that wasn't fair. It wasn't her fault she was beautiful and knew how to act like a woman in front of a man like Slade. Jill might as well spit and grab her junk as much as she considered how she looked in front of Slade. Would it even make a difference? Glancing down at her paint-covered, and dirty t-shirt, what little breast that filled out the t-shirt and ripped jeans, Jill knew the answer to that question. She was a hot mess.

"Ma'am," the woman was saying.

Jill almost looked behind her to see who she was talking to. Ma'am? "Hmm?" Jill said, snapping out of her thoughts.

"If you go to the chair with the blue curtain, I'll take your picture." She gave Jill a sad little smile.

Ignoring what that smile might mean, Jill frowned. "Don't I have to pay something?" What the fuck happened, did she black the hell out?

"The gentleman took care of it." She nodded to Slade, the sexiness back in her voice.

Looking over at Slade, who was watching her closely as he put his wallet back in his pocket, Jill grabbed her stuff without taking her eyes off Slade. "How much was it, Slade?" Jill reached into her pocket, pulling out a small wad of bills. "I was going to pay."

"Put your money away. The Council pays." Slade moved toward the chair where the woman waited behind a camera.

"Oh, you carry the Council's wallet?" Jill frowned as she passed him to flop into the metal chair. When the woman told her to smile, Jill wanted to punch her. Instead, she just tilted her head giving her a 'take the fucking picture' look and the woman did…quickly.

"It will be just a few minutes," the woman stated, not to Jill, but Slade.

When Jill snorted and walked away, Slade thanked the woman and followed Jill, who was leaning up against the wall. She had her head tilted back and eyes closed.

"I think you might have a concussion." Slade's voice washed over her tired body.

"Nah, just tired." Jill still didn't open her eyes. "Need sleep."

"Jill about before…" Slade sighed.

Now, that popped Jill's eyes wide open. Was he seriously going to do this here? Break it to her in the damn DMV that…that…oh, hell, no!

"If you are talking about me shooting you in the ass, then talk away, but if you are talking about anything else, I don't want to hear it." The look on his face indicated that it wasn't her shooting him in the ass that he had been referring to. Jill's eyes narrowed at him as the woman called her name. Snapping her mouth shut, she marched over to get her temporary license.

The woman was staring at Slade, not her, with a longing Jill totally understood. Welcome to my world, she wanted to shout at the woman, but didn't. Instead, she leaned over whispering to the woman who smiled so brightly Jill almost squinted. The woman hurriedly wrote something down on a small piece of paper, handing it to Jill. Turning, Jill marched back to Slade. Before he could tell her it just wouldn't work out with them, she'd give him an out.

"There is nothing about *before* that we need to talk about." She slapped him in the chest with the money she still held in her hand along with the woman's phone number, and then gave him a push, which didn't budge him an inch. "I'll make it easy for you." Without another word, she slammed out the door.

She didn't look back, because if she had, she would have been terrified at the look on Slade's face.

Chapter 11

Jax walked up to Caroline's house, or actually her parents' house, and rang the doorbell. He could hear people talking, and then the door opened.

"What are you doing here?" Sid looked behind Jax. "Has something happened?" He grabbed his phone out of his back pocket, checking his messages.

"I'm picking up Caroline," Jax responded, wondering how this conversation was going to go.

"Why?" Sid frowned, putting his phone back in his pocket.

"Are you her father?" Jax's smartass question was met with narrowed eyes.

"No, but her father will ask the same damn question," Sid shot back.

"Can you tell her I'm here?" Jax really didn't want to have an argument with Sid, so he decided to play nice.

"I probably would if she was here." Sid stepped aside. "Come on in."

Jax walked through the door into the house. Lana spotted him. "Hi Jax." She walked up, looking from him to Sid. "Has something happened?"

Before Jax could answer, Sid stepped in. "No, he's here to pick up Caroline."

"Why?" Lana frowned, looking almost identical to Sid. It was actually scary.

"I'm taking her out to dinner." Jax absolutely hated to answer to anyone, but he figured this was her sister. Actually, he was kind of surprised Caroline hadn't said anything.

"Oh, okay." Lana looked a little confused. "Let me call her."

Sid and Jax made small talk about Warrior business while Lana was calling Caroline.

"That's weird." Lana tapped her phone to her chin nervously. "It went straight to voicemail. Are you sure it was tonight? She never said anything to me about it," she asked Jax with hope.

He took his phone out and dialed. "Yes, it was tonight." He put the phone to his ear. "I texted her to make sure we were still on." He clicked his phone off when, as Lana said, it went straight to voicemail.

"When did you and my sister start dating?" Lana's tone was worried and curious.

Jax just stared at her before answering. "It's dinner, Lana. Try again," Jax said, nodding toward her phone, a bad feeling nagging at him. Caroline didn't seem like the type to stand anyone up. He watched Lana as she did try again, but she pulled the phone away without having a conversation.

"I'm worried," Lana frowned.

"Worried about what?" Lana's mom walked into the entranceway, noticing Jax. "Oh, hello."

"Ms. Fitzpatrick," Jax nodded, figuring that's who this beautiful older woman was.

"Mom, have you talked to Caroline?" Jax knew Lana purposely took the worry out of her voice so not to upset her mother.

"I talked to her at lunch today." Melanie Fitzpatrick smiled, looking at each of them, and then frowned. "Why? What's happened?"

118

"Because she was supposed to have dinner with Jax tonight." Lana's face once again bloomed with worry. "She never said anything about it to me and she would never not show up."

"She said she had to stop at the apartment to pick up a few things after work." Her mother's eyes widened. "You don't think Rod…"

"No, I'm sure she's fine and lost track of time," Lana replied, but her eyes clearly indicated when she looked at Sid that she didn't believe that for a minute.

Jax watched Lana's reactions, reading her like a book. He and Sid made eye contact. "What's the address? I can stop by and see if she's there."

"We'll go with you." Lana went to grab her stuff. "Just keep dinner warm, Mom. We'll be right back."

"You be careful and call me." Her mother stood, wringing her hands. "Your father is picking up Jamie from soccer practice and should be home any minute."

"It's fine, Mom." Lana gave her mom a reassuring smile. "She probably got caught up in doing something and forgot to turn her phone off silent. You know how she is about that."

Her mom nodded, but didn't seem to believe it.

As they walked out the door, Jax headed for his car. "I'll follow you guys."

"It's just about five minutes from here," Lana said, half running toward her car.

Jax had driven his car instead of his bike for his dinner date with Caroline. Pulling out behind Sid and Lana, Jax's bad feeling began to grind at his gut, and his gut was usually not wrong. His finger tapped the steering wheel. Sid drove, running a few red lights in less populated areas, with Jax right behind him. Finally, they pulled into a nice apartment complex, weaving through different lanes until before pulling up in front of a row of apartments.

"Is that her car?" Jax asked, once Sid and Lana joined him on the sidewalk. When Lana nodded, Jax took off. "Which apartment?"

"104." Lana hurried up beside him. Once at the door, she pounded loudly. "Caroline?" she called out.

"Don't you have a set of keys?" Jax asked impatiently.

"Rod hated me," Lana replied, knocking again, and then tried the doorknob, which was locked. "This is only the second time I've been here."

Jax didn't like hearing that at all. He looked at Sid. "You wanna do it or should I?"

Sid moved Lana out of the way before lifting his foot and kicking the door in. Jax and Sid plowed into the apartment ready for anything, Lana coming in behind them.

"Dammit!" Lana looked around, the apartment was in shambles. Sid pushed her back as they slowly made their way deeper into the dark apartment.

A noise down the short hallway drew their attention. Jax held his finger up as he crept that way, cocking his head listening closely. Sid and Lana were close behind him.

Without any warning at all, Caroline jumped into the hall with an iron skillet in her hand swinging with everything she had. "You son of a bitch!"

Jax caught the skillet before it made contact with his head. "Caroline!" he shouted as she fought him in panic mode. "It's Jax."

She looked up, her eyes focusing with realization. The skillet dropped from her fingers, hitting the floor with a loud bang. His eyes searched her face and a rage so deep flashed throughout his body. Her eye was swollen with the beginnings of a bruise coloring her pale cheek. He tilted her chin up, looking at her neck, which had markings of a perfect choke grip. Her lip quivered, but she tilted her head, putting on a strong front. "I'm fine." She glanced behind him to see Sid and Lana. "You just scared me."

He knew that to be true, feeling the shaking in her body. "Where is he?" Jax's tone was deadly and meant business.

Caroline looked away, her strong front crumbling. "It doesn't matter."

"The fuck it don't." Jax turned her face toward him again. "Are you hurt anywhere else?"

"Hurt?" Lana pushed past Sid and Jax, trying to get to her sister. Once she was close enough, she saw her face in the darkness of the hallway. "Jesus, Caroline. What did that bastard do? I'm going to kill him."

"I'm fine, Lana," Caroline repeated, pulling away from her sister. "It's my fault. I should have known better than to come alone, but I never thought he would do something like this."

"What happened?" Lana led her out into the kitchen where broken dishes were scattered everywhere.

Caroline, folding her arms around her body, looked at the mess. "Damn him."

"I'm not worried about the mess, Caroline." Lana frowned. "We'll clean it up. I want to know what the hell happened so when I call the police—"

"Lana, just leave it alone," Caroline snapped. "It's over."

"Bullshit I'll leave it alone," Lana snapped back. "Have you seen your face?"

Caroline looked at Jax, then back to Lana. "Just leave, Lana." Caroline turned to walk back down the hallway. "I don't need you turning cop on me."

They all watched Caroline disappear into her room, slamming the door behind her. Jax looked down at the kitchen counter and saw Caroline's phone. He had to power it up which explained exactly why her phone had gone directly to voicemail. Turning it over, he noticed the crack in the back of the case. Only hard force would crack a case like that. He searched through her incoming calls. There were over 200 missed calls from one number yesterday. Memorizing that number, he switched to text messages. The last text message was half an hour ago from the same number. Anger so raw gripped him. Whoever this son of a bitch was he needed to be taught a lesson, a very painful lesson.

"This is why she doesn't want anyone involved." He laid the phone down, pushing it toward Lana and Sid.

Lana picked it up with Sid reading over her shoulder. "He threatened my little sister?" Lana was livid.

"If she got any of the family involved or the police." Jax looked at Sid and a silent message passed between them.

"Caroline should know better." Lana smacked the phone down on the counter.

"And you would do the same thing she's doing." Sid looked down at Lana. "You know it and I know. I've never seen a family as close as yours. Caroline not wanting to go against him in order to keep your sister and family safe doesn't surprise me."

Lana sighed long and hard. "I know. You're right."

Jax left, walking down the hall. Knocking on the door, he opened it without waiting for an answer and walked in. Caroline was on her hands and knees tossing things out of the closet.

"Lana, I don't care what you say," Caroline huffed as more clothes and shoes came sailing over her head to a big heap on the floor. "I just want to get the rest of my stuff, this mess cleaned up and forget I ever met the jerk."

Jax walked over, picking up a pretty red nightgown she had tossed over her head. Cocking one eyebrow, he held it up. "I'll let Lana know that when I see her," Jax said, then grinned. "I thought you were a teacher."

Caroline gasped when she turned to see Jax holding the red nightgown. Her eyes continued to stare at it. "Teachers aren't saints." Caroline's lip trembled. "Some are even called whores."

Jax dropped the nightgown and helped her off the floor. Damn, he sucked at this shit. Here he was trying to make her feel better; instead, she was on the verge of crying.

"Hey." Jax leaned down in her vision and cursed at the unshed tears. "Listen, smack me if you want. I suck at trying to make people laugh."

Caroline did look at him as a sad grin tipped her lips. "I'm sorry." She shook her head. "I'm usually not like this."

"What happened, Caroline?" Jax led her to the bed, sitting her down. The more he looked at her bruised face, the more pissed he became. Not wanting to scare Caroline any more than she was, he had to control the deep rage he felt at her being mistreated by a piece of shit scumbag.

"We have to get our stuff out by tomorrow morning." Caroline looked around the room. "We agreed he would get his stuff out over the weekend and then I would come after work this week to get the rest of my stuff. Rod sounded fine about it, until I didn't show up on Monday after work. He called me and was yelling, telling me I needed to get here to get my stuff. It just went on and on."

"Then why in the hell did you come alone today?" Jax didn't sound angry, just confused.

"Because I'm too trusting and stupid." Caroline rolled her eyes, then grimaced at the pain it caused her. "He told me the reason he was upset was because he wanted to talk to me, try to work things out and I ruined it by not showing up. He said he had to go out of town for work, which he did a lot. So I believed him. Today, I knew I had to come and get the rest of my clothes and the few dishes that were left. When he showed up, he laughed, saying I was stupid to believe he was going out of town, which I was. I should have known it was a lie."

Jax sat quietly, letting her go at her own pace, even though every instinct he possessed urged him to get up, walk out, find the fucker and kill him.

"He told me that if I didn't work it out with him, he would call my work and get me fired with lies, but I wouldn't budge. I told him to go ahead and give it his best shot." Caroline frowned. "Then he…"

"He what?" Jax urged, keeping the growl out of his voice.

"He accused me of seeing someone. I told him I wasn't, which isn't a lie. I mean a dinner is just dinner." Caroline glanced up at him, her pale cheeks blushed beautifully. "Anyway, he grabbed my phone and saw your message. He went crazy."

Jax went deadly still. Reaching over, he again tilted her face to his so he could see the bruising against her soft skin. "He hit you because of my text." It wasn't a question.

Caroline shook her head. "I don't think that's the only reason. He just went out of control. Even as far as threatening my younger sister, Jamie. Said his brother had taken a real liking to Jamie." Anger flashed across her eyes. "His brother is much older than Jamie. I know it was a threat to scare me so I won't tell anyone. He knows how much I love my family. I still can't believe how he treated Lana when I wasn't around and I never knew."

The text Jax saw on her phone must have been a reminder threat to her. "Nothing is going to happen to Jamie." Jax stood, pulling her up with him.

Caroline stood, looking around at all of her clothes then back at Jax. "Thank you, and I'm really sorry about dinner. I have to get this done and well…" She touched her swollen face.

"You are beautiful, Caroline." Jax wondered briefly who the hell possessed his body because the intense need to make this woman more comfortable was overwhelming. "Never doubt that. We'll do dinner another night."

"You're too sweet." Caroline smiled, reaching up giving him a hug. "Thank you."

Jax hugged her back, suddenly feeling uncomfortable as hell. Jax Wheeler was not sweet, what the fuck was happening to him? Pulling away, he led her toward the door. "Come on. Talk to your sister," Jax grumbled, a frown plastered across his face.

"Don't like being called sweet, huh?" Caroline chuckled, walking out the door ahead of him.

"Not at all," he responded, his eyes running down her body. Okay, this was the Jax Wheeler he knew. Watching her womanly hips and ass sway as she walked away was more his style. Thinking of what he wanted to do with that body was more on his level, no matter what she went through. Yeah, this was more of who he was, not that sweet shit.

"You know where this asshole hangs out?" Jax asked Sid while the women talked.

"No, but I'm sure we can find him." Sid's smile was evil in anticipation of finding the bastard and making him pay for what he'd done to Caroline.

"He's mine when we do," Jax warned Sid, dialing his phone.

"No sharing, huh?" Sid laughed, looking over his shoulder at the women.

"Hey, I need you to run a number for me and find me an asshole," Jax said on the phone, keeping his voice low. "Oh, yeah, well, bite me. And if you call me chief one more fucking time, I'm going to tomahawk your ass and take your scalp. Yeah, I need it now. I do have someone else I can call if you can't handle it. Uh-huh, fuck you, too. All right, hurry up."

"Nice," Sid smirked. "Do most people do you favors when you threaten them?"

Jax nodded with a serious stare. "Yeah, they do."

"Awesome, isn't it?" Sid nodded in total understanding.

"This guy can skip trace anyone. He's a pain in my ass, but is good at what he does. I just threaten him and then I get what I want." Jax switched the phone to his other ear, then glanced over at the women who were cleaning the broken dishes in the kitchen. His eyes met Caroline's. He could really get lost in her gorgeous eyes.

Sid saw the look that passed between the two. "You know, double weddings are really popular now." Sid's tone took on a serious note, but then he blew it by being a smart ass. "It would mean everything to me to call you brother, as in brother-in-law."

"Fuck off, Sid," Jax growled.

"Ah, that's a new one," Sid laughed. "Fuck off, Sid, has a different ring to it."

Jax just stared at Sid. "Is it your job to piss people off?"

"Actually, no, but it would be fucking awesome to get paid to piss people off." Sid's eyes opened in fake excitement. "I'd be a rich son of a bitch."

"That you would." Jax couldn't help but laugh; something he rarely did. Jax held up his finger when Sid started to say something else. "Yeah. Got it. Keep an eye on it and let me know if he moves within the next fifteen minutes." Jax hung up and then gave Sid a smirk without saying a word.

Nodding, Sid headed toward Lana. "Babe, we're going out for a few." He kissed her forehead. "You going to be okay here for a while?"

"Where you going?" Lana didn't hide the suspicion in her voice.

"What happened to my door?" Caroline stopped Sid from having to lie to Lana. She walked over staring at her broken door.

Sid pulled out his wallet, and then handed Lana a card. "When you didn't answer, I kind of kicked it in," he explained. "That's the company I used when Slade and Jill went through their phase of throwing people through walls."

"Thanks." Caroline gave Sid a small smile, and then looked at Jax. "Both of you."

Jax simply nodded before walking out the door. Lana followed them out.

"Kick his ass for me." Lana reached up kissing Sid. "But stay out of trouble."

"You see, this is one of the reasons I love you." Sid grabbed her in a hug, kissing her breathless.

"You can tell me the other reasons later." She nuzzled his neck before letting him go.

"I'll call you later." Sid gave her a promising wink before

following Jax to the car. "So chief, you really have a tomahawk?"

"I *really* hate you." Jax glared at him over the top of his car before getting in.

"Yeah, I get that a lot." Sid gave his famous 'don't give a shit' grin before climbing in the car. "Now, let's go find this fucker."

Chapter 12

Slade sat at his desk looking through faxes, papers, yet nothing was making sense. All he could think about was Jill and wanting to make sure she was okay. If she did have a concussion, she should be woken every few hours if she fell asleep. He knew she was tired and probably sleeping at this very moment. Even though she was part vampire, being human still made her susceptible to the dangers humans faced.

"Ah, fuck!" Slade stood up, pushing away from his desk. Running his hand through his hair, he stared at nothing. One thing he definitely missed about being human was sleeping so he could escape his own damn thoughts.

Throwing up his hands in surrender to his nagging thoughts of Jill falling asleep only to never wake again, he threw open the door and walked out. Dammit, he knew she was trouble. No, wait a minute. He was a doctor. It was his responsibility to check on her. "Yeah," he said to no one since he was alone and talking to his damn self.

By the time he made it to her room and knocked, he had a full conversation with himself coming to the conclusion that this was just a doctor thing, his oath to take care of the injured. The door had been fixed, but opened a crack with his knock. Pushing it open a little further, he spotted her curled up on the bed. She had a pair of shorts and was wearing a hoodie. The hood was pulled up over her head and he could see she had her red 'Beats' on listening to music, but was fast asleep. Walking deeper into the room, he just stood, watching her sleep.

He'd had many women in his long life, but none, not even one compared to Jillian Robin Nichols. Glancing around her room, he spotted her drawing pad she usually always had with her. Curious about what she drew, he walked over to the drawing pad, then glanced her way to make sure she was still sleeping. Reaching out, he flipped it over and was shocked. His penciled face stared back at him. Picking it up for a closer look, he fingered one of the rough spots as if the paper had gotten wet. It was discolored and rippled. There were identical spots in a couple of other places. And then it hit him like a punch to the gut. Tears. The spots were dried tears. He continued to look through the book realizing how good of an artist she really was. There was one with her two dogs. He turned back to the one of him, the only one with tear stains.

"You know that could be considered creepy." Jill's soft tired voice floated to him in the silence. "What are you doing here, Slade?"

Setting the drawing pad down, he turned to look at her. She was still in the same position except her eyes were open and sleepily staring at him. "I wanted to check on you."

"I'm good." She yawned. "Just very tired."

"And that's what worries me." Slade frowned, walking toward the bed.

"I've got some human in me, Slade. Before I was turned, I could sleep all day," Jill sighed, closing her eyes. "Don't you have a date or something?"

Slade frowned down at her, not liking that dig. "If you are referring to the phone number you handed me, you little smartass, it's on the DMV floor."

Jill opened one eye to look at him. "She was pretty and obviously into you."

"Yeah, well, it seems I'm preoccupied by a pain-in-the-ass woman who seems to constantly want to piss me off," Slade growled. "Now sit up and let me check your head."

Jill slowly pulled herself up. "I'm not the one who ran off like a little bitc—"

"Watch it," Slade ordered with narrowed eyes as he sat on the edge

130

of the bed. Gently, he used his fingers to pry her eyelids open wide so he could check her pupils. "Look up at the light." He repeated the action with the other eye. "And I didn't run. Does that hurt?" He pushed on her head in different positions after he was done checking her eyes.

"Well, you walked out pretty quickly." Jill was looking up at him, and then grimaced when he hit the sore spot on her head.

"I needed to let off some steam." Slade pulled his hands away.

"You said it was a mistake," Jill countered, not giving in.

"No, I said it shouldn't have happened," Slade corrected her.

Jill carelessly shrugged one shoulder. "Same thing."

"And once again, no." Slade shook his head trying not to smile. Usually, women who continued with the same issue over and over again got on his last nerve and he'd find any excuse to split, but Jill was entertaining when doing it. "A mistake is something I would never want to do again."

That seemed to stump her. She opened her mouth to say something then snapped it shut, looking away as she hugged her legs to her chest, putting her chin on her knees all the while looking at the wall. "So you would want to do *that*…again…with me?"

Slade's lips curved up in a grin. "Listen, Jill. This is complicated."

Her head snapped back toward him. "No, Slade, it's not. You either want me or you don't. That's not complicated. It's a simple question requiring a simple answer."

The pressure of wanting to do the right thing had Slade itching to punch something. He wished it was that simple, but it wasn't. She didn't understand what was at stake.

"And your silence tells me all I need to know." Jill lay back down and curled up. "Close the door when you leave."

"You don't understand," Slade growled, struggling to contain his frustration. "I'm doing this for you."

"Excuse me?" Jill swiftly stood, actually standing on her bed and threw her hands on her hips. "You're doing what for me? Driving me fucking insane?"

Slade also stood, making them eye-to-eye. "Yeah, well, welcome to the world of the insane." His angry tone matched hers. "You think this shit is easy for me?"

"Oh, what, coming in and fucking me, getting your jollies off and then walking out?" Jill put her finger to her lip as if thinking really hard. "Hmmm, let me think. Yeah, asshole, I think it's easy for you."

Don't smile, Slade told himself. Damn, but she was cute as hell when pissed. "My jollies?" He couldn't help repeating.

"Don't you dare make fun of me." Jill pointed at him in warning. "How would you feel if I came into your room, fucked the hell out of you then ran out as if it was the biggest mistake I'd ever made?"

"First of all, don't ever ask a man that question, because…well, just don't, and I didn't run out," Slade ended on a sigh. This was not getting them anywhere. But he did know one thing, if she was to come to his room and fuck the hell out of him, she would go nowhere, but he kept that to himself since she didn't seem in the mood to listen. She was revved up for a fight.

"Yeah, keep telling yourself that, Doc," Jill hissed. "Let me make this easy for you—"

"What? You going to give me more women's phone numbers?" Slade shot back.

"No, that *was* a mistake," Jill sneered. "I wouldn't want to do that to another woman unless she was my enemy."

Slade crossed his arms to keep from grabbing her, which is what he wanted to do, but not to harm, unless it was a bare ass spanking. A pissed-off Jill was sexy as hell. Her skin flushed, her eyes bright with anger, chest heaving as she shouted out; her quick wit turned him on like nothing else ever had. He wondered how far he could actually push the little wildcat.

"Listen, baby…" It looked like the fires of hell flamed her eyes, answering the question of how far he could push her. Not very far apparently.

Jill threw out her hand, the force pushing Slade toward the door. "Do *not* call me baby!" She gave a hard push with her hand, her eyes still on fire with anger.

Digging his heels in, he fought against her power. Slowly, he lifted his hand, pushing with his power against hers. "Don't forget, I've got the same power and I know how to use it."

Frowning as her feet moved backward on the bed, Jill visibly tried to push back harder, but it was no use; she was moving quickly toward the wall. Slade followed by stepping up on her bed as if it was just a small step. She struggled with everything she had, but it was no use. He had her plastered against the wall, both hands up above her head without him even touching her, only his power kept her prisoner.

"What are you going to do now, badass?" Slade tilted his head, looking down at her. When she struggled to move, he smiled. "The things I could do to you right now."

A fire of a different kind lit her eyes, before a smirk curved her lips. "Go for it, Warrior." Her voice lowered in a sexy timbre. "Then you can run out when you're finished." Her voice changed to sarcastic in a flash.

"One of these days, I'm going to smack that sweet ass of yours."

The smile never left his lips and his eyes promised he would do just that.

"Promises... Promises," Jill responded as if she couldn't care less, but her harsh breathing told him otherwise.

"Listen, and listen good, Jillian." He bent so his mouth was close to her ear, but his eyes still stared into hers. "Once your initiation is over, you are *mine*. Make no mistake, I will have you again and again, but for now, you focus on getting through initiation."

She sucked in her breath, biting her lower lip.

"If you'd keep that mouth of yours closed and listen, this whole situation would be different." He breathed in deeply, inhaling her scent; his cock hardened painfully in his jeans. "But then again, that mouth of yours has its benefits because without it, I wouldn't have you exactly where I want you."

"And where..." her voice cracked, causing her to clear it, "where's that?"

"Plastered against the wall under my total control." He moved his head around, their lips brushing against each other as he made his way slowly to her other ear. "And that...*baby*...makes me hard." He pushed into her, showing her exactly how hard he was. The flare in her eyes let him know she liked being in his control, which made it that much sweeter.

He could feel her body tremble, could smell her need and wanted nothing more than to fulfill that need, but she was going to have to learn to listen and not automatically think he only wanted one thing from her. Oh, he wanted nothing more in the world at that moment than to sink deep into her tight warmth, but Slade wanted her and he was done hiding it, but she was going to finish the program before anything more happened between them.

"But—" Jill's voice was harsh with need.

"There are no buts, Jill. I'm your trainer. That is most important right now," Slade replied before she could even finish her sentence. "This is the way it is and the way it will be. Finish the program and then we will see where we go from there."

Their faces were inches apart, breath mingling and Slade had control…until her wet, pink tongue snaked out to moisten her lips. Pushing away from her, he released his power, turned stepping off the bed, heading for the door. Jill followed him.

"So that's it?" Jill stood on the end of the bed. "You're leaving…again?"

Slade turned enough to look at her over his shoulder. "You heard what I said, Jill. Finish the program." His eyes ran over her body; his mind, as well as his hard cock, demanding he walk back and take her, ease his misery and hers, but he was stronger than that. He meant what he said. He would not be the reason she failed or got killed. He was her trainer first and foremost, and at that moment, he hated his fucking job.

Walking out of the room was probably the hardest thing he had ever done. Before he could take a step, something big hit the door behind him. He smiled, shaking his head. Yeah, he was going to pay for this stunt, but their focus needed to be on her training and nothing more. Taking a step, he groaned, looking down, but first he needed to take care of his need. Damn that woman was going to kill him or drive him insane. His mind quickly wondered how she would ease her need. "Fuck!" He shook the thoughts from his head, and walked faster to his room. Yeah, he was going to go insane.

******

Walking into a weight gym, Jax realized he had been right. The guy was a muscle head. "You see him anywhere?" Jax asked Sid, looking around.

"No." Sid walked over to the counter where a cute girl with a preppy ponytail and tight workout clothes stood at a computer. "Hello."

She looked up, her eyes widening at Sid, then shooting for Jax. "Hi." She smiled, putting on her best sales face. "You guys interested in a membership?"

"Hell, no," Jax grumbled.

"Actually, I am." Sid laughed loudly, rolling his eyes. "And I'm trying to talk my buddy into joining with me, but he's being a hard-ass thinking he don't need it."

The girl's eyes ran up and down Jax, and from her expression she agreed; he didn't need it. Then her sales' face returned. "You are in great shape." The girl nodded at Jax. "But this is a great gym with all the state-of-the-art equipment to help you stay in great shape."

"That's what I told him," Sid sighed, shaking his head before looking back at her with his biggest smile. "So, can we take a look around before making the decision?"

"Sure!" Her excitement at a possible bump in salary by signing two new memberships had her grabbing papers. "I'll get everything together on this end. You guys go check it out. I know you won't be disappointed. Plus, we are the only twenty-four hour gym in the area."

"Thank you." Sid smiled down at her, making her blush. "I'm sure we won't be disappointed in what we find at all."

Jax had already taken off. It was pretty empty since it was two o'clock in the morning. The place was big, and as Jax was about to give up finding the bastard, Sid chuckled, pointing toward the back corner.

"He really is a douchebag," Sid smirked. "He's going to be so happy to see me."

Looking to where Sid was pointing, Jax spotted the man immediately, standing in front of a mirror that covered the whole wall while pumping weights and looking at himself before flexing. "He's mine," Jax reminded Sid.

"Just got your back, brother." Sid nodded, looking slightly disappointed as they made their way toward the iron-pumping asshole.

Rod was too busy looking down at his muscle to notice two figures behind him in the mirror, but once he looked up, it was a photo moment because the look of shock on his face was classic. Sid with his crooked 'you're getting your ass beat' smile and Jax's 'I'm the one beating your ass' glare couldn't be misconstrued.

Dropping the weights, Rod tried to make a run for it, but had nowhere to go. Jax grabbed him by the back of the neck, forcing him down on a weight bench.

"What do you want?" Rod's voice didn't fit his body image. He sounded like a scared girl, his voice high with fright. "I didn't do anything to Lana." His eyes shot to Sid.

"And you're very lucky for that," Sid growled down at him.

"You like hitting women?" Jax smacked him on the back of the head, hard. "Does it make you feel like a man, you piece of shit?"

"No, it was an accident." Rod's lie pissed Jax off even more, making him smack the back of his head harder.

"Try again, motherfucker," Jax sneered down at him. "Do you know what my tribe did back in the day to men who abused their women?"

"No." Rod's voice shook almost as bad as his body. "And I didn't abuse Caroline."

Jax grabbed Rod by the throat, getting in his face. "You're not even fit to say her name."

"Ah, Jax." Sid tilted his head, watching Rod's face change colors. "I was hoping to prolong his suffering for a while; it's more entertaining that way."

With one last squeeze, Jax shoved his neck away. "A woman should be honored, not beat on by little pricks like you." Jax knelt down in front of Rod so the bastard could see the truth behind his words.

"So what did your tribe use to do?" Sid sat down on a weight bench next to Rod. "I'd *really* like to hear the story."

Jax's smile turned evil as his fist clenched tightly; his piercing black eyes never left Rod's. "First, after the bastard was found, he was tied to a tree. The elders allowed all the women to inflict punishment, but not kill. When the women were finished, the woman who had been abused had her turn, and it wasn't pretty. Indian women could be more ruthless than the men."

"Go on." Sid leaned closer as if really getting into the story, which was fucking with Rod's head.

"Once she was finished, the women would go back to their daily routines while the men took over." Jax's face took on a menacing look. "If it was rape, his cock was cut with expertise off his body. The shaman would sew him back up to make sure he would live so every day he could see his rotting raping cock hanging from the woman's camp."

"Holy shit. Can someone really live without their dick?" Sid leaned back, really thinking about that. "Then again, who the fuck would want to?"

"If it's done right, they can, and believe me, our shaman had it down to an art and even showed men in the tribe how it was done so the punishment would live on after he was gone." Jax watched the sweat roll down Rod's terrified face, a primal satisfaction filling his body.

"Let me guess." Sid snapped his fingers and pointed at Jax. "You were one of those men the shaman taught."

"I didn't rape her. Is that what that bitch said? She's fucking lying." Rod went to stand up, but was slammed back down.

"Shut the fuck up and listen," Jax warned, his eyes black as night.

"Yeah, I want to hear the rest, *Rod.*" Sid's face indicated he was loving every fucking minute of this.

"In my tribe, the punishment reflected the abuse," Jax continued. "If a man hit a woman, his hands were removed. If he bit a woman, his teeth were removed, and not in a pleasant way. Everything was done so that the bastard would live with his punishment and disgrace, every day."

"So what if they called her a bitch?" Sid asked, using his head to point at Rod.

"Then the nearest male would punch him in the mouth." Jax did just that before pushing Rod all the way back on the weight's bench. "This is your only warning. If you ever come near Caroline or her family again, I will hunt you down, and believe me, you don't want me hunting you down because once I find you, and I will find you, I will relive my roots and deal out every punishment I've ever learned. It will be painful and you will be hideous, but you will live. You understand me, motherfucker?"

Rod nodded, tears rolling out of the side of each eye. He tried to answer, but choked on the blood from his mouth. "Yes," he finally muttered past his broken teeth and swelling lips.

Sid walked over with a bench lift bar loaded down with weights, setting it down across Rod's chest. "I'm kind of impressed, Rod. If I was you, I'd be scared enough to piss myself." Sid let go of the bar so all the weight kept Rod immobile, before he looked at Jax.

"Hey, didn't you guys scalp people also?"

"Yes." Was all Jax said as he pulled out a butterfly knife, opening it with flare. "Our knives were a little bigger, but this would do."

Sid nodded, and then looked down at Rod's crotch as his red shorts became darker with piss. "And there it is," Sid grinned. "Figured that would do it."

Jax leaned over Rod. "Remember, you cannot hide from me."

Rod nodded and squeezed his eyes shut, a low keening coming from his throat.

As Jax and Sid walked toward the exit, Sid grinned. "Now that was fun."

Jax mumbled, still in his rage-mode.

"So what tribe were you with?" Sid glanced at him sideways.

"The one you didn't want to fuck with, white man." Jax pushed his way out the door.

"Point taken." Sid nodded with raised eyebrows, and then smiled. "I'm going to like you, Chief. Now let's go home and I'll fix you up some grub."

"That's cowboy slang, dumbass." Jax turned his head away so Sid couldn't see his half smile. This fucker was nuts, but funny as hell.

Chapter 13

After hours of lying awake, Jill headed to the kitchen, grumpy and sexually frustrated. She had thought of many nasty, painful ways to torture Slade. After a cold shower, which didn't help her one bit and proved the belief that cold showers helped a sexually frustrated individual was total bullshit, her ways of torture turned even more evil.

"Well, hello, sunshine." Steve smiled at her from the table.

Ignoring him, other than a growl, Jill headed for coffee. Grabbing the biggest cup she could find, she poured and poured, dumped half a bowl of sugar in and took a long drink, loving the burn going down her throat. Bringing the cup down, she sighed then looked around at everyone staring at her.

"What?" she glared, not in the mood.

"You want some food with your cup of sugar?" Sid eyed her closely.

Shaking her head, she poured more coffee and sugar into her cup and walked to the table to sit down across from Steve. Jax sat on one end drinking coffee. Adam had just walked over with food falling off the edges of his plate and sat down.

"So when do your stripping lessons start?" Adam dug into his food, waiting for her to answer.

Pulling the hood up around her head, Jill frowned. "Tessa texted me this morning. I have to meet them around noon at the bar."

"Good." Sloan had walked in on the conversation, followed by Jared and Slade. "That will give you plenty of time to practice your driving. Congrats on passing the written. Monday you test for your driving permit and you better be ready. I had to pull in a few favors to get you in before your required time."

Well, that sure as hell didn't add any pressure. What she really wanted to say was 'can't I even drink a full cup of coffee before you're on my ass about something',' but instead, responded with, "Yes, sir." Seriously, she wanted to live, but was just having a minute to relax too freaking much to ask?

"Who's free this morning to go with her so she can practice driving?" Sloan looked around.

"Ah, well, I ah…" Adam about choked on his egg when Sloan's eyes fell on him.

Jill glared at him, the ass. God forbid, he let her drive his precious piece of crap.

"I'll do it," Jax said, surprising everyone. Draining the rest of his coffee, he stood, looking at Jill. "Let's go."

"Dun Dun Duuuuunnnnn," Steve mumbled before taking a bite of food.

Jill snatched a sausage link off Adam's plate, hitting Steve between the eyes with it before standing up and taking her cup to the sink.

"Hey!" Steve frowned, before looking at the sausage and taking a bite.

Jill rolled her eyes when she turned around to see Steve eating the sausage she threw at him. Passing Sloan and Slade, she nodded, but kept her eyes off Slade, because suddenly, all the torture techniques popped into her head again. Yeah, she needed to get out of there.

Heading outside, she saw Jax walking toward a cherry red Mustang GT. Holy shit, if she wrecked that car, she would be a dead woman. She wondered briefly if stress could actually kill a half-breed. "Hey, if that's a stick, I can't drive it."

Jax laughed without turning around. "There is no way in hell I would let you drive this car." He popped the trunk, getting something out. "We're taking one of the other cars."

Okay, that settled her stomach a little bit. Still, it rolled and pitched thinking about getting behind the wheel while the person who hated her and wanted her to quit the program sat next to her. This was going to be a total fail.

They went to one of the old cars, a Nissan, the Warriors used for different occasions. He threw the keys to her. Jill got in, put her seatbelt on, started the car and sat there staring out the window.

Finally, Jax glanced over at her. "Please tell me you know how to put the car in gear."

Jill nodded. "I just don't want you to start yelling because that's just going to make me more nervous."

"Don't give me a reason to yell and I won't yell." Jax's response was pretty much to the point, but didn't help. Jill gave him a sideways glance. "Okay, I will only yell if you are about to plow someone down. Better?"

Again, Jill nodded as she put the car in reverse. Pulling out fast, and then slamming on the brakes, Jill watched out of the corner of her eye as Jax's upper body flew forward and then slammed back against the seat. She waited…ready.

Slowly, he turned to look at her. "And the reason for that was?" He cocked his eyebrow at her.

"Just wanted to make sure you weren't going to yell before I actually got out on the road," Jill shrugged.

Jax nodded slowly, still eyeing her. "Well since we have *that* cleared up, are you ready to stop fucking around and get this over with?"

"Yep." This time, Jill pulled out carefully and headed for the exit of the compound driveway. Flicking on her blinker, she looked for traffic and pulled out, smiling at herself for getting that far without killing them. As they travelled down the road, Jill kept a death grip on the wheel, her eyes going all over the place looking for obstacles she could murder with the car.

Leaning over, Jax looked at the dashboard and sighed, "How about pushing on the accelerator a little harder, Jill. It shouldn't take us a half an hour to go a block and a half."

Frowning, Jill did as he said. She should have said no yelling *and* no being a smartass. "Where to?"

"You know how to get to the bar?" Jax looked at his watch.

"Yeah." Jill continued to drive and everything seemed to be going smoothly until someone pulled out in front of her. Jill slammed on her brakes barely missing the car. "Are you serious! Watch where you're going, asshole!! Are you freaking blind?" Jill screamed, blaring her horn. "Come on. Can we go faster than two miles an hour?"

Jill flipped on the blinker, getting in the other lane to pass. As she passed, she and Jax looked into the car. A little old man, who was absolutely adorable and could barely see over the steering wheel, glanced at them, giving them a grandfatherly smile.

Jax slowly looked at Jill with a frown. "I suggest, if that happens during your test, do what you did, minus the blaring of the horn and screaming threats at old people in a fit of road rage."

Jill shifted on the seat, frowning, but nodded. "Understood."

"Make sure you use your signals all the time." Jax sat back, relaxed, as if enjoying the ride. "You missed a few. I'm not sure how many points that will be. Have you ever parallel parked?"

Stopping at a red light, Jill glanced over at Jax. "No."

"Never?" Jax frowned and cursed. "Okay, no big deal, but we need to practice that. You're okay driving when you're paying attention. Find a street that cars park on."

Driving up and down streets, she finally found one. Seeing a parking spot between two cars Jill slowed down. "Is that a good one?"

Jax looked at it and actually got out for a closer look. Walking back to her side of the window, he bent down. "Get out and let me do it first. Stand over there and watch."

Getting out of the car, Jax pulled her aside as someone drove past. Heading over to stand, she watched what Jax did and shook her head once he was in the spot looking at her. After pulling back out into the street, he got out and waved her over.

Shit, there was no way she was going to be able to do that. "There is no way," Jill spoke her thoughts out loud.

"Yeah, well, you have no choice now, do you?" Jax looked back at the spot where he had parked. "When you test, they will have cones, not cars."

"What if I hit one?" Jill still stared at the spot as if it was her worse nightmare. Hell, it was pretty damn close to her worse nightmare.

"You won't." Jax opened the door for her.

"But if I do?" Jill sat in the driver's seat, staring at the spot before looking up at Jax.

"Then you get to tell Sloan and he'll have to call the insurance to fix whatever you fuck up." Jax laughed at her horrified look. "Now, pull up like I did. Then turn the wheel and start backing up slowly. It's really common sense and I do know you have common sense."

Waiting for Jax to step out of the way, Jill closed her eyes, said a quick prayer, put the car in drive and pulled up."

"Open you damn eyes, Jill!" Jax yelled.

"Don't yell at me!" Jill yelled back.

"Then keep your eyes open!" Again Jax yelled back, shaking his head with a roll of his eyes.

Once Jill pulled up, she braked and put the car in reverse. Turning around in the seat so she could see, she started backing up in jerky movements.

"Use your mirrors," Jax instructed. "And stop slamming on the brakes."

Jill mumbled to herself, her neck hurting from jerking her head around to each mirror. Once she had the car backed in, she put the car in drive, turned the wheel and started moving forward.

"That's good, Jill." Jax walked closer, watching. "Cut the wheel more. You got plenty of room up here."

"Please don't let me hit the car," she said to herself. "Please don't let me hit the car. Please don't let me hit the car."

"Okay, now cut the wheel again and put it in reverse. Take it slow." Jax walked to the back of the car.

"Please don't let me hit the car," Jill continued the chant since it seemed to be helping. "Please don't let me hit the car. Please don't let me hit the car."

"Good, Jill, now straighten the wheel and pull up a little." Jax waited until she was good and held up his hand. Walking to her side of the window, he smiled down at her. "Congratulations on your first parallel park."

"Really?" Jill's smile was huge. Slamming the car in park, she got out and stared at Jax with a happy look on her face. "I really did it."

"Yeah, you did good." Jax grinned with a nod. "Now, do it again."

"Okay." She hurried to the car, excited, but then stopped, turning to Jax. "Why are you being so nice to me?"

"Hell if I know," Jax grumbled, but when Jill continued looking at him, he frowned. "I figured I was being pretty hard on you. Don't worry, I'm sure I'll be back to my asshole self soon enough."

"Thank you." She smiled at him before getting in the car. "I appreciate your help."

"Yeah, well, let's see what happens Monday before you get all sappy and shit." Jax motioned for her to do her thing. "Come on. I don't have all day."

Jill parked five more times before Jax was happy enough to leave. Once they were in the parking lot of the bar Tessa worked at, Jill picked two cars to park between. It wasn't parallel parking, but close enough. Once parked, Jill switched off the engine and sat, sporting a huge grin.

"Pretty proud of yourself, aren't you?" Jax wore a half-grin on his face.

"Yes, I am," Jill sighed, handing him the keys.

"Well, you should be, except for the moment of road rage, you did well." Jax looked at the keys, but didn't take them as he got out of the car. "Keep them. You're driving back."

"Sweet!" Jill stuck the keys in her pocket, and then walked into the bar and froze. Not only were the women there, but Damon, Sid, Jared, Duncan and Slade, as well as Adam and Dillon. The only two missing were Sloan and Steve. Okay, so she thought the parking spot was her worst nightmare and how wrong was she on that. The stripper pole actually took on a shape of horror as it

147

zoomed into her vision.

"How did the driving go?" Sid asked as she passed him.

Jill didn't even look at the guys, just gave him a thumbs up as she passed. She couldn't talk if she wanted to. Tessa smiled at her until she saw her face.

"What's wrong?" Tessa frowned. "Did you wreck?"

Prying her eyes off the stripper pole, she looked at Tessa. "No, I didn't wreck, but I wish I would have." She lowered her voice. "What are they doing here?"

"We thought it was best if you had an audience to get you used to…you know," Tessa replied, and then wrapped her arm around Jill.

"No, Tessa, I don't know." Jill pulled away in total freak-out mode. She was seriously going to have a panic attack. Looking over her shoulder everyone was sitting around talking, not paying them any attention except when her eyes hit on Slade; he was staring right at her. "I can't do this."

"Just ignore them, Jill." Nicole walked up, hearing their conversation. "Now, come on. We don't have much time."

Tessa pulled Jill over to the pole. "Can you dance?"

Jill nodded. "Yeah, I guess so."

"Thank God," Pam sighed. "That would make this so much harder."

"We got some clothes for you, but won't make you put them on right now with all the guys here." Tessa grinned excitedly. "You are going to look awesome."

"I'm going to be a stripper." Jill frowned at their excitement, even Angelina was beaming. "Not a beauty pageant contestant."

"A gorgeous stripper." Caroline rubbed her hands together. "I'm doing your makeup and wig."

"Wig?" Jill was sure she was going to vomit. How in the hell was she going to pull this off? Then she really looked at Caroline's face. Her cheek was bruised and swollen, her eye black. "What happened?"

"Nothing." Caroline waved her off. "And yes, a wig. A beautiful long, black wig."

"Yeah, so you can whip your hair around." Angelina did just that, getting a whistle from Adam, which made her blush.

"Okay, we are each going to do a little on the pole so you can watch." Tessa walked over behind the bar and turned on some music. Warrant's "Cherry Pie" blared throughout the bar. Tessa walked right up to the pole, kicked off her shoes and took control with the sexiest dance Jill had ever seen.

Mouth opened wide, she watched Tessa, who was a full-bodied, beautiful woman, dance like she had never seen a woman dance. 'Holy shit,' Jill mouthed, looking at Lana who was grinning at her, and then nodded toward Jared. Jill glanced at Jared who had walked closer and simply stood staring at his mate as if no one else was in the room and Tessa was dancing just for him. The heat in his eyes almost burned her. When the song ended, no one said a word.

Tessa straightened her hair, her clothes and walked off toward the bar like a boss, giving Jared a sexy wink. Once at the bar, she looked toward the other women. "Next."

"If one of you motherfuckers even has a hard-on, I will kill you," Jared warned as he stalked toward Tessa, taking her in his arms before disappearing in the back storage room of the bar.

"Jared, I have to stay out here and help," Tessa laughed as they disappeared.

"You will, this will only take…" Jared's words faded as they disappeared.

"I'll get it," Angelina laughed, running to the radio.

Nicole also laughed before winking at Jill. Grabbing the pole, she tossed Damon a mischievous grin and danced her ass off. Damon walked right up to the small stage, standing directly in front of Nicole, as if trying to block anyone from seeing her.

"You're blocking everyone from seeing," Nicole said over the music as she swung by him on the pole.

"And I don't give a fuck. No man is going to watch you dance like this." Damon's warning was said loud enough for all to hear and hear they did. Jill looked and everyone was suddenly looking busy with anything other than looking toward the stage.

Nicole snorted. "What are you going to do? Decapitate them?"

"Yes, if need be," Damon replied. He sounded so serious that even Jill was afraid to watch Nicole dance. When Nicole was finished, there were audible sighs and grunts of relief throughout the room.

As soon as it was Lana's turn, Sid stood up, heading toward the stage. Once he was before Lana, he turned around to look at his fellow Warriors. "I suggest you fuckers get busy doing something. If I catch anyone watching her, other than the women, Jared and Damon will look like pussies compared to what I will do to you."

Lana rolled her eyes, but smiled. As soon as the music played, she danced and obviously only for Sid, because Jill looked and every single Warrior respected Sid's wishes and looked elsewhere. As soon as the dance was over, he grabbed Lana around the waist for a kiss that melted even Jill. 'Holy shit' moments were happening like crazy. Sid grabbed the pole, giving it a shake, before he looked up to where it was attached, then down to the floor.

"What are you doing?" Lana also looked up and down the pole, confused.

"Seeing how this thing is set up because one is going in our room." Sid gave it one more shake, nodded as if it was a done deal and walked back to his seat with the other Warriors, but not before giving Lana a wink.

On and on it went. Pam danced only for Duncan, and well, her of course, but during Pam's dance, Jill felt uncomfortable watching when Pam got off the stage and pretty much gave Duncan a standing lap dance. The more everyone danced, the more Jill realized she was royally fucked. Angelina was the last one and once her song was completed, everyone looked at Jill.

"There is no way in hell I can do that." Jill held up her hands giving a nervous 'no fucking way' laugh. "You guys are amazing, sexy and, well, I'm not any of that, so maybe Steve would have been a better choice for this job. Don't they have gay night or something?" Jill knew she was rambling, but the more she rambled, the longer it would take for them to get her near that pole.

Tessa finally came out of the back room with Jared looking flushed and satisfied, walked over and pulled her toward the pole. "You can and will do this." Tessa smiled, putting one of Jill's hands on the pole, which Jill pulled away as if it bit her. Tessa ignored her and repositioned Jill's hand. "Start the music."

Nickelback's "Something In Your Mouth" played, a song Jill loved and knew, but her body was frozen. She couldn't move, not one single muscle. Tessa waved toward Angelina, who turned the music off.

"I got this." Caroline walked up to Jill. "You need to think of this as a job, Jill, because it is. Close your eyes and listen to the music. You said you knew how to dance, so dance. No one will laugh. The Warriors are counting on you, Jill."

Jill's eyes searched the Warriors who were watching her closely with expectations she didn't think she could live up to. "It's just…"

"Listen to me," Caroline whispered. "I know you have something for Slade, so use it. Show that Warrior what he's missing out on. Close those pretty eyes of yours and let loose. If Sloan and the guys didn't think you could do this, you wouldn't be doing it. The only one in this room who doesn't believe in you, is you."

Jill looked at her and knew she was right. She was being asked to do a job, and by damn, she needed to do it. She drove without killing herself, or Jax, and parallel parked. And how many times had she danced to this song? Hundreds at least. She just had to make it…sexy. "Okay," Jill nodded.

Caroline smiled. "You got this." Caroline turned, walked away and nodded to Angelina to start the music.

The last person Jill saw as the music started and she closed her eyes, was Slade. Maybe, just maybe she could use this to torture Slade in some small damn way for payback, the ass. Yeah, this was a new torture technique she could use against the sexy Warrior who was driving her insane. Her body moved with the beat. She tried to use the pole, but banged her head. Fuck that hurt, but she didn't stop, didn't see the grimaces on the faces of everyone. Soon, her body took over. She didn't think, just let go, not caring who was watching because honestly, she didn't know, didn't want to know. Finally, the music stopped, her eyes opened slowly. It was eerily silent as everyone stared at her; the women with shocked looks and the men with angry glares. Slade's eyes were narrowed and she could actually see the tick in his jaw from where she was standing.

Jill found Tessa whose shocked face was turning into a huge grin. "What?" Jill whispered, not sure what the hell was going on. Did she suck that bad?

"You slut!" Nicole laughed, clapping her hand. "That was awesome! Where in the hell did you learn to dance like that?"

"Really?" Jill gave them a nervous disbelieving smile.

"Honey, I was about ready to go slap Jared, you were so good," Tessa laughed, hugging her. "You are going to rock this."

"But I didn't use the pole that much." Jill frowned and rolled her eyes. "And I banged my head on it. I don't think that's too sexy."

"Hell, that's something we can work on," Tessa grinned excitedly.

Jill smiled, looking back toward Slade, but her eyes caught Caroline who was standing by Jax. Caroline gave her a wink and a thumbs up. Before she knew what was happening, she was surrounded by women giving her instructions for the pole and finally felt like she could accomplish a job that could help the Council.

Taking one more peek, she watched as Slade stood, shoving Dillon halfway across the room before slamming out of the bar. Her eyes met Jax's who gave her a smug look. Jill quickly turned her attention to what was important, and that was being a VC Warrior. Nothing else mattered; at least that's what her head said. Her heart had other plans.

Chapter 14

Alice sat in the limo, staring at her ring. Soon she would be the Mayor's wife, Mrs. Alice Ferguson, the First Lady of the city of Cincinnati. Now, *that* had a nice *ring* to it. Alice laughed, her mind already decorating the office she would soon be getting. She was tired of having to use Tom's office. He was an idiot. She should be the one sitting behind the Mayor's desk, but she was fine running things from the back of her limo. For now.

Her plans were already taking shape in a way even she never dreamed, and all she had to do was suck the Mayor's small, limp cock and she was given anything her heart desired. In order to get the building to house half-breeds, all she had to do was let the pervert Mayor do nasty things to her and every wish she had was given to her. Nothing had been easier; hell, some of it she enjoyed. Her main plan was in motion: get rid of half-breeds. It was time to put her next plan in motion and that was to take out the Warriors and their small band of breeds who were protected by law. That one was going to be a little harder. As much as her fiancé hated the VC Council, he was still a pussy when it came to decisions about them, but she had plans. She actually had an epic plan to replace *him* with someone who had a set of balls. The door to the limo opened, bringing Alice out of her thoughts.

"What do you have for me?" Alice was eager to get things in place.

"A lot." The man looked Alice over, a cocky grin curving his lips. "What do you have for me?"

Slowly slipping her expensive coat off her shoulders, she stared at the handsome undercover detective who was in her pocket. He was her kind of man, sexy, buff, with a 'fuck you' attitude. She loved when his eyes traveled over her breasts that spilled out of her tight dress. "This is just a hint of what I have for you, but first, why don't you make me wet by telling me what you have." She loved human men. They were so easy and thought with their cocks, and Detective Jim Daniels had a big cock.

154

His eyes flamed at what was to come. Handing her a folder, he grinned. "I think you'll be happy."

"I hope so." She opened the folder and the first thing she saw was that little bitch half-breed, Jill, with Adam, Steve and another breed who Alice thought looked familiar, but wasn't sure. There were different pictures of them with the Warriors. One caught her eye. "Why were they at a paintball arena?"

"Well, it seems that they are getting ready to be initiated into the VC Council." The man sounded proud of his find.

"Shit! I didn't know they were doing that now. I thought it was next year." Alice shuffled through the pictures faster. When she was a part of the Warriors as a donor, she knew everything that was going on. Since leaving, she was left in the dark. God, she hated them, every single one of them and their bitch mates. "We can't let that happen. The little bitch will be protected for life."

"The little bitch?" Jim grinned. "Is this a personal vendetta, Mrs. Mayor?"

Alice laughed. "Yes, against that little bitch, it is personal."

"So what's the plan, boss?" Jim leaned back, waiting for his orders as his eyes feasted on her full breasts and long legs.

Liking the hold she had over this man, Alice thrust her breasts out with a sigh. Men always liked to think they were in charge. Most didn't like taking orders from a woman, even though they were paid well in both money and favors. "I'm not sure, Jim." Alice put her finger near her mouth, running it back and forth across her full lips. "I do know one thing I want done, and that's for the Warriors to be shaken up a bit."

"Consider it done." Jim's eyes slid back and forth with her finger. "I've got enough man power to fuck with them."

"Well, I don't care what you do or who you kill, but…" She held up Jill's picture, "she stays alive. There will be a big bonus for her."

"Yes, ma'am," Jim nodded, taking the pictures before tossing them to the other seat across from them. "Any other orders?"

"Yeah, there's a new Warrior; he's American Indian," Alice sneered, remembering the bastard in Tom's office. She hated him almost as much as she hated that little breed bitch. "If he happens to get a silver bullet between the eyes, there will be another bonus."

"Yes, ma'am." Jim's grin turned menacing. "Will definitely be on the lookout for him."

"You do that." Alice gave him a flirty smile. Pulling out an envelope, she handed it to him. "You can count it."

Tossing the money onto the pictures, Jim shook his head. "I trust you." His eyes went to her breasts.

Alice could hear his desire in his heartbeat. Slowly, she slipped the dress down her shoulders; baring her breasts, and then pulled her dress up, exposing the fact she was not wearing underwear. "Your bonus for the pictures."

Jim reached out, grabbing one of her breasts with one hand, then pulling her closer with the other one. "Honey, I can't wait to see what my bonus is when I bring the Warriors to their knees."

Looking out the window as Jim nipped down her neck, Alice's eyes turned black as night. "You do that, Detective, and you may become my head of security with daily bonuses."

Moaning, Jim made quick work of dropping his pants and plunging into her. Alice bared her fangs, sinking her teeth deep into his neck, sucking until he was spent inside her. She didn't know what excited her most; his cock deep inside her or the fact that the Warriors were about to get their due.

******

Caroline walked up to Jax as everyone got ready to leave the bar. She had really enjoyed helping Jill who, thank God, knew how to dance. The poor girl was a mess of nerves, but did really well.

"So, teach, why didn't you dance?" Jax smiled, but his eyes were intense.

Self-consciously, she brushed her hair toward her bruised cheek. "No one wants to see me dance," she laughed, rolling her eyes.

"I wouldn't have minded seeing you dance. Was actually looking forward to it." Jax winked. He reached out, gently brushing her hair back. "And don't hide your face."

"It's gross." Caroline blushed with a frown. Realizing she used one of her kids' words, she smiled. "Like *totally*," she added with a laugh.

Jax grinned, cocking his eyebrow. "Hanging around kids too much?"

"You don't even know," Caroline snorted, shaking her head. Looking at the clock on the wall, she wondered if she should ask. *Ah, what the hell*, she thought. "So you want to do that dinner? It seems you've been holding up to your side of the bargain." She glanced back at Jill who was talking with Jared.

"I have Jill with me." He frowned. "I helped her with her driving and parking today. She takes her test Monday for her license. I promised her she could drive back to the compound."

"Oh, well, that's okay." Caroline looked away a little embarrassed, but did grin. "You really are holding up to your end of the bargain. Even going above and beyond just being nice."

"Yeah, well, who knows how long it will last." Jax rolled his shoulders, looking uncomfortable. "It's totally against my nature."

"So how do you think Jill did with her dance?" Caroline took pity on him and changed the subject of how nice he was being, since it obviously made him uncomfortable.

"Don't know." Jax stood, towering over Caroline. "Didn't watch her."

"But why not?" Her eyes widened. "She did really well."

"Watching Jill use a stripper pole would be like watching my..." Jax caught what he was about to say and cursed.

"Your sister. I knew that's why you were treating her like you have been." Caroline finished for him, putting her hand on his arm when she saw the hurt those words caused him. "Jax..."

Jax jerked his arm away without even looking down at her. "Jill, let's go," he yelled out, heading toward the door.

"Jax." Caroline followed him outside. "I'm sorry. I shouldn't have said—"

"You're damn right, you shouldn't have." Jax turned so fast he startled Caroline, making her stumble back. "I told you not to mention her to me again!" His control snapped, making him bellow at her.

They stood staring at each other for a second until Jax growled, turned and walked off. Caroline watched him walk away. "I know," she whispered to no one, at least no one anyone else could see. "Dammit, I'm going."

Caroline marched across the parking lot. "You have got to deal with this." Caroline stopped right behind Jax. "It's eating you alive and you have to deal with it. Talk to your sister."

His head fell back as if trying to control himself; it didn't work. "She is fucking DEAD!" He turned on her. "What the fuck do you *not* understand about that? You and your so-called gift is a bunch of bullshit. You are a fake! She is dead!"

"I am not a fake, you stubborn son of a bitch," Caroline yelled back. "Just because you are too closed-minded to listen to me and your sister, who yes, is dead, but right here talking to me and now looking like a nervous mess because you are acting like a lunatic, doesn't make it not true."

"Get the fuck out of my face now, before I do something I'll regret!" His fists closed tightly as he stared down at her.

Caroline's eyes shot to his hands, and then back to his face. "What are you going to do, hit me?" Caroline snorted. "You are the one who is a liar and a fake. Feeling all sorry for me was a lie."

"No, but now I understand why he might have—"

She not only smacked him once across the face, but twice, without saying a single word. She turned, storming off, a knife twisting in her gut. He sure as hell was not who she thought he was. She sure sucked when it came to reading living people, not that he was actually living, but he wasn't a damn ghost either. Caroline made it to her car before the tears started to fall.

******

Shaking, Jax stood staring at the ground, trying to regain control. Looking up, Jill walked right up to him.

"I know you didn't mean what you just said to her." Jill frowned, glancing back at Caroline, who ran, jumping into her car.

"Yeah, I did." Jax also glanced in that direction, his voice not sounding very convincing.

"Then why do you look crushed?" Jill tossed him the keys. "I'll find my own way home, but I think you better go after her. That was a pretty dick move, even for you."

Caroline peeled out of the parking lot, spraying gravel everywhere. "Dammit!" Jax cursed as he quickly sat in the driver's seat before slamming it into reverse.

She was a few cars in front of him, but he was catching up. "Fuck!" He cringed when she flew through a red light, a car barely missing her. Racing up beside her after maneuvering around cars, he blared the horn. She actually looked, before flipping him off. Rolling down his window, she rolled hers up. "Pull over, now!" Her response was to flip him off again and sped up.

"Piece-of-shit Nissan," Jax cursed, slamming his hands on the steering wheel as if that would make it go faster. This would not be an issue if he was in his GT. Jax had the pedal to the floor, yet he was losing her. Seeing the light turn yellow, he glanced to see if she was preparing to stop. She did hit the brake a few times, slowing down enough that he was able to catch back up to her. Slamming the pedal, he maneuvered slightly in front of her, wedging her toward the curb. He was shocked when she actually went up on the median and kept going. "Are you fucking kidding me?"

Okay, she wanted to play. Jax jerked onto the median, stopped the car and jumped out. With a step, he was off and running, catching up to her faster than any car could. Running up beside the passenger's door, he tried to open it, but she locked it, looking at him as if he'd lost his mind. "Open the door!" he yelled, but she shook her head and told him to go to hell. "If you don't open this fucking door, right now, I'm going to tear if off."

He watched Caroline's hand hover over the lock button before she finally hit it, unlocking the door and slowing down, but he didn't wait. He opened the door and swung himself in, slamming the door shut...hard. "Pull the goddamn car over."

"Get out of my goddamn car," Caroline shouted, swiping tears away. "Or I'm going to call the police."

"I am the police...more or less, and I'm pulling you over for about ten driving violations." Jax growled, and grabbed the steering wheel as he kicked his leg over, moving hers out of the way to control the gas and brake.

Caroline smacked at his arm. "What are you doing?" She smacked again, her eyes frantically looking for danger of being hit. "You're going to kill us."

"Oh, that's classic." Jax pulled into an empty parking lot, slammed the car in park and took the keys. "You almost got t-boned back there running a red light. Jesus, Caroline, you could have been seriously hurt."

"Like you would give a shit. Now, give me my keys." Caroline snatched at them, but he pulled them away. "Fine." She got out of the car and started walking.

Jax got out, jumping in front of her. "Listen, I'm sorry and yes, I would give a shit if you got hurt."

"You're sorry?" Caroline snorted, swiping at a tear. "Well, I don't accept. And honestly, I don't even know why I care what you think about me so much. I must have brain damage from Rod, which I probably deserved, in your demented mind." She threw that at him, flipping him off again.

"Will you stop flipping me off and listen," Jax sighed, grabbing her arm to stop her. "I didn't mean what I said. I was wrong to say that, Caroline. I would never lift a hand toward you in anger and I absolutely don't think it was right that he did. I even made damn sure he would never do it again."

Her body was still turned away from him, listening, but his last sentence made her turn around. "What did you do?" she whispered, but still eyed him with distrust.

He shook his head. "I didn't kill him if that's what you're thinking. I wanted to, but just believe me when I say after Sid and I were finished with him, he won't ever bother you again."

Looking away from him, she nodded. "Thank you." Holding her hand out toward him, she sighed, "Now, can I have my keys back so I can leave?"

His phone rang as he answered her, "No."

Caroline dropped her hand, gave him an evil glare, her face red with anger as she passed him to lean against her car.

"What?" Jax growled into his phone. "Yeah. No, she's fine. Just take the Nissan back to the compound for me, okay, Sid. Yeah, that's it on the median. Dammit, I said she's fine." He hung up.

"Why can't I have my keys, Jax?" Caroline gave him a sideways glance.

"Because I want to talk to you…" Jax swallowed, looking away, "about my sister."

Chapter 15

"Oh, shit's gonna hit the fan." Jared glanced at Slade with a grimace as Jill and Dillon walked into Sloan's office, laughing.

Leaning against the wall, Slade glanced up then away.

"You get his feet and I'll take his arms." Sid acted like he was ready to pounce.

Slade closed his eyes briefly, keeping control; he had to keep control. Sid and Jared weren't making it easy, the fuckers.

"Do you have a fucking phone?" Sloan's voice boomed, making Jill jump.

"Ah, who me?" When Sloan just stared at her and Dillon, Jill nodded. "But I was driving and didn't get the group message until we were almost here."

"I sent the message an hour ago." Sloan still stared between the two.

"Well, I was driving and, ah…" Jill's eyes went to Dillon for help.

"And we stopped for some pizza," he added, nodding toward Jill.

"Pizza?" Steve frowned. "Well, thanks a lot for asking, assholes. I want pizza."

Sloan rubbed his forehead as if trying to scrub his frustration away.

"Just makes you want to scream, don't it?" Sid leaned toward Sloan, but was shaking his head at Jill and Dillon.

"I'm going to remove my hand, and when I do, you better be away from me, Sid," Sloan warned.

"Done." Sid nodded, straightened up and moved a step away.

Sloan did remove his hand, but his eyes zeroed in on Jill. "You stripper ready?"

"Ah, that's an odd way to…" Jill stopped, nodded and cleared her throat when he sneered at her. "Yes, I think so."

"What the fuck do you mean, 'you think so'? Either you're ready or you're not." Sloan looked at Slade. "Is she ready?"

"Yes, she's ready." Slade did his best to keep the growl out of his voice and sneer off his face.

"Well, she better be. Tomorrow night is the night." Sloan rummaged around his desk. Finally finding what he was looking for, he handed Slade a picture. "This is the mark. His name is George Groper."

Sid opened his mouth, shook his head and looked at Sloan. "Seriously?" Sid ignored Sloan's glare. "I'm sorry, but how classic is that. I mean, we are doing a sting in a strip club and the mark's name is George Groper. Nobody could write this shit."

"You done?" Sloan looked up at Sid, his eyes narrowed.

"Yes." Sid thought for a moment and nodded. "Yes, I am."

Slade grabbed the picture out of Sloan's hand, and then passed it around. "What if he doesn't show?"

"Then we go back until he does," Sloan responded. "Me, Slade and Duncan will be in the surveillance van."

"Why am I in the van?" Slade's head snapped up.

"Because I said so," Sloan replied with his 'no budging on this' tone. "Jax and Damon will be inside, so you two make sure you have your suits. This is a high-class club. Sid and Jared will be stationed outside the building, ready for assistance if needed."

"What about us?" Steve frowned, looking around. "What do we

do?"

"Take the night off." Sloan didn't even look Steve's way. Reaching in his desk drawer, he pulled out a box. "Jill, you will wear this at all times. It has a small camera and microphone. We will be able to see what you see and hear what you hear."

Jill took the box and opened it, pulling out a beautiful studded choker with a pendent. "Okay." Jill nodded, putting the choker back in the box, then lifted something else out. "What's this?"

"It will go with the outfit the women picked out for you, and that is your earpiece so we can tell you what to do. It's small enough that it won't be detected by anyone, no matter how close they get." Sloan looked up at her. "You won't be alone in this, Jill."

"I know." Jill smiled, putting on a brave front.

Slade watched Jill and knew she was nervous, even as hard as she was trying to hide it. His protective instincts kicked in and he wanted to assure her she would be fine. He wouldn't let anything happen to her, but that was going to be damn hard when he was in the fucking van. Yeah, he and Sloan would have a talk about that after everyone left.

"Any questions?" Sloan looked around, then frowned. "Where the hell is Jax?"

"He had car trouble," Sid answered with no more information. "We'll fill him in," he told Slade.

"I have a question." Jill's voice shook. "How am I supposed to get there? I don't test for my license until Monday."

"Shit." Sloan frowned, tossing down his pen.

"I can take her." Dillon stepped up.

"No, she can drive. Jax said she did fine, and as long as she's careful, there will be no problems," Slade answered, glaring at Dillon.

"Yeah, but—" Dillon started again.

"And I said no, she can drive." Slade's eyes darkened. "You have a fucking hearing problem?"

"No," Dillon snapped back, glaring at Slade. "I'm just trying to help."

"Yeah, well don't," Slade warned. When Dillon started to open his mouth again, Slade took a step forward, his eyes deadly. "I said...don't." The deepening of Slade's voice warned everyone in the room that shit was about to get real.

Sloan's head was going back and forth between Slade and Dillon. "They seriously don't pay me enough for this shit," he sighed. "Next on the agenda is initiation. Wednesday is the start of your initiation. We will have a short meeting beforehand, which no one better be late for or I'm going to beat the hell out of you, so be on fucking time. I hope to hell you guys are ready for this."

Steve, Adam, Jill and Dillon all voiced their readiness and each looked nervous as hell.

Sloan stood looking at Jill. "Have you fed?"

"Not in a while," Jill answered honestly.

"You need to feed so make sure you do that before tomorrow night," Sloan warned her. "I suggest you all feed before initiation."

"Are there any donors...?" Jill looked embarrassed. "I still don't have a donor."

"I thought I told you to take care of that?" Sloan frowned down at her.

"You can feed from me," Dillon replied with the innocence of a

166

total idiot.

"Oh, hey…" Sid and Jared both stepped up next to Slade. Sid actually hooked his arm on Slade's shoulder until Slade shrugged it off. "You're on your own, kid." Sid gave Dillon a sad look.

"No, she can't fucking feed from you." Slade's eyes flashed black with a darkening red rim. "Neither can she have pizza with you, and you sure as hell cannot drive her anywhere."

"What is wrong with you?" Jill frowned at Slade, then glanced at Sloan who was watching the scene closely.

Slade couldn't help it; his control snapped and fuck it. He was done hiding his feelings and was ready to let any male within ten miles know that Jill was his before he killed someone.

"Everyone out!" Sloan yelled, and then leaned against his desk with his arms folded. "Except you three." He indicated toward Slade, Jill and Dillon.

Once everyone was gone, Dillon spread his arms wide. "What did I do?"

"First off, I spent ten minutes sitting next to you in the bar listening to your remarks about Jill as she danced," Slade growled, trying to get a grip on his raging anger. "And they are things I will not repeat."

Dillon shrugged. "Hey, can I help it if she turned out to be hot."

"Eww, Dillon." Jill looked at him, shocked, before smacking him in the arm. "You're like a brother to me."

Dillon actually laughed. "Sorry, Jill, you're gorgeous, but it's cool." He looked up at Slade. "I didn't know you and the doc had a thing going. I mean, I wondered why you were glaring me to death, but it's all good."

"Now, you know." Slade's voice was deep with warning. He could see Jill's eyes open wide in shock, but he didn't look at her. "She is off limits."

"I swear, I will only look at Jill as a sister." Dillon tugged her hair. "See."

"Ouch, you jerk." Jill elbowed him in the stomach.

"Truce?" Dillon stuck out his hand toward Slade.

Slade took his hand in a strong grip and nodded, but his eyes gave the kid one last warning.

"Both of you get to the warehouse." Sloan nodded toward the door.

Once Jill and Dillon were out the door, Sloan turned his attention to Slade and laughed.

"What the fuck is so funny?" Slade frowned, not finding anything about the situation humorous. When Sloan continued to laugh, Slade eyed him cautiously since Sloan rarely laughed. "What in the fuck is funny?"

"Oh, hell." Sloan held his stomach. "I haven't laughed that hard in a long time."

"Well, glad you find the situation funny," Slade grumbled, wondering if Sloan had finally lost it.

"I've been waiting for this moment." Sloan laughed again, then cleared his throat. "And for it to happen because some kid gets a hard-on for Jill and I was here to witness you losing it."

"Hey, you didn't hear the shit he was saying when she was dancing." Slade pointed toward the door. "And he's no kid."

"Yeah, probably nothing we haven't said in our years of watching strippers," Sloan grinned.

"Jill is not a stripper," Slade hissed.

"No, she's not. She's a beautiful young woman with a badass attitude and is going to make one hell of a Warrior." Sloan nodded, but his grin faded quickly. "You need to claim her, my friend, because I can't have you going around threatening every male who even looks her way."

Slade didn't say anything; he just nodded. Pausing, he looked at Sloan. "You knew the whole time, didn't you?"

"Probably before you did, you dumb bastard." Sloan straightened up, walking behind his desk.

"I can't wait for the day a woman wraps you around her finger," Slade grumbled. "I cannot fucking wait."

"Not going to happen, so go to hell," Sloan growled. "Now get out of here and do your job before I have to fire your ass."

"So Jill is safe? You're not going to kick her out of the program?" Slade headed for the door, but needed to make sure he didn't just kill any chance Jill had in the program.

"I'd be a fool to kick her out. I figured you two were going to happen. I would ask you to wait until after her initiation, but I don't see that happening. I'm not kicking you or her out no matter what I said, not that you'd listen to me anyway." Sloan turned more serious. "But you need to keep a cool head, especially tomorrow night, and let her do her job without interference because some guy might run his hand up her leg or some shit. It could be dangerous for her if you have another fit."

Slade sneered, but agreed, "I've got it handled."

"Well, I hope to hell you handle it better than you did a few minutes ago," Sloan warned, but laughed again.

Walking out of Sloan's office hearing laughter ringing out behind him, Slade knew without a doubt if Sloan was making fun of him, Jared and Sid were going to be relentless. "Fuck!"

******

Training had been brutal, but Jill welcomed it. Of course, Dillon gave her shit for not telling him about her and Slade, but in all honesty, she hadn't really known. Or at least she wasn't for sure. Damn him. He confused her and she had no way of talking to him during training.

Stepping out of the shower, Jill toweled off quickly. Tossing the towel on the floor, she walked out of the bathroom determined to get dressed, find Slade and ask him if he'd lost his mind.

"You need to start locking your door." Slade's voice snapped her head up, making her jump.

Slade stood against her wall in old ripped blue jeans, no shoes and a white sleeveless tank that fit him like a second skin. 'Holy shit' was all that came to her mind. She knew her nipples automatically reacted to the sight of him. Turning, she started to go in the bathroom.

"Don't!" His command stopped her.

Slowly, she turned back around and stood before him. His eyes roamed her body, setting her on fire. She wondered briefly if she could actually bitch him out while standing before him completely naked.

"What in the hell was that all about in Sloan's office?" Yeah, she had no problem with it. "Sloan is probably clapping in glee just waiting to see me so he can throw me out. Did you tell him we...you know...also."

Slade lifted his eyes to hers and smiled. "First of all, I don't think Sloan has ever clapped in glee."

170

"I don't find any of this funny, Slade." Jill frowned at his joking. She did turn then, went into the bathroom, grabbed a towel and walked out, her body covered.

Eyeing the towel wrapped around her body, Slade frowned. "Oh, Sloan found it really funny."

"No, he didn't." Jill's tone clearly called Slade a liar. "And why did you act that way toward Dillon? He's just my friend."

"Dillon was not looking at you as a friend at the bar." Slade took a step toward her. "He needed to know he had no chance with you. If you would have hooked your little finger at him, he would have followed you in the back and been balls deep inside you in a heartbeat."

"Okay, that was crude." Jill held the towel tighter against herself. "I don't look at Dillon that way."

"Crude but absolutely true, and good thing for him you don't," Slade growled, his eyes narrowed. "And no, I didn't tell Sloan anything other than you are mine."

Jill's eyes widened. "You told him that?"

"I also told you that. My exact words to you were, 'once you are mine, it will be body and soul'," he reminded her.

"But I didn't know if I was yours or not, Slade. You're a very complex man and…" Her stomach dipped as she shivered. This man had such an intense stare, as if he could see into her soul. "… you confuse me." She swallowed hard.

Slade smiled without humor. "Oh, you are mine, Jillian." He held his hand out, the towel ripping away from her body. "Never doubt that."

Jill made a grab for the towel, but missed. Again, she stood naked before him. "It's hard not to doubt when you run after touching

171

me."

"I didn't run." Slade took a step closer, but still didn't touch her. "And I did a hell of a lot more than touch you."

It was so hard to hold a conversation with him while she was naked and he looked like a sex god with his muscles bulging out of that damn shirt. She was a sucker when it came to tight white muscle shirts; there was nothing sexier. He looked so at ease standing in her room, like he was ready to relax on a Sunday morning with his faded jeans unbuttoned. Hell, she didn't notice that before, and his bare feet.

"I thought nothing was going to happen between us until after the initiation?" Jill dragged her eyes up to his, the smile on his lips was pure male.

"I lied." He reached out, grasping her waist. Slowly, he pulled her to him. His grip tightened as he lifted her up his body.

"Thank God," Jill sighed, loud enough for him to hear. She put her hands on his shoulders as he lifted her as if she weighed nothing.

His eyes left hers as he lifted her above his head, his mouth hovering over her breast. When his tongue snaked out to lick one nipple, she thought she had died and gone to Heaven. Throwing her head back, she hissed in pleasure. He continued to torture her, going back and forth from breast to breast. He lowered her, making Jill want to cry; she didn't want the sensations to stop.

"Wrap your legs around me." His demand sent a shot of desire through her core, turning her on more, if that was even possible. She was more than happy to follow orders. As soon as her swollen lips made contact with his hard stomach, Jill moaned, her head falling back.

His large hands moved down to her hips, sliding her down so she rested against his hard cock. More moans escaped Jill's throat. Slowly, his hands moved her hips up and down his hardness, pressing her swollen lips against his jean-covered cock carefully, but with enough pressure to pleasure her. Her breath gasped out; she gripped his shoulders, riding him with the help of his hands. She managed to look at him, his eyes, black with passion, watched her intently. He slowed her down, before speeding up. It was enough to drive her fucking insane. All she wanted was sweet completion.

"You like that, don't you?" His voice was harsh. His hands tightened on her hips and ass. "Come on, Jill. Let go." He dipped his head low enough to bite her nipple, sending Jill over the edge.

His mouth crashed over hers, swallowing her scream, one hand held her against him, the other found her swollen nub and he worked it with expertise, prolonging her pleasure to the point she thought she was going to faint. Slade's hand moved from her nub, up her stomach to cup her breast, before making its way to her neck and then to the back of her head. Grabbing her hair, he pulled her mouth from his and smiled. "Good girl."

Jill opened her eyes and did her best to focus. Blinking repeatedly as she tried to catch her breath, Jill's body shuddered once more. "That was…" She couldn't even find a word to describe what her body just went through.

"Yeah, it was," Slade responded, the pride in his voice unmistakable. "And there will be more of…*that*…after you feed."

Unhooking her legs, she tried to slide down, but he shook his head. Licking her lips, her eyes moved to his neck. "I know you said you're in charge, but I have a request." Jill didn't know exactly how this dominance thing worked, but it was so worth a try to ask.

"And what would that be?" Slade cocked an eyebrow, an amused grin playing against his lips.

"I mean, I'm not sure how this works." Jill felt stupid. She needed to do more reading, more research.

"I'm not a practicing Dom, Jillian. I am demanding, but my main purpose in the end is to make sure you have the pleasure you desire. I may smack your ass red if you need it. I may tie you to the bed and make you beg as I torture you with pleasure until you scream, but you will always be taken care of in every way, in and out of that bed." Slade's eyes became intense. "Now, tell me your...request."

Yeah, like she could actually form words after having Slade tell her his main purpose was to give her the pleasure she desired and torture her with pleasure. Hot damn, she almost came again by just listening to his words. Clearing her throat, she glanced at his neck again. "I want you inside me when I feed." Her eyes shot up to his as soon as her desire was spoken aloud. The heat in his eyes seared her.

Slade slid her down his body. "Undress me."

Before he even finished those two words, she was already working off his shirt. Glancing up at him with lowered lashes, she placed a kiss against his hard stomach making her way up to his chest. Her lips following the progress of his shirt. He didn't even flinch, but stood still as stone. Her mouth found his nipple and with a quick lick, she nipped lightly, making him hiss. He was so much taller than her; she had to tiptoe to bring the shirt over his head. He kept his arms down to his sides so the shirt just went around the back of his neck. Now, that was fucking hot as hell. Deciding to leave it like that, she ran her hands slowly down his body, loving the sensation of his muscles beneath her hands.

His jeans were already unbuttoned. Slowly, she unzipped them and his cock sprang forward as if thanking her. Never having performed oral sex before, Jill had an overwhelming urge to start now. Without thought, her tongue flicked out.

"Ah, Goddamn woman!" Slade jerked away, pulling her up.

"But I..." Jill looked back at his hardened cock, disappointed.

"And you will, believe me, you will." Slade lifted her chin. "But not yet." He leaned down, kissing her as he managed to take his jeans off the rest of the way.

Jill tried to keep her eyes up, but they had a mind of their own and traveled down the path to paradise. His hands grasped her waist again, but one made the journey down, touching her as he slipped one finger inside her and then another. Her legs wobbled. His other hand held tighter so she didn't collapse to the floor. Her eyes closed in sweet surrender.

"You are more than ready for me." His harsh spoken statement sent chills over her body.

Opening her eyes, she took one more look at his length. "I could say the same to you."

He chuckled as he picked her up. "Honey, I'm always ready for you."

Slowly, to the point of actual torture, he lowered her on his hard cock. A hiss of erotic pleasure escaped them both. Jill wrapped her legs around him once again, and used her strength against his tight ass to bring her all the way down his length, but he wouldn't allow it. He continued his slow pursuit of filling her. Jill had been looking down between their bodies watching the erotic play until finally he was deep inside her. Raising only her eyes, she looked into his and knew she could no longer lie to herself; she loved him, truly loved this man, yet the courage to say those words escaped her.

"Feed." His quiet demand shook her to the core.

Lowering toward his neck, she placed a soft kiss where she would take his blood. Slowly, she opened her mouth and gently sank her teeth into his hard flesh, taking long sweet pulls. He let her feed for a few short seconds before he started pulling her off him. Then with more force, he lowered her back onto his rigid cock, causing erotic sensations to pour over her. When Jill moved against him,

Slade once again stopped her.

"Feed and feel, Jillian," Slade whispered, cupping her ass as he set a rhythm of true bliss. "Let me do the work for you."

Oh, and feel she did. Every sensation seemed tripled as she drank his Warrior blood. On and on it went. His rhythm went from gentle and slow, to hard and pounding, bringing her closer and closer to the edge. Drinking her fill, she pulled away after licking the two small puncture wounds closed. Wrapping her arms around his neck, she licked her lips and let go. She had to move, her body wouldn't stay still any longer, which he allowed. With everything she had, she met him thrust for thrust. It became almost violent in their need.

In three strides, Slade walked to the bed and lay her down without crushing her as they kept their frantic rhythm. Picking up one leg, he kissed her calf as he brought it over his shoulder. Jill knew she was close, but tried to control her release, not wanting the connection to end, ever.

"What are you doing?" Slade smiled down at her as he slowed.

"Isn't it obvious?" Jill eyed him, moving against him, but damn, even his chuckle was sexy.

"You trying to hold out on me?" He plunged in harder, and then held still, fully inside her.

"Maybe," Jill sighed, trying to get him to move, but he wouldn't budge. "I just don't want it to end."

"I can make you explode any time I want, Jillian." Slade pinched her nipple, sending that delectable zinging sensation straight to her pussy. Slade hissed as she tightened around him. "And it just means we can start all over again."

"I like the sound of that." She gasped when he pulled all the way out only to plunge back in. He repeated the motion relentlessly, moving her up the bed by pure force.

His fingers found her sensitive nub, and with a few strokes, he pinched, sending her past the point of caring about anything, not even the scream that surely shook the compound. Slade kept pounding, not even trying to hide her howl of ecstasy. His search for release ending only seconds later.

Slade collapsed, using only his elbows to keep his weight off her. Tilting his head, he ran his tongue slowly across her soft lips before kissing her breathless. "You okay?" He lifted, looking down into her eyes.

Before she could answer, someone pounded on the door. Fear of what happened the last time shadowed her face.

"I'm not going anywhere," he promised, kissing her on the forehead. "But I'm seriously considering getting us an apartment."

"Jill, is Slade in there?" Sid pounded again.

Slade jumped up, pulling on his jeans. "Cover up," he warned her before walking over to open the door, enough to shield Jill from being seen. "This better be good and not you trying to be a fucking hero," Slade sneered at Sid.

"Someone took a shot at Jax." There was no humor in his voice. Sid was in full Warrior mode. "We need you and Jill downstairs, now. Bring your sketch pad, Jill," Sid called out before heading down the hall.

Jill was already up and getting dressed. Slade pulled his shirt over his head. Grabbing her sketchpad, Jill followed Slade out of the room, practically running to keep up. He reached back and grabbed her hand. One thing she knew, having a Warrior shot at was serious business for the VC Council. Dread and a tinge of fear crawled up her spine as she held tightly to Slade's hand.

Chapter 16

Jill's hand in his felt right. Even when they walked into Sloan's office, he didn't let go. Everyone stood, looking tense.

"Were you hit?" Slade looked Jax over as well as Caroline, who sat, looking pale.

"No," Jax responded as Caroline shook her head.

"What the hell happened?" Slade asked, ignoring everyone staring at their hands. He held her tighter. He knew Jill kept shooting Sloan nervous glances.

"We stopped to grab something to eat and took it to a park," Jax responded, his voice hard with anger. "We had just sat down and started to eat when Caroline flew across the picnic table tackling me to the ground. In the next second, I heard a gunshot, so I rolled over onto Caroline to protect her when the tree behind me exploded with splinters, right where my head had been."

"His sister screamed in my head," Caroline answered the unasked question. "I just reacted, not really knowing what was going on."

"Guess you're a believer now." Sid's eyes opened wide with a 'holy shit' look.

"I can describe the shooter." Caroline looked toward Jill. "Can you draw him?"

"Yeah," Jill replied, opening her sketchpad as Slade fetched her a chair.

"You saw the shooter?" Jared's eyes narrowed, ready to go after the bastard now.

"No, I didn't, but Jax's sister did." Caroline looked at Jax, then down to the floor.

"You didn't go after him?" Steve asked Jax with a frown.

Jax looked his way. "I was not leaving Caroline unprotected," he replied as if Steve should have known the answer to that.

Caroline looked at Lana. "Can you see her?" she asked Lana. "I'm still pretty shaken up and don't want to miss anything."

Lana nodded, walking up closer. "You sure you feel up to this right now?"

"Yeah, I'm fine," Caroline answered, looking toward Jill, who nodded that she was ready to go.

Slade watched Jill work as Caroline and Lana threw descriptions at her. To many, this would seem strange, but to him and the other Warriors in the room, it was the norm. They had seen so many fucked-up things; that two women talking to a dead woman and a half-breed vampire sketching a profile pic for them to go on was pretty much the norm.

"Was his moustache bushy or thin and did he have a beard with it?" Jill looked up from her sketch.

Caroline looked at Lana. "Like a porn 'stash?"

Lana nodded and looked at Jill. "No beard."

"Porn 'stash?" Steve snorted. "You even know what a porn 'stash is, Jill?"

Jill focused on her sketch a few more minutes before looking up at Steve. "Yeah." She pointed at him with her pencil, moving it back and forth. "Kind of like what you're trying to grow there."

Steve's hand flew to his mouth, covering his puny moustache. "That was cruel. This is not a porn 'stash."

Jared looked closer when Steve dropped his hand. "I had an aunt who had a fuller moustache than that."

"Where is all the 'stash hate coming from?" Steve frowned, using his finger to smooth it down while looking at Jared. "You're just jealous you can't grow one."

Slade grinned at their back-and-forth bullshit. It actually broke the tension and had Caroline smiling, which seemed to put Jax more at ease. Everyone waited patiently for Jill to finish. Jill stood, walking toward Caroline and Lana.

"Is that him or at least a good resemblance?" Jill stood back, crossing her arms, waiting.

Caroline and Lana looked at each other. "Alisha said it's identical to who she saw. She also said...you are very talented."

Jill's eyebrows rose. "Oh, well, tell her..."

Lana laughed. "We know it's weird, but it is what it is."

"Tell her thank you." Jill smiled back.

Jax took the sketch from Caroline and examined it, memorizing it before passing it to Sid, who also looked and passed it around. After everyone had studied the sketch, Jill took it back and tore the page out, handing it back to Sloan.

"Could I have a minute with the Warriors, ladies?" Sloan asked, giving them a weak smile. "Thank you for your help."

"Wait for me," Jax warned Caroline as she stood. Nodding, she followed Lana out.

Jill started to go, but Slade stopped her, shook his head and leaned down. "He didn't mean you."

He chuckled when her eyes popped open and her mouth formed a complete circle. "Oh." She rolled her eyes.

Once they were gone and the door shut, Jax picked the picture up again. "I want this son of a bitch caught." Jax's calm front disappeared as soon as Caroline left. "She could have been shot."

"Have you ever seen that guy before?" Damon nodded toward the sketch.

"No." Jax frowned. "I don't even know anyone here except for you guys."

"So no one you've pissed off here or maybe in the past that could have followed you. Someone with a score to settle?" This came from Slade.

Jax eyes snapped to Slade's. "I've pissed off thousands of people, some on a daily basis."

"Or this might not be personal," Sloan added.

"You mean somebody might be gunning for the Warriors?" Adam finally spoke up, looking around the room. "Wouldn't that be suicide?"

The room was silent, everyone deep in thought.

"I think it's personal," Jill spoke up, glancing up at Slade, then to Jax. "No one really knows you're here, yet you were at a place that none of the Warriors go with Caroline, which means you were followed."

"But we were all at the bar." Jax motioned around at everyone.

"Yes, a public place even though it was closed." Jill shrugged. "Maybe I'm wrong, but if it was a Warrior thing, and maybe it is, why did they follow you and not a Warrior from this area?"

"That actually makes sense." Duncan stepped up. "We would have more enemies than Jax, so why wasn't one of us followed."

"Who have you pissed off since you've been here?" Jared frowned, looking at Jax, and then turned to wink at Jill. "Good thinking by the way."

"Other than you guys, nobody." Jax glanced down at the picture again.

"Didn't you pay a visit to the Mayor's office?" Slade's gaze went to Jax.

Jax's eyes went black. "That fucking bitch!"

"I think the Mayor's a dude," Steve added.

"No, you dumbass. His whore," Jax spat.

"Alice." The name echoed in the room.

"Fuck!" Jax slammed his hand down on Sloan's desk.

"I take it the meeting with the Mayor and Alice didn't go well," Sid snorted with an angry glint to his eyes.

"I thought it went really well," Jax sneered. "Guess they didn't think so. I walked in on her sucking his dick and didn't back out of the room with a 'sorry'. I also believe I called her a whore a few times."

"Well, if Alice is involved, then we all need to watch our asses," Sloan warned, and then looked toward Steve, Adam and Dillon. "Looks like you guys are on tomorrow night."

"Yes!" Steve hissed, pumping his arm up and down. He then stopped. "What are we doing?"

"I don't want anyone without back-up." Sloan looked the room. "Dillon, I want you to stay here and keep an eye on things. I don't think there will be a problem, but I'm not going to take any chances, and Lana will be here, also."

"No problem," Dillon nodded.

"Adam, I want you and Steve to follow Jill to the Club. Once she pulls in, you guys keep going and then head back here. We will all be in place by that time."

"Done," Adam replied, glancing at Jill then back to Sloan.

"Jax, I'm going to switch you and Duncan." Sloan shook his head even before Slade could say a word. "You are not going into the club, Slade, so save your breath. Jax will be in the van with us. Damon and Duncan can handle the inside, while Sid and Jared are posted outside the club."

Slade wanted to argue, but kept his mouth shut for now.

"Are you good with this, Jill?" Sloan asked, putting all his focus on her. "Are you ready?"

"Yes, sir." Jill nodded, looking him directly in the eye. "I'll do my best for you guys."

"We know you will." Sid stared down at her before sighing dramatically, glancing at Slade's hand on her shoulder. "Okay, if no one else is going to say anything, then I guess I'll whip my balls out and say it."

"Jesus!" Sloan slammed back in his chair, closing his eyes as if praying for patience.

"I'm sure he'd be interested, too." Sid glanced at Sloan before turning his attention back to Slade and Jill. "So, is this official now?" He pointed back and forth at Jill and Slade.

Slade rolled his eyes while squeezing Jill's shoulder. Sid was such an asshole. "Yeah, you got a problem with it?"

"No, other than..." Sid held both hands up with his palms out, "pay up, bitches!"

Slade watched as everyone dug deep into their pockets. "You fuckers bet on us?" Not that it really surprised him. Even when shit was going down, no matter how bad it got, the Warriors took it in stride, did their jobs and had fun in-between. So yeah, this was also very normal.

"Oh, yeah, did they ever. But I tried to tell them…shit, who am I kidding." Sid snorted with a grin. "I bet these losers that you'd be an item before Jill got her Warrior status. And well, as you see, they decided to bet against the king of gambling."

Slade watched, surprised, as Sloan slammed money into Sid's palm. "Even you?"

"I did every fucking thing in my power to make sure I won this bet." Sloan frowned at Slade. "Just four more days, that's all you had to wait, dammit."

"I'll be damned," Slade cursed, looking down at Jill to see how she was taking it. She seemed nervous as hell as she watched Sid.

Even after everyone paid up, Sid still held his hand out. "Feels a little light." He raised and lowered each hand as if weighing the money. Jill dug into her pocket, slamming down twenty bucks.

"You bet?" Slade's eyes narrowed. "Are you fucking kidding me?"

The laughter in the room was deafening as Slade stared at Jill. An unbelievable grin then spread across his face.

"What?" Jill frowned at him.

"I can't believe you bet against us." Slade shook his head, trying to look pissed, but his grin continued growing.

"I thought it was a sure bet and needed some cash. I actually bet it wouldn't happen at all, so I was for sure I'd win. You were pretty adamant that there would never be anything between us." Jill shrugged. Turning, she glared at Sid with the evilest glare she'd ever given.

Sid just smiled at her. "If you can't take the heat, then don't place your bet with the king."

******

Jax followed Slade and Jill out of the office. Still shaken, his eyes searched for Caroline. He still couldn't believe she threw herself at him. When he found the motherfucker who took that shot, he would kill him in the most painful way he was taught in the ways of his tribe.

Caroline stood from where she and Lana were sitting on the steps, giving him a weak smile, but then saw Jill and headed her way. "Jill," Caroline called out. "I'm going to stay here tonight since it's so late. You want to start getting ready around noon?"

"Yeah, that would be great." Jill smiled and proceeded to roll her eyes when Sid walked out with a big grin, counting his money.

"What is that?" Lana frowned, trying to swipe it from his hands.

"Oh, no, woman." Sid pulled it away. "As a matter of fact, pay up."

"For what?" Lana put her hands on her hips.

Sid nodded toward Slade and Jill. "It's official."

"Dammit," Lana hissed, digging into her pockets, glaring at Jill and Slade. "Couldn't you have waited just four more days?"

Slade crossed his arms, looking disgusted. "Did everyone in the damn compound bet?"

"No." Sid thought for a moment. "Little Daniel didn't have the cash."

"I don't have any money on me." Lana spread her arms out.

"That's okay. I'll collect interest on you." Sid winked and then took Caroline's money. "Thank you."

"You guys are so wrong." Slade frowned, grabbing Jill's hand, leading her up the stairs.

"But it feels so right," Sid laughed as he and Lana followed them.

Jax shook his head, watching Sid. "He's an idiot."

"But he's good to my sister." Caroline smiled, watching Sid chase her up the stairs.

An awkward silence filled the entryway. Jax was not comfortable in these situations at all. Give him someone who needed an ass kicking and he was on it, but this, yeah, so not his thing.

"Well, I guess I'll go up." Caroline turned to go.

"Wait a minute." He grabbed her arm, turning her around. "Thank you."

"You're welcome," Caroline responded and laughed. "Wow, that was really hard for you, wasn't it?"

Jax gave her a crooked grin. "Yeah, it was. I'm not used to thanking people."

Caroline gave him an understanding nod. "Maybe after things calm down, we can have that dinner and talk."

"Sure, sounds good," Jax replied, his mind going a mile a minute before his eyes drilled into hers. "I'm going to find who put you in danger, Caroline. And without sounding too much like an asshole, don't ever put yourself in danger for me again. You could have been killed."

"As you could have been. I'm sure those were silver bullets," Caroline replied, searching his eyes. "I have a feeling not too many people have done things for you, Jax Wheeler, but know this. If I had to do it all over again, I would in a heartbeat." She tiptoed up, kissing his cheek and gave him a smile before turning away.

Jax watched her go. She was right. No one had ever done anything like that for him. She had literally saved his life and that was something he would never forget.

Chapter 17

Jill fidgeted as Caroline fixed her wig, Nicole painted her toenails and Pam applied her press-on nails. It was crowded in Jared and Tessa's room, but it was nice being with the women.

"Stop moving, Jill," Nicole sighed, looking up at her.

"I'm sorry." Jill frowned. "I fidget when I'm nervous."

Trying to take her mind off what she was getting ready to do, Jill thought about the previous night. Once she and Slade got back to her room, he actually laid her across his lap and smacked her ass good for betting against them, which lead to other things. A grin slipped across her face at the thought. But the best part was afterwards, when he took her in his arms and held her the rest of the night. Hardly any words were spoken, which was fine with her. She savored that moment because for the first time in a long time, she didn't feel alone.

"Okay." Caroline walked in front of Jill, reached over Nicole to fluff Jill's bangs and smiled. "Perfect. And that wig is going nowhere, so if you and Slade want to do a little role-playing afterwards, you'll be good to go." Caroline gave her a wink.

"Wow, you look amazing with long hair." Nicole looked up at her.

Jill wrinkled her nose. "I like my short hair. It doesn't get in the way and is a breeze to fix."

"Okay, toes done." Nicole stood, stretching. "Let them dry for a few minutes."

Pam affixed the last nail. "Where's Tessa with the choker?"

"Here I am." Tessa came running in. "Had to get Slade 'cause I couldn't find it. And doesn't he seem like a happy man this morning."

Jill blushed, not saying a word, and then noticed them all looking at each other. "What?"

"Okay, we're dying to know." Tessa walked over after grabbing a covered clothes hanger with Jill's outfit. "Is he, you know…"

Jill laughed. She quickly realized they were all serious; even Angelina was on edge waiting for her to answer. "I'm not going to talk about Slade like that."

"Ah, you suck," Nicole grumbled. "You know he's just too good-looking. I bet he isn't all that in bed and he probably has a little…"

"I can hardly walk this morning, so if he's little, I'd hate to see a big one," Jill jumped to Slade's defense. "And he makes damn sure I'm taken care of."

"Ha! I knew it." Nicole pointed at her.

"Is he demanding?" Tessa grinned.

"Very." Jill nodded, grabbing the hanger from Tessa. "And that's all I'm saying."

"Damon's the same." Nicole's smile was that of a satisfied woman.

"So is Jared." Tessa added with a sigh, "Drives me crazy sometimes, but I love it."

"All these Warriors are alpha, girls." Pam sat down, pulling her feet up under her, glancing over at Daniel who was fast asleep on the bed. "And we got the best of the best."

Jill smiled until she pulled the paper away from the hanger and saw her outfit. "This is it?"

"That's it." Nicole grinned, admiring the outfit. "Beautiful, isn't it. Go on, try it on. I'm dying to see you in it."

"This is a job. This is a job. This is a job," Jill repeated to herself as she headed toward the bathroom, eyeing the tiny strip of cloth in horror.

Once in the bathroom, she closed the door. Laying the outfit on the sink, since it was no bigger than a washcloth, Jill caught her reflection and jumped. "Oh, my God." She looked at herself, leaning closer. Caroline was damn good with makeup and her black wig looked real. Reaching up, she touched her face, her eyes going to her dark-red fake fingernails. Her lips were painted the same dark red. Jill had never worn lipstick, but she had to admit, her lips looked amazing.

Stripping out of her clothes, she stood naked, staring at the tiny white outfit as if it was a living being she was afraid to touch. "Just put it on, Jill," she griped.

It really was pretty. The top was a draping soft cloth that connected at the neck by golden rings. She thought she heard Tessa say it was a cowl top, whatever that meant. All Jill knew, there wasn't much to it and it barely covered what breasts she had. Though as she turned this way and that in the mirror, it did make her boobs look pretty good. It cut all the way down to her navel where the cloth gathered in a V-shape. When she moved to put the white boy shorts on, her boob popped out. "Are you kidding me?"

After stuffing her boob back in, she continued to pull the shorts up. Just below her belly button, three gold rings matching the top stretched across the shorts. The mirror was too high for her to see the shorts. Twisting, she tried to see her ass, but couldn't. She did put her hands back there and felt a good amount of cheek. With one last look in the mirror, she headed out the door.

"Well, if my boob is supposed to pop out as well as my ass cheeks, then this should do just fine." Jill looked up and stopped in mid-stride. Every Warrior was crammed in the room and every eye was on her.

"Holy fuck!" Jared choked out, but shut up when Tessa smacked him with the back of her hand.

"Yep, girls, we did it," Nicole laughed and clapped her hands. "We have created a stripper. Damn girl, you are rockin' in that–"

"No fucking way in hell are you wearing that!" Slade's voice cut off Nicole as it boomed throughout the room. Daniel started to cry.

Duncan went over to pick up Daniel. "How about we give them a minute." Duncan passed Slade, giving him a 'you poor bastard' look.

"I've got tape for your top to keep your boobs in," Tessa leaned in to whisper to Jill before Jared could pull her out.

Jill watched the emotions cross Slade's face. "It's just a job, Slade. At least that's what I keep telling myself."

He rubbed his hand across his eyes, a deep scowl tightening his lips. "I seriously don't think I can let you go in there."

Instead of getting mad, Jill walked up to him. "I know this isn't easy for you, Slade, but I have to do this and you have to let me. I'm going to be a Warrior. I want to be a Warrior and I want you to support me as a Warrior."

Slade looked her over again, anger blazing in his eyes. Putting his hands on her shoulders, he set her back a few steps, turned and punched the wall, not once but twice. Rolling his shoulders, cracking his neck back and forth, he finally turned around.

Looking at the two holes in Jared's wall, Jill frowned. "You feel better?"

"No." His eyes roamed her body again. "Jesus, you're beautiful. Though the wig can go."

Jill blushed and actually felt beautiful. "Please support me in this, Slade."

He nodded without saying a word, but cupped her face in his

hands.

"I'm really nervous." Jill's eyes searched his. "I don't want to let you down, the guys down."

Something flashed in his eyes, but was gone. "You won't."

Suddenly, the door burst open and in walked Tessa, Nicole and Pam. "You know what, Warrior." Nicole pointed her finger into his chest with each word. "You're not the only one a little upset about this mission. Our guys are going into a strip club with beautiful women. Do you think we're happy about that?"

"No, we are not," Tessa added, then glanced at her wall. "What in the hell did you do to my wall?"

"You guys—" Jill tried to break in, but they weren't having it.

"She is going to do this because it's her job, just like it's my man's job to walk into a room full of beautiful women, who I know will be all over him." Pam frowned, looking upset. "So you just need to get over it."

Slade frowned at the women before looking back at Jill. Taking the studded choker from Tessa, he turned Jill around and placed it around her neck. Turning her back to face him, he took her into his arms and kissed her hard. "Stay safe and know I'll be with you." He tapped the choker and turned, just as Jared looked through the open door.

"You ready?" Jared looked at Slade. "We have to get moving."

Slade didn't say anything as he left the room, but Jared spotted his wall.

"What the hell did you do to my wall?" The men's voices faded as they got further away from the room. "You will fix that, fucker."

Jill stared at the empty doorway, the reality of what she was about to do hitting her like a sledgehammer to the stomach. "I think I'm going to be sick." She ran to the bathroom, slamming the door shut.

"Ah, crap." Nicole headed after Jill. "Get the makeup out for touch-up.

"Get the tape, too." Jill shouted from the bathroom. "My boob keeps falling out."

They laughed until they heard the retching from the bathroom, then they groaned.

****

Everyone was in place, except for Jill who wasn't due for another half an hour. Slade felt trapped in the surveillance van, but Sloan had been right. He couldn't be trusted to be inside where he could reach out and beat the fuck out of anyone who even dared touch Jill.

"She's going to be fine, man." Jax was watching him. "She's smart and thinks things through."

"If I didn't think she could pull this off, I wouldn't have asked her in the first place," Sloan added.

"And don't think about how hot she looked," Sid said through their earpieces. "She's not really a stripper."

"Sid," Sloan said as he checked the monitors.

"Yeah, boss," Sid's voice crackled.

"Shut the fuck up and pay attention to what the hell you're supposed to be doing." Sloan's voice deepened with meaning.

The airway went silent until Sid's voice broke in again. "What the hell crawled up his ass now?"

"I can still fucking hear you," Sloan growled.

"Dammit, I hate these fucking things. I never know when the fuck they're on or off," Sid grumbled.

Even as anxious and on edge as he was, Slade grinned when Jared laughed through their earpiece.

"Fuck you, Jared," Sid hissed. Once again, the airway went quiet.

Silence continued as they waited. It was part of their job, patience for what was to come.

"Hey, guys?" Jill's voice filled the van, but it was distorted.

"Is something wrong with her mic?" Slade leaned closer trying to hear.

"I think she's still too far." Sloan turned some knobs. "Jill, can you hear me?"

"Yes." Her voice was clearer. "I'm getting ready to turn in. Who am I supposed to ask for? I'm sorry. I forgot."

Sloan and Jax shared a look. "It's all right, Jill," Sloan reassured her. "Hailey Ayres. She is expecting you. And Jill…"

"Yes." Jill's voice was crystal clear, indicating she was close.

"Breathe," Sloan said. "You're not alone."

"Yes, sir." A big exhale of breath came over their earpieces, making them smile except for Slade. His eyes were glued to the monitor.

Finally, they saw the black Nissan pull into the lot. "We have eyes on Jill," Jared confirmed. "Steve and Adam just drove past with no signs of being followed."

Slade watched Jill get out of the car dressed in dress slacks, heels and a loose fitting shirt. "I can't believe I'm saying this, but open your blouse a little more. The collar is blocking some of the view," Slade told her as he watched the other monitor that was connected to her choker. He waited until they had a clear shot. "That's good."

Jill suddenly stopped before opening the door. "Did you give them a name?"

"Shit," Sloan hissed, holding his hand over his mic. "Okay, hurry and think of a name."

The door opened before they could handle it and a man stood there looking at Jill. "You lost, honey?"

Everyone in the van held their breath.

Jill gave a girly laugh. "No. I was just getting ready to open the door." Jill walked past him with a flirty grin. "Thank you."

"My pleasure." The man grinned, closing the door. "Now, how can I help you?"

"I'm here to see Ms. Hailey Ayres." Jill looked around, giving the guys a great shot at the inside.

He picked up the phone. "Who should I tell her is here to see her?"

"Lola." Jill gave him a large smile.

"Lola?" Sid whispered in the earpiece.

"Shut up, Goddammit," Slade hissed. "You're doing great, Jill."

An older woman headed toward Jill, a frown on her face. "I'm Hailey. How can I help you?"

"It's nice to meet you, Ms. Ayres." Jill stuck out her hand. "I was told to be here at four and ask for you."

"Oh, but I thought your name was Jennifer." The woman's eyes went to someone behind Jill.

"Shit." Slade looked over at Sloan who was watching the monitor closely.

"I'm sorry, it is, but Lola is my stage name." Jill laughed nervously. "I'm so nervous. I've never worked in such a beautiful place and I want this job so badly."

Everyone held their breath waiting for the woman's reaction. Everyone breathed easier when she gave Jill a proud smile. "Thank you." She also looked around. "I've worked hard to make this a respectful place."

"Obviously, all your hard work has paid off," Jill responded appropriately.

"Now, Jeremy told me you were a half-breed. I'm so sorry about what's going on out there. Believe me, I don't believe in what they are doing with your kind." The woman patted her arm. "We do not discriminate here."

"I appreciate that," Jill replied. "I've stayed low key and under the radar. Hopefully, all of this passes quickly. We're not all bad."

"Oh, I know that, honey." Hailey smiled, grabbing her hand. "I've got all different types of girls here, human, vampire, but you are the first half-breed. Men are going to be all over you."

Slade's fist tightened at that, but Sloan pointed at him and mouthed, 'Calm the fuck down, now'.

"Do you allow them to touch your girls?" Jill asked worried.

"Oh, heavens, no," she laughed. "I meant they will all want to be at your table. Now, come on. Let me get you with the other girls and they will get you going."

Sloan covered his mic, leaning toward Slade. "I swear I will shoot your ass if you even make a move toward that door. She is doing fantastic."

Slade nodded, glaring at the monitor, his body primed to protect, yet he was fucking stuck in a van. This had to be the last time this happened, because he honestly didn't think he could take it again.

They watched as Jill walked past a room, following the woman. Damon sat in a corner, a woman dancing in front of him on a table with a pole. He turned, making eye contact with Jill. Opening a door, Jill followed the woman into a room full of half-naked women.

"Girls, I'd like you to meet Lola." Hailey smiled, pulling her more into the room. "This is going to be her first night here so show her the ropes and treat her like your sister."

"Hey, Lola," the women greeted with smiles.

"Hello." Jill's voice held strong.

"I've got her." A beautiful redhead walked up and took hold of her hand. "Stick with me and you'll survive your first night."

"Holy shit," Jax whispered, watching over Slade's shoulder. "Too bad Sid's stuck out there and can't see all these gorgeous naked women."

"Don't need to see shit, my man," Sid shot back. "I've got me a beautiful mate waiting for me at home."

"Who has a large gun and knows how to shoot," Jared cut in.

"There is that," Sid added, the seriousness in his tone not missed by anyone.

"Shut up!" Slade hissed. "And keep this line clear, dammit."

The three apologized with 'sorry' before the line went silent.

Chapter 18

"I'm Cherry." The beautiful redhead grinned, and then flipped her red hair. "I know, not very original, but the men love it. So, is Lola your stage name?"

Jill nodded. "Not very original." She scrunched her nose with a smile.

"It's fine," she laughed, rolling her eyes. "Most of these men don't care what our names are anyway, but if they like you, then they request you by name."

Jill sat on a small stool, setting her bag down. "So how does this work exactly?" When Cherry looked over at her, Jill cleared her throat. "I've worked at some pretty shitty clubs, nothing compared to this."

Cherry nodded. "It's very different. Unless you have a request right away from a regular, you get assigned. Men will either request you to dance on their table or Hicks will assign you a table."

"Hicks?" Jill asked, her eyes roaming around watching the women get ready and wondered if she should also. Talk about feeling out of place. This was so far from her comfort zone, Jill felt like she was having an out-of-body experience.

"Yeah, you'll meet him." Cherry frowned, rolling fishnet stockings up her legs. "He's okay, but likes to touch."

"I thought no one was allowed to touch us." Jill frowned, not liking this at all. If someone actually touched her, she would have to keep control by not kicking his ass.

Cherry laughed. "We have security out there." She nodded her head the way Jill had come in. "But back here, we fend for ourselves with some of the staff. Though Hicks might not mess with you."

"Yeah, well, I hope not." Jill stood back up, nervous energy flowing through her body.

"Hey, Pixie!" Cherry yelled.

A pretty girl with long blonde hair turned, her golden eyes glowed. "What?"

"Hicks bother you anymore?" Cherry turned, focusing on adjusting her boobs.

"Not since I threatened to tear his throat out." Pixie smiled, baring sharp fangs.

All the women laughed and Pixie winked. "You'll be fine, breed, just flash him some fang. He'll leave you alone."

Jill gave a shaky laugh.

"You'll be fine," Cherry grinned. "Just don't get caught back here alone. Now, get changed. We're about ready to go on."

Her stomach pitched violently and she prayed to God she didn't vomit again. "Where's the bathroom?"

"Back there, honey, but hurry." Cherry fluffed her hair. "Hailey hates when we go on stage late."

Jill nodded, hurrying toward the bathroom, trying not to kill herself with her damn high heels. Why women wore the damn things was beyond her. She was going to burn them as soon as she was finished with this job and enjoy every minute of it. Once inside, she locked the door and wobbled to the sink to glare into the mirror, her stomach pitching violently.

"Jill, you okay?" Sloan's voice sounded in her ear.

Before Jill could say anything, nausea hit her hard and she turned, running to the toilet. The groans sounding off in her ear let her know they were getting an awesome look and audio of her vomiting. Once she was finished, she went to the sink, rinsed her mouth out before checking her makeup.

"Jill…" This time it was Slade's voice.

"I'm fine." Jill smoothed her hair down, unbuttoned her blouse and began to undress.

"Well, I'd just like to say I'm glad I missed that little performance with the toilet bowl on the monitor, yet still, it sounded absolutely disgusting." Sid's voice filled her ear.

"Hey, Sid." Jill kept her voice low.

"Yeah, hon." Sid's voice turned serious as if he was there if she needed him.

"Shut the fuck up." The laughter made her feel better, as if they were in the room and everything was going to be okay. "And, Sloan, I want a raise…a big one when I start getting paid."

Laughter echoed in her ear as she opened the door and walked out. More women, who Jill figured had been out the front dancing when she came in, filled the back dressing room. A large man stood in the middle holding a sheet of paper, his eyes scanning the women.

"Hot damn, Lola." Cherry pulled her over after Jill shoved her clothes in her bag. "I love that outfit. Where'd you get it and what colors did it come in."

"You can talk girl crap after your shift, Cherry." The man had walked up, his eyes checking Jill out as if she was his next snack. "Who are you?"

"Lola." Jill kept her voice firm. She knew this guy's type. He fed on the weak.

His eyes grossly ran over her body again before searching his paper. "You take table six. Everybody else has their regulars except for Monica who is at table three, and Pepper you're at table eight."

"Ah, sorry about your luck." A woman, with short black hair patted her on the arm. "He's in rare form tonight."

"George?" Cherry frowned, shaking her head. "Well, hey, he might be good for your first night to break you in. He doesn't demand much other than talking."

"Talking?" Jill acted like the newbie she was. "We didn't do much talking with the customers at the other clubs I've worked for."

"These men are rich and pay good money, so if they want to talk…we talk. They want us to dance…we dance and if they want us to fuck…we fuck, but after hours and away from here." Cherry laughed at Jill's face. "Got to pay the bills, honey. But that last part, the fucking part, is not required."

"Good to know," Jill nodded, following the women and wondering briefly if Sloan somehow managed for her be at George's table. If so, he was damn good.

"Hey, don't knock it," a woman who was walking past grinned. "And Monica, you've got a gorgeous vampire at your table. I tried the *fucking* thing after hours with his hot ass, but he didn't bite. No pun intended."

The women laughed. Jill joined in, knowing she was talking about either Duncan or Damon.

"I'm up for the challenge." Monica pushed her boobs up, fluffed her hair and licked her lips. "Once you go vampire, it's hard to find a good fuck with your own kind."

"You ready?" Cherry smiled at her.

"Yes," Jill replied, smiling back, but her hands were clenched so tightly, she felt one of her press-on nails bend.

"You'll do great, girl, and remember security is thick out there, so any problems, just let them know." Cherry squeezed her arm before they exited the back room and walked onto a stage.

Jill followed, but stopped when Cherry did. The women were all positioned on the stage. A man's voice filled the room and Jill had no idea what he was saying, nor did she care. She did, however, place a sexy smile on her face as she scanned the room. She found Duncan and Damon right away; they were both looking at her. She followed Damon's eyes as he looked away toward a man, George Groper. The tables they sat at were round and large, with a gold-plated stripper pole going through the center to the ceiling. Every table had one chair with one man. Small steps were placed for the girls to climb up on the table.

As the women moved, Jill once again followed. She watched closely and imitated Cherry, swaying her hips provocatively, praying she didn't fall on her face. She really should have been trained to walk in the damn shoes.

"Just follow me. Your table is to the right of mine," Cherry said over her shoulder with a smile. Soft, sexy instrumental music played as they walked down the steps from the large stage and to their tables.

Jill sashayed to her table, her eyes meeting George's for the first time. He picked his glass up, taking a long drink, his eyes looking her up and down. He looked younger than in his picture and actually handsome, but there was something about his eyes that bothered her. A somewhat haunted look.

Climbing the three small steps carefully, Jill glanced to see the other women posed on the pole and stand perfectly still. She followed, doing the same thing. Looking down at George, he had his phone out sending a text. Her eyes shot to Damon, who glanced away from the woman at his table to her, but for a brief second, his eyes shot to George then away. Within seconds, the music started.

It was a seductive beat of music. Jill began to move her body, but she felt like she was going to hyperventilate.

"Jill, slow your breathing," Slade's voice soothed in her ear. "You are doing great. Try to bend so we can get a shot of his phone when he has it out."

Nodding, Jill cursed when she made eye contact with George. He was probably wondering what the hell she was nodding at. She gave him a shy smile, but he didn't smile back. She had no clue how long she danced, but in all honesty, she had to respect the women around her. This was damn hard work. Some songs were slow and seductive, while others were fast and grinding. Thinking she was surely failing big time at this mission, she felt a hand on her leg. Looking down, George waved someone to bring a chair. Jill carefully stepped down, her feet throbbing as George stood, holding the chair out for her. She noticed a few other girls sitting talking with the men they were dancing for.

He downed the rest of his drink, raising the empty glass to the waitress before sitting down. "What's your name?" he asked.

"Lola," Jill said in her sexiest voice, smiling shyly, wondering if he liked the shy-girl routine. Until she figured it out, she'd play that part.

"Nice to meet you, Lola. I'm George." He nodded at her, and then looked at his phone. "What would you like to drink?"

Looking up at the waitress, Jill frowned, not knowing what to order.

"All the girls have a two drink maximum." She smiled down at Jill, realizing she was new.

"Oh, I'll have what he's having." Jill didn't know what else to say unless she ordered a diet Pepsi, and well, that wasn't sexy and didn't inspire a man to open his soul to her.

George raised his eyebrow to that, but he didn't say anything.

Jill felt sweat bead across her forehead. She honestly didn't know what in the hell to say and suddenly wished she was back on the table dancing, which was saying at lot.

"Tonight your first night?" he asked, placing his phone back down before looking at her.

"That obvious, huh?" Jill thanked the waitress when she put her drink in front of her.

"No, not at all. You're very…talented," George laughed, lifting his drink up and taking a swallow. "It's just I usually get the new girls."

Following suit, Jill took a large gulp of the drink the waitress sat in front of her and about spit it back out. Her eyes watered and her throat burned like fire. "Holy shit," Jill sputtered as George chuckled, patting her on the back.

"Jesus, Jill, slow down on that stuff," Slade's whispered voice echoed in her ear.

"Are you okay?" George leaned toward her, his smile genuine.

Jill nodded, trying to smile her sexy smile, but failed miserably. "What is that?"

"Jack and Coke," he laughed, shaking his head. "More Jack than coke mind you. Just take smaller sips and it will go down nice and smooth."

Touching her throat, Jill laughed, "Packs quite a punch."

"That it does." He lifted his drink up with a grin, taking another long swallow.

Once Jill regained her composure, she smiled at George. "So why do they give you the new girls? Why don't you just find one you like and ask for them?"

"No, I'm fine with the new girls." He glanced around. "Just gives me someone new to talk to who doesn't give a shit what I'm saying."

"Well, George, my feet are killing me, so thank you for asking me to sit," Jill gave a teasing grunt, putting her elbows up on the table, leaning in.

Giving her a small smile, he texted something else on his phone, a large frown playing across his face. Jill did her best to see, but the angle wasn't right. He slammed his phone down hard on the table then took another drink, almost draining the glass.

"Sorry, I don't mean to be rude, but work is driving me crazy," he sighed, his eyes searching hers as if looking for some answer to an unasked question. "So what made you decide to do the half-breed gimmick? Good job on the fangs by the way; they look real."

Okay, she was stumped. She heard cursing in her ear, which indicated they weren't going to be much help. Well, this could go one of two ways; he could take her in for being a half-breed or he could not give a shit. She was hoping for the not give a shit.

"They probably look real because this…" she waved her hand over her face, "is not a gimmick." The cursing in her ear stopped, replaced with dead silence.

"Ah, shit." George scooted away from the table. "You need to…you shouldn't be at my table. Do you know who I am?"

Well, shit, that didn't go over well. "No, actually, I don't. Should I?" She played dumb.

"I'm Mayor Ferguson's Deputy Mayor." He reached over, draining his glass, motioning for another.

"Ah…" Jill frowned, also taking a drink, but a much smaller

mouthful. This time, she savored the burn in her throat, because she was about to either blow this mission all to hell or open it up for a victory in their favor. "So you're one of them. Yeah, maybe I need to switch tables or is that what you've been doing on your phone, calling in the breed round-up team?"

He slammed his glass down, gaining attention from those around them. Jill's eyes shot to Damon who was ready to stand, but she shook her head slightly. George leaned in toward her. "I'm not like that son of a bitch or his cunt of a fiancée."

Jill remained silent, listening to Slade in her ear wishing he would be quiet so she could think. This ear thing was a really bad idea. "Dammit, Jill, be careful."

He waited until the waitress set down his drink and left before turning on to her. "I should have been Mayor, not him."

"And you would have done it differently?" Jill chuckled, shaking her head, hoping to hell her hunch about George paid off. "This war on half-breeds has ruined my life. Why do you think I'm slinking around at night working in dark clubs, dancing for strangers half-naked? I had a great job working in a finance office, but because of your boss, the Mayor's 'Stop the Breeding of Half-breeds' campaign, I can't even walk down the street without the fear of being locked away."

When he didn't say anything, but simply stared at her, draining his glass, Jill figured she'd blown it big time. Dammit, she read him wrong and she'd failed; Sloan was going to be so pissed.

"When I signed on with Tom Ferguson, he was actually a pretty stand-up guy." He glanced down at his phone before continuing as Sloan snorted in Jill's earpiece. "We believed in the same things, wanted the same things for the community and he was a shoe-in to win because of his affiliation with the police force. He talked me into supporting him as his Deputy Mayor. I figured it would help me in my future pursuit in politics, but it only feels like I've sold my soul to the devil."

Jill took another sip of her drink, ignoring the warning from Slade to slow down, but she needed this drink. It was easing her nerves tremendously. "Why do you say that?"

"Because that's who I feel I work for now." George laughed without humor. "I'm so stuck in deep shit; I don't know how to get out."

"So quit, resign or whatever a Deputy Mayor would do." Dammit, she wanted to dive deeper into the 'sold his soul' comment, but didn't want to sound too eager and clue him in.

"I'm in too deep for that now." True fear flashed in his eyes. "No one leaves unless told to leave, and that doesn't happen either. They just disappear."

"What changed everything?" Jill leaned back, taking the drink with her. "You seemed to be on track with the Mayor during his campaign."

"His fiancée happened," he hissed, pure hatred coloring his face. "Once she came into the picture, everything changed and the whole half-breed campaign began. It was her way or no way. I tried everything I could to talk to Tom, but she had him wrapped around her finger. She actually cornered me, telling me that if I was a good boy, she'd take good care of me…meaning sex, but if I crossed her, I would disappear."

"I'm sorry." Jill took another drink, setting it down, then placed her hand on his arm. "You seem like a real great guy, wanting to do right."

"Yeah, real great guy," he snorted, draining another glass.

Jill couldn't believe he was still able to talk after drinking so much. "What I don't understand is where the VC Council is in all of this? Have you gone to them?" Okay, this was the big one; she just tossed out the big guns.

"I'm watched all the time because that bitch doesn't trust me." George frowned, fingering his glass. "This is the only place I can escape to, but I know someone is in the parking lot or nearby ready to follow me. If I even glance at anyone on the VC Council, I'm a dead man. She has a real hard-on for those guys. Plus from what I understand, she has a traitor high in the ranks there; that's how all the paperwork and meetings went through to Washington without the Council ever knowing until it was too late."

More cursing from every Warrior with a mic overwhelmed her hearing. George's cussing brought her attention back to him.

"What in the hell am I telling you all this for." George's voice was shaky with fear. Small beads of sweat broke out across his forehead. Nervously, he grabbed a napkin, wiping the sweat from his brow.

"George," Jill tried to break into his freak out.

"Jesus, I need to quit drinking." George took another gulp of the drink the waitress kept filled. "I must be out of my damn mind telling you all that."

"George!" Jill said with more force. When he stopped and looked at her, Jill gave him a comforting smile. "I'm a stripper and a half-breed. Even if I wanted to tell anyone anything, who would believe me," she laughed, trying to calm him down.

He nodded, trying to gain control. "I'm afraid, with no way out." He looked at her, his eyes turning serious. "You need to be careful, Lola. Alice hates your kind for some reason and will stop at nothing to get rid of all of you."

Jill knew exactly why Alice hated her kind. Hell, Alice hated her the most and the feeling was more than mutual. "Have you been in their so called half-way house?"

A haunted look shadowed his eyes. "Yes, and do whatever you can to stay out of there. It's a nightmare."

"What do you mean?" Jill pushed. "Are they being mistreated?"

When he didn't answer, Jill straightened up, trying her best to keep her anger at bay.

"Just stay away from there," he warned. "I did my best to stop it, but I'm only one person and this is way bigger than me. She has hired a bunch of…well, I don't know who they are, but they are a cruel looking bunch who does her dirty work."

"I have friends in there," Jill lied, but then again, she realized she may not be lying at all.

George looked at her with pity. "I'm sorry." He sighed, "Really I am."

Glancing at Damon and turning to take a peek a Duncan, Jill made a decision that probably wasn't hers to make. Her eyes went back to Damon and he narrowed his eyes at her as if he knew exactly what she was about to do.

"Jill?" Slade's voice filled her ear. "What are you doing?"

Ignoring his voice and Damon's stare, Jill looked back at George. She better not be wrong on this, but so far, she had been dead on. "What happens if the Mayor and his fiancée go down? Do you take over as Mayor?"

His eye flashed to hers. "Yes, but–"

"Listen, I may know someone who can help you, but you have to help them." Jill tried to read his reaction, but couldn't. "Would you be willing, even knowing the risks? Do you really want to make a difference or is that just you talking through your Jack and Coke?"

"Son of a bitch!" Sloan shouted in her ear. "Jill, stand down. You do not have authority…"

Jill acted like she was fixing her hair, but pulled the small hearing device out of her ear. Glancing at Damon, who she could see better than Duncan, he leaned back in his chair rubbing his ear clearly indicating that Sloan was telling him to warn her to put it back in so he could bitch her out more. She opted not to do that. This time, Jill took a big swig of her drink; she was going to need it.

"There is no one who can help me," George said, but held a glimmer of hope in his gaze.

"Actually, you're wrong, but it's your call." Jill shrugged as if she couldn't care less what he did. "I think it would be wonderful if someone actually stepped up against the Mayor and his fiancée, but unfortunately, proof is what they need and can't get, but you can."

He sat back in his chair, staring into the distance. Jill allowed him to soak it in. Hailey walked over at that moment. "Mr. Groper, is there something wrong?" She cast Jill a dark look. "I can get you another girl if you'd rather. Lola is new."

George snapped out of his daze. "No, she's absolutely fine. Thank you."

"Oh, okay." Hailey smiled first at George and then at Jill. "Just wanted to make sure my best customer was being treated fairly."

Once she walked away, George turned to Jill. "You're not really a stripper, are you?"

Knowing that even though she took out her earpiece and couldn't hear anyone, they could all hear her. "No, I'm not." She looked him in the eye. "But I do know someone who can help you."

"Give me a lap dance." He scooted away from the table.

Okay, now that confused her. "Ah…what?"

"In my right suit pocket is my card." He fanned his suit jacket out, plastering a fake smile across his lips. "I think my cell is tapped, but if you call about decorating my house, I'll know it's you and the bastards listening will ignore the call."

Jill finished off her drink and then grabbed his, finishing his off, numb now to the burn. Standing, she walked toward him, straddling his legs. She began to move her body, touching him. Her hand slipped into his pocket feeling cards, taking one, she pulled her hand out, but crumbled the card as small as she could to hide it in her hand; she had nowhere else to put it. Glancing sideways, she saw Duncan head her way, and brought the card up to George's shoulder, waiting for him to pass, knowing what he was doing. He stumbled right when he got to them, running into the chair. Their hands touched and the card disappeared from hers.

"Hey!" She tried to right herself. George's hand kept her steady. "Watch it."

"I'm sorry," Duncan replied drunkenly, but kept on heading toward the men's restroom.

Jill continued her dance. Leaning down close to George's ear, she sighed, "You really need to stay out of places like this when you become Mayor."

"Can I really trust you?" he whispered back as she started to pull away.

"About as much as I trust you." She smiled down at him. "Trust goes both ways."

Chapter 19

Jill headed toward the car barefoot. Those damn freaking shoes were going to burn the first chance she got. Putting her earpiece in, she frowned; this was going to be painful.

"Hey," she said, waiting for the fallout.

"Hey? Hey!" Sloan yelled, making her grab her ear. "That's all you've got to say is fucking HEY?"

Swallowing hard, Jill glanced around the parking lot, digging in her bag for her keys. "Actually, no." She opened the door, getting in; okay, she actually fell in. Maybe those last two drinks with the girls in the back was a bad idea. "I don't think I should be driving."

"Jill, what's wrong?" Slade sounded pissed, but not as pissed as Sloan.

"I've got a slight...buzz going," she giggled. What the hell, she didn't giggle...ever, and why she found that funny was beyond her.

"Shit," Slade hissed in her ear, but he sounded funny.

"I got her." Sid's voice interrupted more cussing. "Jill, you see that dumpster to your left?"

Jill looked, rising up to see over the car parked next to her. "Yup."

"Pull up next to that. I'm going to slide in," Sid ordered.

"Roger," Jill snorted, wondering what the hell was wrong with her. She'd pissed Sloan off. Slade didn't sound too happy, yet she was giggling like a girl. She had never been drunk before and it wasn't like she was stumbling drunk, but she felt pretty damn good and kind of funny; ha-ha funny. She laughed again.

"Jill, how much did you have to drink?" Jared chuckled.

"Only a glass and a half." She started the car, putting it in reverse. "Of Jax and Coke."

"Jax?" Sid replied, his voice muffled, indicating he was on the move. "What the fuck is Jax and Coke."

"I think she means Jack and Coke," Jared snickered.

Jill pulled up to the dumpster, slammed the brakes too hard and waited. Her door opened, causing her to jump. "Shit, Sid, you scared me."

"Scoot." He used his butt to push her over and took off. "Got her."

"Everyone, get your asses back to the compound, now." Sloan's order was harsh and loud.

Jill pulled out her earpiece, closing it up in her palm. "Why is he such an asshole?" Jill frowned.

"I can still fucking hear you. Goddamn people! Learn how to quiet your mic before you start insulting me," Sloan growled loud enough that she heard him through her hand where she held the earpiece.

Jill's eyes shot wide open as she looked at Sid in shock, pointing to her hand in disbelief. "How did he hear me?"

Sid was laughing so hard he couldn't answer, but pointed at her neck. When she raised her hand her fingers touched the choker and her face comically shifted to horror as she realized what she had done. Reaching around, she pulled off the choker, shoving it in her bag.

Pulling into a gas station, Sid looked over at Jill who had laid her head back on the seat. "I would suggest you not do that. You need to stay awake and alert." He grinned, shaking his head. "I'm going in to get you some coffee so you can fully understand the ass-chewing you are about to get. Lock the door."

Jill raised her head as soon as Sid spoke. Once he slammed the door, she locked it. "Drinking is way overrated." She rubbed her head, which was starting to hurt. Taking her wig off, she shoved that in her bag also. Lowering the sun visor, she pulled out the hair clips Caroline had used, and then peeled her fake lashes off. "And dammit, it hurts being a woman."

She hit the unlock button for Sid. He slid in, handing her coffee. "Drink up."

"Where's the cream and sugar?" Jill opened the lid, blowing on the coffee.

"Black is best." He grinned at her as he backed out, and pulled onto the road.

"I have to have sugar." Jill went to put the lid back on.

"Jill, I'm telling you the truth here. You want to be sober and on your toes, because Sloan is pissed." Sid laughed when she groaned.

"I hate coffee without sugar," she griped, but drank it anyway.

Pulling into the compound, Jill sighed. "How bad is it going to be?" she said once they got out of the car.

"You just better hope that this works out with Georgie boy." Sid shook his head. "Took balls doing what you did, that's for sure."

Jill headed up the walkway to the door, but stopped. Slade leaned against the wall, his arms crossed as only Slade did as he waited for her. She took another sip of her coffee watching as he nodded to Sid, but his eyes never left hers.

"You okay?" His voice was deep, without emotion.

Nodding, Jill slowly walked toward him. "Are you mad at me, too?"

His lips twitched, but he didn't smile. "We'll talk about that later."

214

He reached out, lifting her chin up, kissing her softly. "Let's get this over with first."

"Okay." When he turned to open the door, she stopped. "Did he really hear me call him an asshole?"

Slade's face turned grim. "That's the least of your problems, Jill."

"Dammit," Jill cursed under her breath. Slade opened the door for her and she walked in, weaving a bit to the left.

"Have you ever drank before?" Slade steadied her so she didn't run into the doorframe.

"Not a drop. I'm still a little fuzzy." Jill grinned up at him. "Fuzzy. Fuzzzzzy. That's a weird word."

As soon as they entered, the women ran out into the entryway. "How did it go?" Nicole grinned.

"Did your wig stay on okay?" Caroline frowned, looking at her wigless head.

"It went great." Jill grinned real big, then swayed when she held up her coffee as if saluting.

Nicole leaned in and sniffed. "Are you drunk?"

"Maybe a little," Jill whispered. "I only had a couple."

"You said you had one and a half." Sid frowned with his hands on his hips.

"Well, Dad," Jill frowned back, "I forgot about the two I had in the back before I left, but they were little."

"Shit. Those were shots, Jill," Sid cursed, glancing at Slade, then Nicole. "Go make up some more coffee. Has she ever drank before?" Slade just shook his head.

215

"And bring the sugar." Jill nodded, pointing at Nicole with her coffee. "Lots of sugar."

"Hey." Damon stuck his head out of Sloan's door. "Come on, so we can get this over with."

"This is going to be ugly," Sid said, looking at Jill. "How drunk are you?"

"I'm fine." Jill grumbled. "I just feel really relaxed and want to smile a lot, but other than that, I'm fine. What's the big deal? So I had a few drinks. Performing barely dressed in front of a bunch of men isn't easy. I'd like to see you do it without drinking, Sid."

"Come on," Damon called out again. "I want to get this shit over with."

"Okay, grumps." Jill headed that way. "Geez, stop being so grumpy all the time."

"Jill." Slade stopped her. "You need to get ahold of yourself. Sloan…"

"Needs to take a chill pill." Looking up at Slade, she smiled. "You are a hot-ass man, you know that, Doctor Slade Buchanan. How about me and you forget about all this nonsense and–"

"Now!" Damon shouted this time.

"Okay!" Jill shouted back with an irritated frown, turned and headed toward the office, but was stopped this time by Nicole and Pam who were trying not to laugh. Nicole poured more black coffee into her foam cup.

"Be careful, Jill. It's hot," Nicole warned.

"I just want to tell you both that Damon and Duncan never once looked at one of those women. I mean they looked, but they fake looked. You two should be really nice…" she slyly gave them the

216

most awkward wink, "to them tonight."

"Jill," Damon growled.

"Damon," Jill growled back and started walking again. "A little thanks goes a long way. I'm helping you out here, buddy."

Everyone became quiet as soon as Jill walked into the room, except for Sloan who was on the phone. Seeing Steve and Adam against the wall, she raised her cup of coffee to them with a goofy grin, then headed their way, squeezing herself between them. Raising the cup to her lips as if hiding what she was saying, she whispered, "What did I miss?"

"Are you drunk?" Adam frowned down at her.

Jill huffed. "No." She held up her cup. "Coffee."

"She's shitfaced," Steve laughed.

Sloan hung up the phone, his eyes going straight to Jill. Okay, that sobered her up a little and actually worked better than the nasty non-sugared coffee she was drinking. He continued to stare at her to the point where Steve started sliding away from her.

"Do you want to explain what the fuck that was all about?" Sloan didn't yell; he didn't growl; he just asked the question with a calm, cool demeanor that scared the shit out of her.

Jill opened her mouth to answer, and then slammed it shut. Looking away, she tried to make the words she wanted to say form in her head so she could answer the question with her numb lips. Looking back, she opened her mouth again and everyone in the room watched in anticipation of what she was going to say. "Ah, which part?" finally came out of her mouth.

"Which part?" Sloan sat back, his stare becoming more intense.

"Yeah, which part?" Jill took a step forward, but when the floor shifted suddenly, she retreated to the wall. She felt herself sliding toward the left, but Adam used his arm to slowly slide her back up. "Why do you always answer a question with a question?"

"What the fuck you doing?" Steve whispered, pushing away from the wall, bending his head to her as he looked at the ground. "Shut the fuck up, Jill."

Anger hit Jill right in the gut, swishing around with the nausea she was feeling, and it wasn't a great combination. "No, I won't shut the fuck up." This time when she pushed herself away from the wall, she walked slowly with concentration to the front of Sloan's desk.

"Jill." Sid actually tried to stop her, but she jerked her arm away. "Sloan, can we do this when she's sober."

"I'm not drunk. I'm just a little fuzzy." She grinned at the word again, but then turned serious. "I did what I felt was right. If it was one of your Warriors with a cock—"

Groans sounded throughout the room. "Here we go again," Sid sighed, but had the biggest grin on his face.

"We wouldn't be having this conversation. Would we? No, I don't believe we would. Believe it or not, Sloan, I can make snap decisions without a cock. Amazing, I know, but I can." Jill saw George's crumpled business card on Sloan's desk and went to pick it up, but it flew out of her hand and landed at Duncan's feet. He picked it up and handed it to her. She tried to straighten it out with one hand since her coffee was in the other. Giving up, she held it out, crumpled, toward Sloan. "This could possibly lead to information we need. I took a chance. I have a brain and I use it daily. I didn't put anyone in immediate danger." She tossed the card on his desk when he didn't take it.

"You broke protocol." Sloan eyed her, but a light of respect gleamed in his eyes.

Jill tilted her head, looking at Sloan "I've come to know all these guys." She threw her hand out with the coffee cup, moving it around to all the guys as Warriors jumped out of the way when the hot liquid flew everywhere. "And I bet…this…ah…this…cup of nasty-ass coffee, they've all broken protocol. Sometimes it may work out and sometimes it may not, but again…I bet this nasty-ass coffee that George Groper will come through for us."

"And what makes you so sure of that?" Sloan's calm was making her a bit nervous.

"Because I saw his fear." Jill put the coffee down on his desk, then looked at her hand, which had started to hurt, small little blisters had formed. She looked away from it to Sloan, not looking drunk at all, but like someone who knew exactly what she was talking about. "I know that fear. I know that feeling of being stuck in something and there is no way out. You will do anything, and I mean anything, to feel safe again. I saw that in his eyes. I felt it in my gut."

No one said a word, nothing. Not even Sloan.

"I trust my instincts. They've gotten me through a lot in my life." Jill blew on her hand. "And instead of yelling at me, which is fine when I really screw up and I *will* really screw up, just trust me on this one. I don't need swats of congratulations on my ass like you guys do—"

"That's football," Jared added with a horrified expression. "Warriors do not swat the asses of other Warriors."

"Whatever." Jill frowned at Jared for interrupting her. "If I'm wrong, you all can stand here and scream or whatever at me, but I know I'm not wrong on this."

God, she was going to puke, or at least thought she was. It was so back and forth like a friggin' war going on in her stomach. Wishing to hell the room would stand still, she took another deep breath, but she had one more thing to say.

"And I swear I will never drink during a job again." Jill groaned when the room tilted. "But I was scared and it helped relax me."

"Jill, none of the Warriors would have let anything happen to you." Sloan sighed, "You need to trust that they have your back."

Jill tilted her head, but wished she hadn't. "No, you're wrong. I was afraid to let you guys down. I wasn't afraid of what would happen to me because I knew none of you would let anything happen to me." Jill smiled with a shrug. "The last two tiny drinks, which I think are the ones that made me fuzzy, were because the girls wanted to celebrate my first night. I've never had that before, so I did, but it will never happened again because I really don't like the feeling I'm having now."

A few chuckles filled the room. Sloan looked toward Slade. "Slade, take her to her room—"

"No," Jill interrupted, picking up her coffee carefully. "I'm kind of upset at anyone with a cock right now. I'd rather go on my own if you're finished."

Sloan's lip twitched. "I'm finished, for now."

Jill nodded as she turned, but the floor swayed. "Steve, you got a minute?"

Frowning, Steve glanced down at his lower body and pointed. "Really?" When Jill looked up at him with pleading eyes, he just threw up his hands. "Ah, fuck it." Rolling his eyes, he hurried to her, wrapping his arm around her waist. He made sure to glance at Slade who nodded his okay.

"Will you please take my coffee? I burnt myself already." She kept her head lowered, looking at the floor as he led her to the door. "And I'm sorry. I know you have a cock, but—"

"Jill don't sweat it. Just please stop saying cock or referring to mine. It makes me really uncomfortable and I don't want Slade killing me." Steve helped her out the door, down the hall and to her room.

Once inside, Jill managed to make it to her bed falling face first into her pillow. "I'm such an idiot," she cried, and then sat up. "And I think I'm going to puke."

Steve sighed, "You're not an idiot. I'm actually proud of you for standing up to Sloan."

"Did I even make sense?" Jill wiped a tear from her cheek.

"Surprisingly, you made perfect sense." Steve laughed, sitting down next to her. "A drunk Jill is a funny Jill with much insight."

"I know I give you shit, but you know I love you, don't you?" Jill leaned over, putting her head on his shoulder. "I really do, Steve, and I'm not just saying that because I'm drunk."

"We're family, Jill. That's what we do, and since you're getting all sappy and shit, guess I will too." Steve leaned his head against hers. "I love you, too, drunkie."

Jill laughed, which quickly turned into a groan. "I'm glad you feel that way because I think I'm going to be sick." Jill raised her head quickly. "And I hate to puke alone."

Steve helped her up and to the bathroom. "Well, I don't know if I love you that much, Jill." When she heaved into the toilet, Steve gagged. "Then again, maybe I do. Damn, what the hell did you eat?"

******

Slade watched Steve walk Jill out the door, wanting to follow, but decided it was better to give her a minute. He was so fucking proud of her drunk ass. He knew at that moment he had found the one. She was definitely the one.

"So what are your thoughts about what happened tonight?" Sloan asked everyone and anyone in the room.

"Hell, Sloan, we've all broken protocol." Duncan was surprisingly the first to speak. "It's not done out of disrespect to anyone in this room."

"Well, I'm damn proud of her." Sid beamed with a satisfied smile of his own. "She's got more guts than a lot of men I know, and she's right. George Groper might be the break we need. She saw something and went for it. Every one of us, you included, Sloan, have done the same."

Sloan nodded. "I'll talk to her more tomorrow and we will try to make contact with this George."

"Sounds like a plan," Jared nodded. "Now, can we go so I can see my woman?"

"Get the fuck out of here," Sloan growled. "You guys are so pussy-whipped it makes me sick."

"One of these days, Sloan, we are going to be saying the same about you," Sid warned with a laugh. "And I cannot wait for that fucking day."

"You'll be waiting a long time, asshole," Sloan sneered. "Now get your ass out of my office."

"I've got forever," Sid laughed as he followed Jared out.

Sloan looked at Slade. "What?"

"She made a good decision," Slade replied, turned and walked out the door.

"Hey, let us know if she needs anything," Sid called out, grabbing Lana who waited for him to come out of Sloan's office.

"Thanks." Slade hurried up the steps and down the hall to Jill's

222

room. Opening the door, he walked in and heard Jill and Steve talking from the bathroom.

"God, I hate to puke, but it feels good afterwards." Jill's groan was miserable.

"Well, Jill, I have to honestly say I hate when you puke, too." Steve made a gagging noise. "You are a dramatic puker."

"What the hell is a dramatic puker?" Jill snorted. "You just puke."

Slade leaned against the wall outside the bathroom door, listening to their conversation, a small grin playing against his lips.

"No, there's different pukers. You got your heavers, your spitters, your gaggers and then there's you, the dramatic puker; all three put together." Steve sounded proud of his observation.

"You know when I said I loved you?" Jill moaned.

"Yeah." Steve's voice held a hint of pride.

"I lied," Jill stated as they both laughed, but then Jill groaned with a heave.

"Oh, God, not again," Steve cried out. "How much did you drink?"

The sound of Jill vomiting made Slade move. Opening the bathroom door, he saw Steve holding Jill's forehead as she vomited in the toilet.

"Thank God." Steve sighed in relief seeing Slade. He stepped out of the way, but still held Jill's forehead.

"Thanks, Steve." Slade took his place. "I've got it."

"No problem." Steve reached down, squeezing Jill's shoulder. "I'll check on you later."

Jill nodded, then heaved again. Slade grabbed a washcloth with his free hand and wet it with cold water. Laying it across the back of her neck, he rubbed her back as she continued to dry heave. Jill reached for the washcloth bringing it around to her face as she sat back on the floor.

"Better?" Slade knelt in front of her. The bathroom was so small; he had to wedge himself between the toilet and wall.

"No." Jill wiped her face, and then rubbed the washcloth across her teeth. Turning on her knees, she curled up and lay on the floor, placing her cheek against the cold tile. "I know this is gross, but it feels so good."

Spotting the small red blisters on her hand, he picked it up to take a closer look.

"I burnt myself with the coffee." Her voice cracked, "I'm sorry, Slade. I didn't mean to embarrass you. I will never ever drink again. This seriously sucks."

Slade kissed her hand and ran his tongue over the blisters to hurry the healing. "You could never embarrass me, Jill." He reached up and turned the shower on. "Piss me off maybe, but never embarrass me."

"Really?" Jill squinted up at him from the floor.

"Yeah, really." He helped her sit up. "You think you can stand?"

"I feel a lot better." She replied, keeping her eyes closed. "I want to brush my teeth." She frowned, letting him help her stand. He moved her in front of the sink and stood behind her as she brushed. He took off his shirt, then his black combat pants.

Jill's bloodshot eyes watched him in the mirror.

Slade laughed at the question in her gaze. "I'm going to help you shower, nothing else." Slade turned her, pulled her shirt off and frowned at the stripper outfit she still wore. Even though she looked fucking hot, he couldn't shake the thought of her lap dancing for another man. It was enough to make him crazy with rage, but he forced himself to remain calm. She didn't need that; plus, he knew why she had done it.

"Wait a minute," Jill hissed when he tried to remove the skimpy top. "They had to tape it 'cause I kept falling out of it."

Slade found the tape and gently removed each strip, not wanting to hurt her. While he was doing that, she had already toed her pants off, leaving only her white boy shorts. He hooked his thumbs in and pulled them down where she could kick them off herself. Wrapping his arm around her, he tested the water before helping Jill in. He steadied her as she leaned her head back, letting the water wash over her face.

Her moans of pleasure made him hard; there was no hiding it. He knew it was a healthy reaction, but he didn't want Jill to think he was a pervert trying to take advantage while she was sick, so he moved his lower half away from her. Handing her the soap, he figured it was best she cleaned herself. The thought of his hands sliding over her slick body was too much to ask of him and his control.

He kept one hand on her waist. The other gripped the wall to keep it off her body as his eyes watched her soapy hands run over her body. His eyes lifted to hers. She was watching him watch her. His hiss echoed in the room when she reached out with her slick hand, grasping him.

"No," he hissed again when she squeezed. "You're—"

"Fine now." Jill's eyes pleaded. "I need you, Slade. My emotions are all over the place, but I know I need you like I never have before."

Slade reached out, cupping her face. "Not as much as I need you, Jillian." He leaned in and their mouths touched with a tenderness Slade had never experienced with a woman. He had never actually made love to a woman; fuck women, yes, but as he picked Jill up, he knew he would be making love for the first time in his life to a woman who held his soul in the palm of her hand.

Chapter 20

Jill headed toward the kitchen after a night of absolute horror and bliss. After his tender lovemaking in the shower, Slade carried her to her bed where they lay and talked for hours. He held her while she slept and woke her up for another round of what she craved, yet there had been nothing tender about it. His intensity had her screaming with pleasure. She stopped in front of the kitchen doors and swallowed hard as sudden fear twisted her heart. She had loved before, but this was different than the love she had for her family. This went much deeper, to the point of actually scaring her. Shaking her doubts away, she pushed through the door, hoping the room was empty.

No, she wasn't that lucky. Everyone stopped what they were doing to look at her. She seemed to have that effect on them lately. Jill felt like the star in a freak show. Heading toward the coffee, she reached out to pour a cup until the smell hit her nose; her stomach rolled with nausea.

"Hair of the dog that bit ya?" Sid slammed down a bottle of Jack Daniels.

Scrunching up her nose, Jill leaned away. "What the hell does that mean?"

Jared walked up, grabbing the bottle and took a big swig. "It means, my dear young friend, the best cure for what ails you is to have more of it." He shoved the bottle at her. "Drink up."

Leaning back, Jill held her nose. "Get that away from me!" She actually gagged.

"You wouldn't be doing that if you were in her bathroom last night while she puked her guts out." Steve frowned, walking in. "It was disturbing. She's a dramatic puker."

"Those are the worst kind." Jared frowned at Jill as if she had three heads.

"You guys are sick." Jill made a beeline past Jared, giving him her dirtiest look. Grabbing a glass, she poured some orange juice. When the smell hit her nose, it didn't make her nauseous so she drank.

Sloan walked in and spotted her from across the room. He crooked his finger at her, indicating for her to come to his office...again. With a groan, she finished off her juice, putting the empty glass in the sink.

"Damn, girl, I think you've broken my record for getting called into Sloan's office." Sid nodded his acknowledgement at her.

"Dude, she isn't even close to that record yet." Jared waved the bottle of Jack at Jill as she passed.

"You're cruel and I hate you," she spat at him, but couldn't hide her grin when she flipped him off.

Sid thought for a minute, then chuckled, "Yeah, who am I kidding? No one is going to break that record."

Jill headed toward Sloan's office, her head pounding with every step she took. She was half-vampire. Shouldn't that make her exempt from having a hangover? The door was open so she walked in.

"Shut the door," Sloan ordered, leaning up against his desk, arms crossed, looking at her.

Jill did, walking further into the room. "Listen, I'm−"

Sloan interrupted her. "I just got off the phone with a close friend of mine, who is one of the highest council leaders." Sloan's voice was deep and deadly serious. "After last night, I called about a possible breech in our ranks. We've had meeting after meeting trying to figure out how laws regarding our kind are being made without our knowledge and consent. It's been confirmed, without a doubt, we do have a traitor. After talking last night, he called a high ranking senate member who confirmed and faxed forged documents of approval for the building of Halfway Houses across the country. Each document was signed by six of our high ranking council members, myself included. The signature was definitely mine, but I did not sign that document."

Jill's mouth dropped open. "But how could that even happen?"

"That's what we're working on now, but as soon as the initiation is over, we're heading to Washington to have the laws overturned, which we were told shouldn't be a problem as long as all six of us have a strong front," Sloan replied, his eyes intense.

"So you mean they'll have to shut down those places and stop rounding up half-breeds?" Jill asked excitedly.

"That's our plan, but I need to get as much information on the Mayor and Alice as I can." Sloan looked away briefly and rolled his eyes. "So I need you to call George and see if your plan worked."

"Give me the number." Jill held out her hand, ready. Hot damn, this was great news.

"Hold on a minute." He actually laughed.

He had been doing that so much more lately, and she liked it. It made him more approachable. Suddenly, she felt bad. "I'm sorry I called you an asshole," popped out of her mouth.

"Jill, I've been called worse." Sloan shook his head with a grin as he walked around to his desk. "And I know for absolute certain that won't be the last time you call me an asshole or worse. Now, where's Slade?"

"He said he had work to do in his office." Jill frowned. "He told me that the half-breed who was being held with Angelina died. He's trying to figure out why and also said he had some calls to make to California."

Sloan nodded as he texted something, then sat his phone down. "I called the DMV. You are going to test at noon today instead of Monday. The Council decided to move the initiation up two days since we are heading to Washington."

"Yes, sir." Jill nodded, but holy shit, that was soon. Excitement and nerves rumbled in her stomach.

"You okay? You went a little pale." Sloan watched her closely.

"I'm good," Jill smiled. "Just ready to get all this over with."

"I don't say this often, but I'm proud of you, Jill." Sloan cleared his throat, looking uncomfortable. "Now, where in the fuck is everyone?" He glared at the door.

"Thank you," Jill replied, mirroring his discomfort.

They both sighed in relief when Damon, Jared, Sid, Jax, and Duncan, along with Steve, Dillon and Adam walked into the room.

"Can I get me a special chair since I'm in here a lot?" Sid looked around as if trying to find a place he would put it before he pointed to a spot next to Sloan. "It actually would go great right there. Right by where all the magic happens."

"Sid, I will jail your ass if one chair delivery reaches this compound," Sloan warned with a sneer. "I mean it."

Slade hurried in, closing the door behind him. Glancing at Jill, he winked at her.

"Awe, isn't that sweet." Sid sighed, fluttering his eyelashes. "Warrior love is so hard to find."

"Why do you always have to run your mouth?" Slade took a step toward Sid. "I swear, one of these days, I'm going to finish that ass whipping I was handing you."

"In your dreams, Doc," Sid chuckled with no remorse.

"Sid, you want me to tell Lana what you said about those women at the club?" Jill glanced over at Sid, her eyebrow cocked.

He snorted, but looked a little nervous. "I didn't say anything."

"Really? I could have sworn…"

"You play dirty." He glared at her.

"Yes, I do, but so do you." She smiled at him before turning back to Sloan. "You ready for me to make that call?"

Sloan nodded, pulling out a phone from his desk and handing it to her. "This number can't be traced." He then handed her the card. "Do you know what to say?"

"Yes." Jill's hands shook a little as she dialed the number, then put it on speaker.

"Hello, George Groper here," he answered after three rings.

"Mr. Groper. It's Lola. How are you doing, sir?"

There was a slight pause before he responded. Everyone became tense in the room. "I'm doing great, Lola. How are you?"

Jill saw Sid roll his eyes. "Been very busy, but finally have a window to meet with you about a few designs I have for your house. Would you be available to meet me soon?"

There was an audible click on the line, one that no human ear could pick up, but everyone in Sloan's office heard it.

"Actually, I was getting ready to call you." They heard his lie. "I really want to get this started and have a few ideas I can bring with me. How about this afternoon around five?"

Jill looked to Sloan who nodded. "That would be perfect and I know I can help you achieve what you want in your home."

After he gave Jill the address, which Sloan wrote down, she hung up the phone.

"His line is definitely being monitored," Jared frowned.

"Okay, let's get ready to do this. It sounds like he has some stuff for us or at least I hope so." Sloan glanced at Jill. "I want everyone ready for anything; this could be a set up."

"Will I have enough time to test?" Jill asked, looking at Sloan.

"Plenty of time, but I want every Warrior staked out around that house an hour prior. It's going to be tricky because it's still daylight, but I know you can do it." Sloan read off the address as each one of them entered it into their phone.

Jill stood, taking the paper with the address from Sloan. "Thanks."

"Good luck." He nodded his dismissal.

Slade took her hand as they walked out, handing her a set of keys. "You taking me?"

"Yes." He smiled down at her.

"But you're busy," she frowned. "I can get Adam to take me or somebody. I don't want to be a pain in your ass."

Slade smacked her ass making her yelp. "You could never be a pain in my ass."

She gave him a 'you want to make a bet' look. "Really?"

"Okay, you can be a pain in my ass, but not this. I want to be there." He opened the car door for her.

Slade's eyes looked tired as she sat in the driver's seat and she felt a sudden wave of selfishness swarm her mind; she had been preoccupied with her own worries. The stress created, trying to figure out what was given to humans to turn them into half-breeds, was evident on Slade's handsome face. Each investigation led to a dead end. Once he was in the passenger seat, she glanced over at him. "Thank you for everything, Slade." She leaned over and kissed him. "I wish I could help you in some way."

"I have the best working on it." Slade touched her cheek. "And we will figure it out, but for now, just concentrate on what you have to do."

Jill smiled with a nod, starting the car. Glancing over at Slade, she asked, "You've never ridden with me, have you?" A playful grin on the cusp of sadistic appeared before Jill revved the engine.

Slade turned from looking out the window to look at her. "Ah, shit." He grabbed the dashboard as she turned and flew in reverse out of the parking spot, and slammed on the brakes.

"Just kidding." She laughed at his look of horror as she carefully drove out of the parking lot and onto the street.

******

Slade paced back and forth in front of the DMV. The cop testing Jill didn't look too happy being called out on a Sunday, but once he saw her excitement, he warmed up to her.

"Son, you're making me a nervous wreck." Jill's dad sat on a bench, watching him.

"Sorry." Slade walked over and sat down.

"Thank you for calling me and letting me know." Chuck Nichols watched the cars passing on the street below. "I haven't been a very good father to Jill."

"Well, it's never too late to start." Slade frowned. "Jill loves you very much, sir."

Giving Jill's father some privacy after seeing him swipe at his eye,

Slade stood back up, glancing at his watch. "Shouldn't they be back by now?"

Composed, her father stood next to him, both watching for the car.

"There she is." Slade stuck his hands in his back pockets as her dad stepped behind the large pillar.

"I don't want to make her nervous." He laughed when Slade looked at him.

Slade nodded, turning to watch as Jill stopped near the cones. The officer got out of the car with his clipboard, walking to the front of the cones. Jill glanced over at him and he gave her a reassuring nod. "She's getting ready to parallel park," he told her dad.

Chuck walked from behind the pillar to peek around the corner.

"Come on, baby. You can do this," Slade mumbled. He watched as she did her maneuvers. Once she stopped the car, coming inches from the front cone, Slade felt such a relief he felt a little weak. It wasn't perfect, but she fucking did it, and he couldn't be more proud.

Jill jumped out of the car and held her crossed fingers up at him as she walked up to the officer. With a smile, the officer handed her a piece of paper. Jill jumped up and took off running toward Slade. He caught her and swung her around.

"I passed." She held him tightly, tears in her voice. "I really did it."

"As I knew you would." Slade pulled her back, kissing her hard, but quick. "Someone else came to congratulate you."

Jill turned her head to see her father standing there with tears in his eyes. "Congratulations, Jelly Bean."

Slade put Jill on her feet and smiled down at her when she looked at him surprised, her chin trembling as tears flowed freely. "Go on," he nudged her toward him.

Jill walked over, taking her father in her arms for a hug. "Thanks, Dad," she cried, then laughed. "I know it's just a stupid license, but I never thought I would ever get it."

"I always told you that you could do anything you put your mind to, even with the battles you had and you've proved that." He smiled sadly. "I'm sorry I didn't help you more."

"I love you, Dad." Jill kissed his cheek. "And you loved me back. That's enough."

"You ready to get that license?" The officer smiled at Jill, holding the door open. "My shift starts in fifteen minutes."

Jill nodded, following the officer inside, but not before turning back toward Slade mouthing 'thank you'. He smiled with a wink.

"I don't know how to ever thank you for what you've helped my daughter with." Chuck looked embarrassed, but his appreciation was in earnest.

"You don't have to ever thank me for anything I do for Jill, sir," Slade responded. "But I do have something to ask you."

"Son, you can ask me anything." Her father gave a nod.

Slade looked toward the door Jill had disappeared through, then to her father. This was easier than he thought.

Chapter 21

Jill drove to the address George gave her, feeling happy and content. After getting her license, Slade had taken her and her father out for a quick bite to eat. Her father was nervous, but excited and proud about her initiation into the VC Warriors. Jill asked about everyone, even her mom, but mostly they talked about what Jill had been going through with her training and her father's health. Her dad also liked telling embarrassing stories about her to Slade.

Slowing down on the street, she looked at house numbers. She had her earpiece in, which Sloan threatened dire consequences if she took it out. She wore a professional dress suit that Nicole gave her and a different choker with a small camera.

"It's the house with the fountain," Jared's voice echoed in her ear. "Black shutters."

Jill nodded, forgetting that they couldn't actually see her. "Okay, I see it."

Pulling into the driveway, she parked behind a gorgeous blue Lexus. "Damn, no wonder George could afford to give me a two-hundred-dollar tip for his lap dance," Jill whistled. "He's loaded."

"He gave you what?" Slade growled in her ear.

Cringing, Jill ignored him and reached for the portfolio case Sloan gave her to make her look more professional. Getting out, she straightened her suit. This time, Caroline had set her up with a short black bob wig. They wanted to make sure if Alice was involved, Jill wouldn't be discovered. Her dark sunglasses also hid her mismatched eyes.

Walking up the marble sidewalk, Jill whistled again. "Nice set up." Juggling the portfolio, Jill rang the doorbell. Within seconds, the door opened. "Hey…"

George shook his head, nodding backward mouthing 'house may be wired'. "Right on time. Come on in."

"Thanks." Jill nodded back, letting him know she understood. "This shouldn't take too long. I know how busy you are."

"I have a few minutes." He laughed and she could tell he was nervous.

Walking into the kitchen, she laid the portfolio out on the table, opening it up. Fake plans were inside. "I'm going to leave these with you."

He picked them up, looking at them, then walked through the house indicating to Jill he also thought there were cameras, not just wired for sound; she was glad she had worn sunglasses. She followed him as he pointed out certain things. She nodded, agreed and played along. They actually made a pretty good team of lying their asses off.

"I think this one is perfect." He smiled handing it to her.

Jill looked at it without seeing it. "Great choice. Just initial it here." She pointed to the corner. After he was done, she slipped it in her case. "As soon as I get back to the office, I will make a copy and have it sent to you."

"That will work." George walked out of the room for a moment, making Jill a little nervous.

"Where the fuck is he going?" Slade's tense voice sounded in her ear. "Keep your guard up, Jill."

"Listen, if you have the contracts and permits, I'll take them now," Jill called out as she closed up the portfolio, but her eyes stayed on the door he disappeared through.

Finally, he came back in with a folder in his hand. "Sorry about that." He handed her a large sealed envelope. "It should all be there, contract, permits and blueprints for electricians and plumbing."

"Great." Jill opened the portfolio back up, sticking it inside, and then headed toward the door. "I will be in touch soon. Thanks for meeting me on such short notice."

"Not a problem." George opened the door for her. "I'll be looking forward to hearing from you."

Jill shook his hand, but froze when Jared's voice sounded in her ear. "Fuck!"

Looking up into George's face, she knew something bad was about to go down. "What?" she hissed.

"Limo pulling in the drive," Jared responded.

"George. Get that fucking look of horror off your face. I'm your decorator, nothing more," she whispered with a smile. "Did they block me in?"

"No," he whispered back.

Jill turned, her eyes going directly to the limo. Someone got out of the passenger side in the front. He was a big man with a military cut, his bulging muscles and a 'fuck you' attitude on his face. He scanned the area before opening the door. Jill gasped when she got a good better look at him. It was the man she drew, the man who took a shot at Jax.

"What is it, Jill?" Slade's voice was calm, immediately settling her.

Turning to look back at George, she smiled up at him. "It's the guy who took a shot at Jax. The man I drew. I know it is."

"Get out of there, now," Slade hissed, but still remained calm.

Jill turned, walking down the steps, flipping her hand up to wave goodbye to George. She made her way down the sidewalk.

"Keep going, Jill," Slade's voice whispered in her ear.

"We all have guns trained on these motherfuckers, especially the big Rambo-looking bastard. If we say run, you run your fucking ass off." Sid's voice was unnervingly calm.

The Mayor climbed out of the limo, his eyes going to Jill first, then George.

"Tom!" George smiled. "What a nice surprise, but what are you doing here?"

"We have an important dinner we're attending and want you to come." The Mayor fixed his suit. "Sorry about the short notice."

"Someone else is in the limo, but I can't ID." Damon's voice now echoed in her ear.

Jill kept walking, hoping the Mayor would ignore her, but she just wasn't that lucky.

"And please bring your beautiful friend." Tom Ferguson's grin was lewd and made her want to gag.

"Oh, no," George laughed, sounding more relaxed. "I'm sorry. That's my decorator. She just brought my final plans out for me to see."

"Mayor." She didn't know if the Mayor would recognize her voice, but she knew Alice would so Jill did her best to change it, adding a twang as she stuck her hand out. "It's nice to meet the man I voted for." Jill smiled, hoping that her fangs were well hidden.

"Well, thank you, ma'am." He winked at her, holding her hand a little longer than appropriate. "Why don't you come with us? George never has a date and I'd like to get to know you better."

"Oh, I can't do that." Jill shook her head. "My boss would

absolutely fire me if I went out with a client, but I thank you for the offer."

"Tom, will you please hurry up," an all too familiar voice yelled from the limo. "Stop flirting with that woman and come on."

Jill's head snapped toward the limo. That was a voice she would never forget. The large man moved slightly and her eyes met Alice's.

"Jill, don't do anything stupid," Sloan warned her. "Say your fucking goodbyes and leave."

Plastering a fake smile, Jill took her hand from his. "It's really was nice meeting you, but I'm late for my last appointment." She turned to look at George. "Mr. Groper, I will have these plans to you by the early part of the week if not sooner."

"Thank you." He smiled and waved.

Jill started back toward the car, but her eyes were on Alice. She was so fucking close she could take her out right now. Her hand tightened on the handle on her portfolio.

"Jill, calm your breathing," Slade ordered. "You're almost there."

As soon as she reached her car, but before she could open the door, Alice opened her fucking mouth.

"Hey, you." She leaned toward the door looking at Jill. "Girl."

"Hey, dumb bitch," the man snapped at her. "The lady is talking to you."

Cursing and growls filled Jill's ear.

Jill looked at the man before turning her attention on Alice. "I'm sorry. I was excited to meet the Mayor, never met one before." Jill tried to sound like an airhead crushing on meeting a well-known political figure.

"Jim, that was rude," Alice cooed. "Apologize to the lady."

"Sorry." He frowned at her, then looked away. Jill wanted to smack the arrogant dick with her portfolio.

"Did I hear you are a decorator?" Alice looked at her fingernails then back to Jill.

"Yes, ma'am." Jill nodded, wishing she could have just one second to redecorate the bitch's face. "Are you in need of one?"

Alice and the muscle head laughed together as if sharing a secret. "Not yet." Jill watched the evilness she had seen in Alice before appear on her face. "But I'll make sure I get your number from George."

"I appreciate the business." Jill nodded, opening her car door. "You all have a nice evening."

Jill got behind the wheel, putting her portfolio on the front seat. Her eyes slowly rose only to see Alice still staring at her. Starting the car, she glanced to see the Mayor and George walk out with George wearing a nice black suit. Putting the car in reverse, Jill backed up onto the street. Taking one last look, her eyes met George's as he got into the limo. "Please let me take the bitch out," Jill hissed, a deep rage building inside her.

"Jill, you need to put the car in drive and fucking go," Slade's voice echoed in her ear.

Jill did just that and took off, her eyes watching in the rearview mirror as the limo pulled out, going in the opposite direction. As Jill turned onto the main road, the van with Slade and Sloan pulled up behind her, Jax at the wheel.

Within twenty minutes, they were pulling into the compound. Jill parked, grabbed the portfolio and got out. Slade was there, opening her door. "You did awesome." He smiled at her.

Jill snorted. "I wanted to beat her ass."

"That's what we were afraid of," Slade chuckled, but then turned serious. "We took a photo off the camera to compare that man to see if it matches your sketch."

"I know it was him." Jill handed him the portfolio.

"Why are you giving me this?" Slade pushed it back at her. "This is your doing. You hand over the evidence."

Jill smiled, feeling excited that she was actually being treated like a true Warrior. It was a good feeling, a feeling of belonging. She may have found something she was actually good at. "Thanks."

"But please, take off that wig." He glared at it with distaste. "Where in the hell does Lana and Nicole come up with these disguises?"

Jill reached up, pulling off the wig. "I don't know, but they're pretty good at it."

They walked into Sloan's office, but he was nowhere to be found. Jax sat texting. "Where's Sloan?"

"Guess he's still outside. He got a call on his cell." Jax glanced up at Jill. "You sure that was the guy from Caroline's description?"

Jill noticed he didn't say his sister's description, so she let it pass. "Yeah, I know it was."

A hardness settled across Jax's face. "Should have taken the bastard out," he growled.

"You want to see my license?" Jill changed the subject; she knew how badly Jax wanted to kill the guy and knew why Sloan had probably stopped him from doing it.

"Of course." Jax reached out, taking it. "How did the parallel parking go?"

"Not too bad. I didn't hit the cones." Jill took her license back examining it. "Does everyone's license picture look as goofy as mine?"

Sid snatched it out of her hands when he entered the room. "Not mine."

"Now, why doesn't that surprise me?" Jill rolled her eyes. Opening the portfolio, Jill pulled out the envelope, laying it on Sloan's desk. Sid handed her license back.

"Good job today." Sid nodded, his tone serious. "That could have been a bad situation, but you handled it like a Warrior should."

Jill beamed at the compliment. "Thank you."

Sloan arrived, heading straight for his desk. He eyed the envelope, but stuck a memory card into the computer then hit a couple of buttons. The printer buzzed in the quiet room. Grabbing Jill's sketch, he laid it on his desk. He pulled the finished picture off the printer, laying them side by side.

"Son of a bitch." Jax, who had stood, slammed his hand on the desk after comparing the two pictures. "The bastard was right there!"

"And there wasn't a damn thing we could do without putting Jill in danger," Sloan added, looking at the picture and sketch. "But we got the fucker now."

"Yeah, we sure do." Jax studied the picture a little longer before sitting back down, his eyes black as night.

Sloan seized the envelope and opened it. Thumbing through the contents, a large smile spread across his face.

"You going to share?" Sid leaned in, trying to see what Sloan was looking at.

Ignoring Sid, Sloan looked up at Jill. "Looks like I owe you an apology."

"Is it good?" Jill grinned, focusing on the papers scattered across his desk.

"There is enough here to get Mayor Ferguson thrown out of office and into prison, along with Alice." His grin widened. "There's more, but I'll have to go through it better, but it looks like we just hit the jackpot."

"That's great!" Jill beamed, filled with pride at successfully helping her team.

"Sounds like we owe George the Groper a steak dinner." Sid shifted through some of the papers himself. "Damn, looks like our Mayor has some explaining to do."

"So does that mean George will become Mayor?" Jill also glanced at the papers, not really knowing what she was looking at.

"Yes, I believe there's a very good chance of that," Sloan replied, making eye contact with her. "Excellent work."

"You know, I think George has a crush on you," Sid winked at Jill. "You'd make a wonderful wife for Mayor Groper, Ms. Jillian Groper."

Slade growled, "Over my dead fucking body."

"Well, I mean, he did give her a two-hundred-dollar tip." Sid shrugged. "He either really liked the lap dance or her, hell, maybe both."

"Yeah, about that." Slade's eyes turned to Jill. "You never told me he gave you a two-hundred-dollar tip."

Jill shot Sid a nasty look. "The girls said that was a pretty good tip on your first night, but normal with regulars."

"Yeah, well, you'll never find out," Slade warned with narrowed eyes, his fist clenching.

"I guess if this Warrior stuff doesn't work out, I can always fall back on stripping," Jill mused, shrugging. "That is pretty good money."

"I think the doc has had enough, Jill." Sid nodded toward him. "If that tick gets any more pronounced, he's going to break his damn jaw."

Jill smiled, heading to Slade. Pulling him down toward her, she whispered in his ear, "I'd give you a lap dance anytime you want. You wouldn't even have to tip me."

Slade's eyes snapped to hers, then to Sloan. "We finished here?"

Sloan, who was focused on the papers Jill obtained from George, waved them off. Taking Jill's hand, Slade pulled her out of the office, leaving the laughter and whistles of the men in their wake. When she wasn't moving fast enough, he picked her up and carried her up the steps.

"The only lap you will ever dance on is mine," He hissed into her ear sending delicious shivers throughout her body.

Oh, she was going to enjoy this.

Chapter 22

The day finally arrived. She could become a Warrior. *No.* She was determined to think positively. She *would* become a Warrior, yet glancing around, she had a small tinge of doubt. She had never seen so many Warriors in one place and they definitely outnumbered the trainees. Her eyes met Slade's briefly. He just gave her a nod of encouragement before scanning the crowd.

She had been doing the work of a Warrior; they all had, but after the initiation, she could earn the title. It was a surreal moment as she stood side-by-side with Adam, Steve and Dillon. Everyone was dressed in black combat clothes; the only difference was, Warrior trainees such as herself, had a vest with a large red X. Talk about standing out. Not all trainees were half-breeds. Actually, she'd only seen two others. Everyone had paintball guns, which she felt great relief about, because until that point, she wasn't sure what would be used.

An older man walked into the crowd, holding his hand up for silence. "In five minutes, the toughest test you will ever take will begin. You have one main objective: stay alive. The course is five-miles long. It may not seem like much to you, but throughout the course, you will have not only obstacles, you will also have highly trained Warriors hunting you. You are all teams of four. Once your whole team reaches the end, you have completed the course." He regarded the trainees before continuing. "On the field, you have the hunters who are identified with a blue X on their vests, while the observers wear the white X. Each team will have one observer. If an observer says you are out, leave the field immediately with hands raised. Anyone with a black baseball cap is a medic."

"The rules are: there are no rules." Once more, the older man looked around. "Each team has been given a confidential word. If you are captured, it is the job of the hunters to get that word from you. If they succeed, your whole team fails. Everyone knows the kill shots. Once you are hit with a kill shot, you leave the field. Each team has a different colored paintball and will be awarded twenty points for kill shots. If you end up shooting each other, it does not count."

A murmur went through the crowd. Jill looked at each of their Warriors. Slade, Jax and Duncan all wore a vest with a white X, indicating them as observers. Slade, of course, was the only one who wore a black baseball cap worn backward, indicating his role of medic, and he looked really hot. Who knew he'd look sexy as hell in a baseball cap. Jill jerked her attention back, trying to focus as she looked at Jared, Sid and Damon who wore a blue X. The other thing she noticed was she was the only female, and that was gaining her a lot of attention.

"Initiates, you have a ten-minute lead. You each have a map to get you to the end safety zone. There are two off-road vehicles placed in different locations. I suggest you look very hard for these bonuses because they are the only ones you will get. I know you have been over everything repeatedly in preparation for today. We do our best to make sure everyone makes it out of initiation in one piece, but death is possible as it is with anything. Be careful out there and good luck." The man's eyes scanned again, this time landing on Jill. "You're going to need it."

Jill glanced at Steve who was looking at her. "Burger flipper is looking more and more like a better career choice."

Sloan walked up to them. "You guys are ready for this. You're as good if not better than any of the others. Work as a team and get your fucking asses to that safety zone."

"Thanks for the pep talk, sir." Steve frowned, glancing around.

Jared, Sid, Damon, Duncan, Jax and Slade all wished them luck. Slade stopped in front of Jill, a hint of worry in his eyes. "Stay safe, no matter what."

"That's the plan." She gave him a wobbly grin.

He looked like he wanted to say more, but turned and walked

247

away. Jill followed Adam as they made their way past the Warriors to the front. Stopping, they waited for the go ahead. Jill stared straight ahead. There was a clearing before them that ended where the thick woods began. Her stomach twisted painfully. On the other side of those woods, lay what she had worked so hard for, what they all worked so hard for.

"I got a plan." Adam glanced behind them, then either side.

"Thank fuck, because for a minute, I thought we were going to wing it." Steve sounded relieved and just plain nervous.

Adam left their group and spoke to each group of trainees. He came back with a smile. "Once we hit the woods, find a good vantage point."

"Vantage point for what?" Steve's nerves were showing in his high-pitched voice.

"Dammit, Steve, be quiet," Adam frowned, then grinned at them. "To take hunters out. Go high if you can."

"Shouldn't we just run straight for the safety zone?" Steve looked at the other trainees who were nodding and looking at Adam. "Shit. Guess not. Fucking crazy if you ask me. I say run like your ass is on fire, but no, not us. We do stupid, climbing trees and shit to shoot highly trained fucking Warriors."

"Shut up, dammit," Adam hissed. "This will work."

Jill nodded. Glancing over her shoulder, she found Slade who stood alone, but watched her. A loud horn sounded. Giving him a small smile, she turned and followed the rest of the trainees into the clearing.

As soon as they went into the woods, everyone dove for hiding spots, scrambling to find a clear shot. Jill scrutinized her surroundings. Staying close to her group, she climbed up a tree. Getting in position, she raised her gun and waited. This was either brilliant or suicide. To make sure she knew where her team was when the shit hit the fan, she scanned the area. Steve was just below her using another tree as a shield and looked like he was praying. Adam was on the other side of her, also in a tree but lower than her, his gun raised. Dillon was further up, kneeling in some brush with a clear view to the field.

Another horn sounded and Jill had a sudden case of fear. She wanted to drop out of the trees and run as if her ass was on fire, just like Steve suggested, but she held strong. Glancing at Adam, who held his hand up, she waited. Looking back at the field, she watched the Warriors arrogantly walk straight into a trap.

"Now!" Adam shouted and the popping sounds of paintball guns echoed throughout the woods. Jill hit three with kill shots. Curses and shouts filled the air as the Warriors realized what was happening.

"Get the fuck out of here!" Adam yelled.

Jill jumped out of her hiding spot. Adam grabbed her as they followed Dillon who had studied the map and was their lead man. Tree branches smacked her face as she raced through the woods. Excitement mixed with fear kept them going. Jill had just turned around to look behind them when her feet hit nothing but air. It was like she was back at the paintball center. What the hell! As her body rolled, hitting small trees and rocks, she realized they had run right off a mountain. After what seemed like forever, the fall came to an abrupt halt. Trying to catch her breath and figure out if anything was broken, she sat up slowly. Okay, that was much more of a fall than at the paintball club. She understood what was meant by dying during the initiation.

Adam crawled toward her. "You okay?" He looked her over.

"Yeah." She looked over at Steve and Dillon, who were also checking over each other.

"So I take it that mountain wasn't on the map," Steve whispered, limping over to grab his gun.

"Dammit." Dillon looked around frantically.

"What?" Adam hoisted himself up, limping toward Dillon.

"I lost the map," he hissed looking around.

They all looked at the top of the mountain. "So how important is the map?" Steve frowned, then raised his hands when they glared at him. "Okay, I get it. It's important."

"We have to find it." Adam frowned. "Spread out, but stay alert."

Jill retraced their tumble down the mountain. Climbing up, she was shocked by how far they had fallen. This was not a good start. Hearing brush rustle, Jill dropped, lying flat. Looking up, she saw two hunters right above her.

"Is that a map?" one of them said.

Shit, this cannot be happening. Jill glanced around, trying to figure out what to do.

"Sure the hell is," the other one laughed. "Poor bastards are going to be running circles out here trying to find their safe zone."

Glancing down the hill, her eyes met Adam's. He shook his head at her, but she knew what had to be done. They needed that map. One thing going for her was they had their backs turned toward her. Slowly and as quietly as she could, she made it to her feet. Aiming her gun, she put her finger on the trigger and pulled. Purple paint exploded on the back of one of their heads.

"Motherfucker!" He grabbed his head, swinging around as did the other one, his gun raised.

"I'm going to need that map," Jill said, praying Adam or somebody had a drop on the guy.

"Looks like we got us a standoff, pretty girl," he smiled, cocking his eyebrow.

The pop of a gun went off. "Son of a bitch." The hunter turned, showing yellow on the back of his head.

Jill carefully headed up the hill to snatch the map out of his hands. "Thank you."

Adam, Steve and Dillon slowly ventured up, guns poised. Jill looked past the hunters to see another team raise their guns to them. Adam waved his thanks.

"Come on." He grabbed the map from Jill, giving it to Dillon. "Don't lose it again."

They ran next to the other trainees who had helped them out, figuring they were stronger in numbers. Popping sounds echoed throughout the woods, making it sound like a war zone.

"We're close," Dillon whispered, scanning the area. "I think…"

A loud rustling sound surrounded them. Jill raised her gun, not knowing what was going on. Glancing over at the trainees they were running with, she watched in horror as they were swooped up in a large net. One of them looked toward them and shouted, "Run!"

Jill did just that, but started too slowly.

"Jill, come on, dammit." Steve was waving his arm at her to come on.

"We have to help them," Jill hissed, spinning around. "You guys go on if you have to, but I'm helping them. They helped us."

"Fuck, is this a girl thing or something?" Steve cursed.

"She's right." Adam came up beside Jill.

The sound of others running toward them had them scattering to find a hiding spot. Adam fell down flat next to Jill. They watched as three hunters walked up to the captured trainees.

"This works every damn time," one of them laughed.

They watched as the hunters dropped the net, releasing the trainees.

Jill frowned as an idea hit. She had no clue if it would work, but it was the only thing she could think of. "You got a plan?" she asked Adam who lay beside her, just to make sure he didn't have a better plan than hers.

"Nope," he whispered back.

"I do, but if it fails…" Jill looked over at Steve, "run your asses off like it's on fire."

"Oh, you don't have to worry about that," Steve whispered back with a snort.

As the hunters were trying to get their confidential word from the trainees, Jill eased herself up. All three hunters held their guns loosely. Jill raised both hands, concentrating like she had never concentrated before. One hunter actually looked down at his gun for a second before dismissing its movement.

"What the fuck are you doing?" Dillon hissed.

"The question is, do you know if what you're doing will work?" Steve cringed, ready to make a run for it.

"I have no clue." Jill pushed her hands forward, and then pulled them back hard. The guns were pulled out of the hunters' hands. Jill threw her arms toward the trainees. The guns flew through the air landing near them.

The hunters and the trainees all stared in shock for a split second until all hell broke loose. Adam stood, taking the first shot, hitting one hunter on the side of the head. Dillon hit another one. Jill's gun jammed as she aimed at the third. Steve took a shot, but missed. The remaining hunter snatched a gun from one of the trainees aiming it at Jill. Knowing her dreams were about to end, Jill frantically worked her jammed gun. The hunter took a shot, and for a split second, Jill prayed she could dodge it, but she never got a chance.

Steve jumped in front of Jill, taking the hit, knocking her over. Dillon and Adam blasted the hunter with continuous shots until they got the kill shot.

"Son of a bitch, that hurts." Steve rolled off Jill.

"Dammit, Steve, what are you doing?" Jill scrambled up, grabbing him, praying he wasn't hit by a kill shot.

Steve looked down at his chest. Jill's eyes saw the unmistakable red splattered over his heart. Their eyes met.

"No!" Jill looked back down, hoping it was just a trick of her eyes, but it wasn't. "Why? Why did you do that, Steve? Dammit." She even tried to rub it off.

"Because you deserve it more than me." Steve fake punched her in the chin with a smile. "Plus, I had to pee, so it's all good. I can repeat next time. I'm not going anywhere."

"I do not deserve it more than you!" Jill sat back, looking at him in shock.

"Fuck." Adam stared at Steve's chest.

"Go on and get your asses to the safety zone." Steve rose, raising his hands. "I really do need to pee."

Jill hugged him hard. "Thank you."

"Don't thank me," Steve grinned. "I've got some things in mind. Paying me back for my hero sacrifice, will be worth it."

"Come on, Jill." Adam grabbed her arm, pulling her away.

"Go kick some ass." Steve spun around, strolling toward the hunters who were walking off the field. "Okay, which one of you shot me? Hell of a shot, but it hurt like hell."

Jill glanced back hearing Steve. She grinned when one of the hunters patted Steve on the shoulder, walking off the field with him. Steve could find a friend anywhere.

Travelling about a mile and a half since leaving Steve, Jill heard what sounded like gunshots, not the pop of a paintball. Stopping, they searched around them, then at each other. "That wasn't paintball guns." Jill stared in the direction of the sound. Suddenly, the horn blew long and loud.

Hunters sprang into action, running out of hiding places taking their vests off. Jill, Adam and Dillon took off following them, knowing that something bad was going on. Five hunters ran up beside them.

"Follow us and keep aware," one instructed as the hunters surrounded them, real guns drawn.

"What the hell is going on?" Adam asked, but as they made their way into another clearing, there was no need for an answer.

Warriors and trainees lay scattered through the field. Warriors surrounded them with guns drawn toward the woods. It looked like a war zone. Cars and motorcycles were flying into the parking area a few yards away. Other Warriors and trainees were making their way toward the wooded area in full-combat mode.

Jill's eyes searched for Slade. Dropping her paintball gun, she rushed through the field. Warriors lay dead, silver slowly killing them, but not one cried out. In their final moments, they lay dying, with another Warrior at their side, giving what comfort they could.

Frantic as the field became more crowded, relief swept through her when she spotted him. He was close to the parking area working on someone. Jill pushed her way through the mass of Warriors, losing sight of him for a second. She knew Adam and Dillon were behind her. Her eyes glanced at the small stone building Slade was next to, using it as a pinpoint to relocate him if she needed to. It took a second for the sign above the door to register.

"No!" Jill pushed her way through, knocking Warriors out of her way as she headed toward the restroom. Slade was bent over Steve, blood was everywhere. "No!" she screamed, trying to get to him, but Duncan grabbed her.

Jill fought with everything she had. Slade glanced toward her quickly; the look on his face told her everything she needed to know.

******

Slade had already made his way to the safety zone. Searching through the trainees already arrived, he looked for Jill. Sloan stood with arms crossed, leaning against a tree.

"No sign of them?" Slade asked, heading toward him.

"Steve is the only one." Sloan nodded toward the crude block building. "He's taking a piss."

"Damn." Slade frowned, hating one of theirs failed the initiation. He continued searching the clearing, hoping to spot Jill soon. Just as he opened his mouth to speak, the sudden sound of gunshots rang out.

Immediately, all Warriors took cover, their training kicking in. Some knocked confused trainees out of the line of fire. As if in slow motion, Slade watched Steve walk out of the building. Turning, Steve looked at Sloan and Slade lying on the ground. His mouth opened to say something as his body jerked hard; he fell to his knees. His shocked eyes found Slade before he fell face first to the ground.

"Fuck!" Slade army-crawled toward Steve. Grabbing Steve by the back of his jacket, he pulled him beside the building, rolling him over. Steve's eyes were opened slightly. "Steve, hold on buddy." Slade ripped his jacket and shirt completely off, seeing the exit wound right above his heart. Rolling him over, he checked the wound on his back.

Jared slid to a stop next to Slade. Seeing Steve, he cursed. "Shit! Is he dead?" Jared looked around, his eyes scanning for danger.

"Not yet, but if I don't get him to a hospital, he will be." Slade pressed his fingers to his neck feeling a pulse, weak, but there. "I can't tell if this hit his heart, but all this blood isn't a good fucking sign."

Suddenly, the gunshots stopped. "Let me get a car." Jared stood, still hunched over. "Keep your fucking head down, Doc. Those are silver bullets."

"Give me your shirt," Slade ordered before Jared left. Tearing Steve's ripped shirt, he pressed his own to the back wound, Steve's to the front, and Jared's he wrapped around Steve's body to hold them in place. Steve's blood pumped out faster than he could control it. The shirt was soaked already. "Dammit!" Slade pressed harder, applying more pressure.

Hearing her voice, Slade looked to see Duncan stop Jill. Her eyes went from him to Steve. The anguish in her face was more than he could take, forcing him to look away. Thank God, she was unhurt. His need to find her almost overrode his job, which was to save as many lives as possible, but since he knew she was safe, he could focus. He had been afraid to look over the field of fallen Warriors for fear of seeing her among them.

Sloan ran over, a look of worry on his face. "I got the van." Sloan helped Slade pick up Steve, and Jared ran over to help.

Slade looked up at Jared. "Keep her safe."

Jared nodded. "You just worry about Steve. I got her."

Once Steve was loaded in the van, Sloan slammed the door and ran to the driver's side. "You're in charge of our group. Keep me updated."

"I will." Jared smacked the van as it drove by.

Steve moaned when the van went over bumps, Slade tried to keep him still. "Hang in there."

"Wasn't ready to go yet." Steve's voice was weak and faint.

"You aren't going anywhere but to the hospital." Slade checked Steve's pulse again, not liking his coloring. "You just fight, you hear me?"

Hissing at the pain, Steve jerked. "Damn, it hurts."

"As soon as we get somewhere safe, I'll give you something for the pain," Slade replied. After a few minutes of silence, Slade figured Steve had passed out since he still had a faint pulse. They hadn't lost him yet. He was startled when Steve grabbed his wrist.

"Please don't let me die as the guy who got shot coming out of the pisser." Steve laughed weakly, then coughed.

"No worries, Steve. Just hold on and you can tell this story however you want." Slade's voice was firm.

A sad smile tilted his lips before he swallowed hard. His eyes met Slade's. "Take care of Jill and Adam. They're my family, you all are."

Slade nodded, watching as the life slipped away from Steve. "Goddammit!"

The van stopped. Slade met Sloan's eyes in the rearview mirror, a silent message passing between the two Warriors.

Chapter 23

Jill, along with Adam and Dillon, sat in shocked devastation. Jared walked over, sitting next to them.

"Slade is going to do everything he can for him. He's a damn good doctor. You know this." He wrapped his arm around Jill, giving her a squeeze. "As soon as we are given the all clear here, we'll head to the hospital."

Nodding, Jill watched numbly. The events and scene around her appeared dreamlike and hazy. She caught her thoughts and grimaced. *No, a nightmare, a horrifying nightmare.* Duncan headed toward them, his face a mask of anger. "They caught two and are bringing them down now."

Jill, along with Adam and Dillon followed Duncan to where five Warriors dragged two bloodied men to the group, tossing them to the ground. Two of the Warriors pulled them up to their knees.

"We told you everything we know," one cried, his frightened eyes scanning all the Warriors surrounding them.

The Warrior closest to him knocked him in the back of the head with his foot. "Shut the fuck up."

"They were hired by a man who works for Mayor Ferguson," one of the Warriors spoke, directing his response to the older Council member who had been in charge of the initiation. "There were ten all together and the others are being hunted as we speak. They were told they would get a thousand dollars each and a bonus if they got her alive."

Every eye went to Jill. Anger so raw and deep hit every nerve in Jill's body. She walked up to the two men, jerking her arm away when Adam tried to stop her. Duncan, Jared, Sid, Damon and Jax stepped up, surrounding her. "What did you just say?" Her voice was low with anger.

"She's talking to you." The same Warrior nudged the man again with his boot. "I'd advise you to answer."

"The guy who hired us doesn't work for the Mayor, but the Mayor's fiancée," the other guy answered, blood dripping from his nose.

"And how do you know this?" Sid asked, taking a step forward, watching the guy closely.

"Dude, you're going to get us killed," the first guy cried out. "Just shut up. They can't kill us. They're VC Warriors. They have to follow the laws."

Damon grabbed the man who spoke, lifting him up off his feet. "Look around this field, motherfucker." Damon shook him. "How many dead Warriors can you count?"

Tension and anger was so thick you could taste it among the Warriors who stared with hatred at the men who had taken down their brothers.

The man's eyes did scan the area before Damon's face was back in his. "There is no law for us to follow now." Damon gave him another hard shake. "So one of you better start talking. If not, you will be the first to die by my hand."

Jill watched from her position in front of the man still on his knees. She had never seen Damon so angry; it was truly a scary sight. She looked back to the other man. Adam moved up close to her. Reaching out, he wrapped his hand around the man's throat. "Start talking, motherfucker, or I will snap your neck with a smile."

"I was asked if I wanted to make some money and told to meet at a house downtown. There were fifteen of us in total. Once we found out what the job was, a few tried to leave, but were stopped." He swallowed, trying to move his neck away from Adam's hand, but Adam gripped harder.

260

"Is he telling the truth?" Sid glanced down at Adam.

"So far." Adam loosened his grip. "Keep talking."

"We were told we would each get a thousand for every Warrior killed." His eyes looked at Jill. "That's when the Mayor's fiancée pulled out a picture of you. She said there was a bonus if we got you alive."

Jill's mind worked frantically. Frustration wasn't close to how she felt, knowing Alice had been in her sights just the day before. Taking a step back, she looked at Adam. "Is that true?" Adam nodded, looking away. "I swear, if my friend dies, I will kill you myself." Jill tried to keep the tears out of her voice.

"If we didn't listen and do what she said, we were going to die anyway. The bitch is determined to see the VC Council go down and has the backing and information on you guys to do it, from what I can tell." The man frowned. "I just wanted to get paid, man. That's all. I don't have anything against you guys."

Jill walked backward through the crowd of Warriors as the two men continued to get drilled. Shouts sounded from the right as more Warriors came forward with more men. As soon as Jill was at the back, she turned and ran toward the parking lot. Looking around frantically, she found a car and prayed she could get it started. She spotted Jax heading toward her from the other side of the parking lot.

"Hey?" He walked up to her. "What are you doing?"

"Trying to find a car I can steal so I can go kill a bitch," Jill sneered, trying different doors, but they were all locked. "Doesn't anyone trust anyone anymore? Fuck!"

"I may be of some help." He jiggled keys in front of her face. When Jill tried to grab them, he pulled them away.

"I'll take you," Jax smiled, heading toward a black BMW. "Here, you drive."

Jill climbed in, frowning. "Where'd you get this car?" She looked at him and wondered about the look on his face, but dismissed it. They had all just gone through hell. "And you are seriously going to let me drive a BMW when you wouldn't let me drive your GT."

"This isn't my favorite car," Jax replied, looking around nervously.

"What's wrong with you?" Jill put the car in reverse, backing out, but eyeing Jax.

"Just a little shaken up, I guess," he replied, giving her a sad look. "I just can't believe what happened. Can you?"

Jill pulled out on the road. "No, I can't," she said slowly, knowing something wasn't right with him, but then again, she felt pretty shaken up too. Her thoughts went to Steve. "Can you call Sloan and see how Steve's doing?"

"How about you shut the fuck up and drive," Jax pulled a gun out, pointing it at her temple.

******

It was a somber sight as the dead Warriors were carefully carried off the field. Sid walked toward Adam and the rest, his face grim. "We got a total of six." He frowned, looking out over the field. "Has anyone heard from Sloan or Slade?"

"Yeah," Jared nodded, then cleared his throat. "He said he wanted us all at the compound as soon as we were finished."

"Fuck, does that mean…?" Adam cursed, his mouth turning into a thin line, his chin trembling. "Fuck!"

"We don't know what that means until we get to the compound." Sid grabbed the back of Adam's neck in a comforting hold. "Don't go thinking shit yet until we hear official news."

Adam nodded without saying a word for a second, visibly pulling himself together. "He took a paintball for Jill right before this happened. Jumped right in front of her because he felt she deserved it more than him. She was so upset, but of course, being Steve…" Adam choked out, "he made us all laugh saying he had to piss anyway."

"Come on. Let's get out of here." Sid put his arm around Adam, and then glanced around. "Where's Jill?"

Dillon walked up at that point. "I just came back from a search and saw her take off with Jax a few minutes ago."

"How in the fuck is that possible?" Sid frowned, turning to look at Jax who stood right behind him. "When he's here?"

Jax stepped forward, grabbing Dillon. "Why would you say something like that?"

Dillon's eyes popped open wide. "How did you do that?" Dillon actually looked spooked, pushing Jax away, and then looked at Sid. "I swear, I *just* saw him leave with Jill."

"By the look on your face, you seem to know what the hell is going on." Sid's voice was low and dangerous. "So I suggest you tell us what the fuck is going on and where Jill is."

"It's my brother." Jax had a look of panic and rage on his face.

"Are you guys twins?" Dillon asked, still looking spooked.

Jax ignored them. Pulling out his phone, he dialed and put it to his ear. "No, we're not. Dammit!" He turned to Sid. "Get Lana on the phone. I need to talk to Caroline. Tell them to meet us at the compound."

"Why?" Sid started dialing.

Looking at Damon, Jax headed toward the compound. "Get as

many Warriors as you can to meet us at the compound."

"Will you tell us what the fuck is going on?" Jared ran toward the parking lot to keep up with Jax.

"That was you getting in the car with her, so if you are not twins, then what the fuck are you?" Dillon glared at Jax. "I know what I saw with my own fucking eyes."

Jax stopped, turning to look at each of them. "Shifter." He spun back around. "And we need to find them now."

******

Slade was just heading out the door, his phone in his hand, trying to get ahold of Jill, yet she wasn't answering her fucking phone. "Shit!"

Caroline and Lana came running in the door. "Where are they?"

"Who?" Slade asked confused.

"Sid called me and told me to get Caroline and meet them here." Lana looked worried. "What happened today?"

Before Slade could answer, Jax raced inside followed by a flood of Warriors. Slade's eyes searched for Jill, not seeing her anywhere. "Where's Jill ?" Slade grabbed Adam.

"She left." Adam looked like he'd been through hell and back.

"What the hell do you mean 'she left'?" Slade shook him.

"I saw her leave with Jax." Dillon, who still looked spooked, glanced at Jax, then Slade.

Slade walked up, grabbing Jax's shoulder. "Where's Jill?"

"That's what I'm trying to find out." Jax shrugged out of Slade's hold.

"Is Alisha here?" Jax looked down at Caroline.

"What the fuck do you mean you're 'trying to find out'?" Slade growled, panic and a rare fear trickled through his system. "Dillon said she left with you, so where is she?"

"Will you give me a fucking minute?" Jax yelled, his face twisted in anger.

Slade went for Jax, but Damon and Duncan held him back. "Hold on, bro." Jared stepped in front of Slade, putting his hand on his chest. "Something funky is going on."

"Somebody better tell me where the fuck she is now before I tear this place apart," Slade roared, making Caroline jump.

Jax cursed, turning on Slade. "She's in grave danger, so shut the fuck up so I can find out what the hell is going on."

"Have you ever heard of a vampire shifter before?" Sid glanced over at Slade.

"There isn't any such thing!" Slade growled, ready to kill something or someone.

"That's what I thought." Sid turned as they all watched Jax closely.

Jax turned back to Caroline. "I need Alisha, Caroline."

Caroline frowned. "She's really upset."

"Why? Why is she upset?" Jax urged, his fist flexing. "Is it our brother?"

"Yes." Caroline grabbed her chest right before she went limp. Jax caught her.

"Caroline!" Lana bent down brushing the hair from her eyes.

Slade shrugged out of Damon and Duncan's hold. "Let me go so I can help her." They did, but before Slade could reach her, Caroline pulled herself up.

"I'm fine." Caroline put a hand to her head and looked at Lana. "Did you see that?"

"Yes, I did." Lana looked at Jax. "What are you?"

That's all Slade heard before he grabbed Jax by the throat. "What did you do to Jill?"

"Stop it," Lana screamed, grabbing Slade. "He didn't do anything."

Warriors pulled Slade off Jax, holding them away from each other. "Does she know where he took her?" Jax yelled over the chaos.

"She's at the Halfway House. Your brother, who looks just like you, took her to the Halfway House." Caroline's shocked eyes burned into Jax's before turning to Slade. "She says you need to hurry."

Chapter 24

Jill drove right through the gates of the Halfway House as if they were guests, Jax's gun still pointed at her head. Something definitely wasn't right with Jax. His hand shook uncontrollably to the point he had to use his other hand to steady it.

"If you're shaking from fear, you're a smart man," Jill hissed at him as she parked where he instructed. "Slade is going to kill you."

"If he can find me," he laughed, jamming the gun harder in her temple. "Now, you are going to get out of the car like a good girl. If you make one wrong move, I am going to kill you and say 'fuck the bonus'."

"You're doing this for a bonus?" Jill looked at him in shocked rage. "Money made you a traitor? You're pathetic. I hope you burn in hell, traitor."

He smacked her in the side of the head. "Just get the fuck out of the car and remember what I said. Even if I somehow miss, we have sharpshooters up on the roof who will take you out."

Getting out of the car, Jill searched her surroundings. She actually didn't want to run, as stupid as that sounded. She had planned on heading to the Halfway House first to find that bitch Alice. Jax grabbed her arm, leading her toward the side entrance. Pulling out his phone, he hit a number. "Yeah, open the door. I'm at the side entrance."

"Not important enough to have a key?" Jill smirked at him. In horror, she tried to jerk away when his face completely changed in front of her eyes. "What the hell is wrong with your face?"

The door opened and he pushed her inside. "Just get in there."

Jill continued trying to look at him, but he wouldn't allow it. She knew his face had…she didn't even know how to explain it. Maybe she was losing it? Maybe the initiation, hell …?" Hell, the

267

past week had just been too much.

He led her past rooms with steel doors that had small openings for what looked like trays. "Stop casing the place." He pushed her faster, the gun still out. "The only way you'll be coming back out is in a body bag."

"Oh, is that so?" Jill egged him on. "You're nothing but a pussy traitor. Having to use a gun on a half-breed girl. Afraid to go one-on-one, Jax? Afraid real Warriors showed me how to kick your ass."

"After I get my bonus, then me and you can have a go around and see who has the biggest dick." He led her to a large two-door room with a camera positioned above it. Before they reached the door, it opened. Jax pushed her into the room causing her to fall to her knees and slide across the floor. Even before she stopped, Jill jumped to her feet, ready.

The first thing she saw was George, sitting in a chair, with the large man from the limo standing behind him.

"Welcome to my party, *breed*."

The most hated voice filled the room making Jill sneer. Slowly, Jill turned her head, seeing Alice through a rage that formed over her eyes. Alice sat comfortably on a plush sofa. "Thank you. I appreciate the invite," Jill said slowly. "Saves me the time of hunting you down."

"Oh, is that right?" Alice laughed, standing; she walked toward her spreading her arms wide. "Well, here I am."

"Yeah, there you are, bitch," Jill hissed, her eyes shooting to George.

"Oh, I'm sorry. Where are my manners?" Alice walked toward George. "This is George. Dear George, who wants my sweet Tom thrown out of office so he can take over. Seems he's a traitor and was giving information to people he shouldn't have." She patted his cheek, clicking her tongue at him.

"You are crazy!" George glared at her. "Tom should never have gotten involved with you, whore."

Alice lifted her hand and Jill knew one blow would be the end of George.

"You still need a decorator, bitch?" Jill laughed loudly, thankful her question stopped Alice's hand from hitting George.

"What did you just say?" Alice turned, her face a mask of rage.

"You heard me. And I do believe you need one for that ugly-ass face of yours. Come closer and I'll decorate that old, wrinkled up mess for you," Jill taunted.

Alice pointed at her, not yet taking the bait. "That was you?"

"Oh, yeah, and we have enough information to…" Jill paused when Alice rushed toward her. They were nose-to-nose. "…take you down." Jill tilted her head as she finished her sentence, a smile playing on her lips.

"I don't believe you." Alice glared, stepping back. She indicated behind her at George. "He doesn't have the balls to do something like that."

"But I do and I can pretty much talk anyone into anything." Jill was practically begging for her to take a swing. "So even if you kill us both, you're still going down. Everything has been given to the Council and very soon, you will be hunted by every Warrior, but not just because of that. The men you hired to kill Warriors talked…a lot."

Alice looked over at the man standing behind George, giving him a glare that proved right there, she was behind it all.

Jill saw a hint of fear in Alice's eyes, just a hint, but it was there and that was all Jill needed. "Your name was mentioned quite a few times and hundreds of Warriors heard it all." Jill smiled, hatred flickering across her features. "You know what happens to people who kill Warriors, especially vampires?"

"Shut up," Alice hissed, baring her fangs at Jill, who stood strong without flinching. "I'm going to enjoy killing you."

"And I'm going to enjoy having you try, you nasty whore," Jill hissed back.

"Before this catfight starts, can I please have my bonus and I'll be on my way, dear Alice," Jax interrupted, looking bored.

"You better take the bonus and run far, you bastard," Jill spat at him.

"You know, I'm getting sick of your mouth." Jax was in her face in a split second. "How about a scare? Hmmm? Maybe that will get you to shut the fuck up."

Jill prepared herself for what was to come, steadying her breathing and body, waiting for the blow she was sure was coming. But as she watched Jax change into another person right in front of her eyes, she stumbled back. What the hell? A man stood before her. He was the same size as Jax, and actually looked similar to Jax, with American Indian heritage, but there was evilness behind his eyes, a hatred directed not just at her, but everything. "Who are you?" Jill asked, staring at him, trying to believe what she just saw. "*What* are you?"

"Well, for starters, I'm not my asshole brother, Jax." He glared at her and smiled without humor. "At least, not right now." The man laughed as he went to touch George, turning into George's twin, and as if showing off, he grabbed the man behind George, changing into him.

"This, you idiot, is a shifter." Alice laughed at Jill's expression.

"He actually came to me with a fabulous idea. After he kills my fiancé, the Mayor, he will pose as him, so it'd be best you die now because your world is about to get rocked."

Jill tried to hide her shock at the man before her being Jax's brother, but she did notice something, and maybe she was wrong. "Okay, well, maybe I'm wrong here, shifter guy, but it looks to me like you need to make contact with the person before turning. How's that going to work when the dead Mayor gets…juicy?" Jill cocked her eyebrow at him and smiled when she read his expression. From the glare he was shooting her, it appeared she was right.

"I'm bored with this conversation," Alice sneered.

"That's probably because you're too stupid to understand the conversation." Jill smirked at her.

"And I really hate her. You want to tag team?" Alice glanced at Jax's brother, holding out her arm.

"Sounds like a great idea." He grabbed her arm and within seconds, he was transformed into a Alice lookalike.

"You have got to be shitting me?" Jill looked between the two, knowing she had to get it together and think about this crazy shit later. She had a feeling she was about to get her ass kicked by not one, but two Alice's. Yeah, that shit just wouldn't do. Tilting her head from side to side, she rolled her shoulders, and then waved them both toward her in a cocky fashion. "Which whore wants their ass kicked first?"

******

Slade stood back with the fifty or so Warriors, his eyes fixed on the building Jill was in. He scanned the place, looking for what dangers he would be facing. As the Warriors behind him made plans, he knew time was running out. His rage out of control, Slade began to walk, then his walk turned into a jog, his focus on getting to Jill.

"Guess he didn't like our plan." Jared ran up beside Slade, yelling behind him, "Take out anyone who tries to stop us. We'll explain shit later to whoever we need to explain shit to."

Picking up his speed, Slade saw an officer raise his gun. His mouth moved with warning, but Slade didn't hear him. He lifted his hand, picking the officer up and throwing him against the iron fence without physically touching him; his gift was strong with his rage. With one leap, Slade sailed over the fence, landing on his feet. Warriors followed his lead, landing all around him. Shots rang out, but Slade continued through the chaos, using his power to toss people out of his way. A young guard stood in front of the door, holding his gun with shaking hands.

"Stop." The man's voice shook. "Please, I don't want to shoot you."

Slade lifted his arm. As the man rose off his feet, Slade pushed forward hard, using the man to crash open the doors. Making his way further into the building, Slade grabbed another guard who was cowering against the wall. He wore a gun, but didn't pull it. "Where is she?"

"I don't know who you're talking about." When Slade picked him up off his feet, the man cried out.

"The Mayor's bitch. Where is she?" Slade growled, his eyes black.

"I can show you." A young girl with mismatched eyes came forward, her red hair flowing behind her. She wore what appeared to be an issued jumpsuit that he noticed other patients wearing.

Slade dropped the man and stared at the girl for a long second. "Who are you?"

"Hurry," she said, ignoring his question as she took off down the hallway, looking behind her to make sure Slade was following. "I think they are going to hurt that pretty girl."

Growling, Slade took the girl's arm. Speeding her along, the girl's feet left the ground.

"It's that door down there," she pointed. Putting her hand on his arm, she whispered, "Be careful. They are bad people."

Slade set her on her feet as he made his way toward the door. Seeing the camera, he pulled his gun and shot it, and kicked open the doors. The first thing he saw was a man standing behind George, pulling his gun. Slade barely gave him notice as he lifted his gun and shot him between the eyes. He continued his search and found her.

"Stop or I will put a fucking bullet in your head!" Slade ordered as he held his gun out, walking toward Jill. His eyes scanned her quickly before he finally noticed Alice and another...Alice. "What the fuck?"

Warriors filled the room, guns drawn. Jax was among them, his eyes going from one Alice to the other. "Long time no see, brother," Jax growled, hatred in his voice.

The Alice on Jill's right faded into a similar image of Jax in front of their eyes. Guns clicked as cries of 'holy shit' and 'fuck' filled the room. "Nice to see you too, Jax."

"Why don't you lie on the floor nice and quiet like, so you don't get shot up with silver and we have us a conversation?" Jax ordered, his eyes never leaving his brother.

"Thank God, you all got here when you did," Alice cried. "That man has been terrorizing me, forcing me to do things–"

Jill punched Alice in the face, knocking her on her ass. "Shut the hell up."

Jax's brother took that opportunity to grab Jill, holding the gun to her head. "I'm sorry, Jax. Would love to chat. Maybe some other time."

"Let her go!" Slade took a step forward, but stopped when Jax's brother clicked the trigger back.

"Careful there, big guy. Don't want to make me jumpy."

"Mika, don't do anything stupid." Jax edged sideways, his gun aimed at his brother.

"What would father think if he could see us now?" Mika gave a sad laugh. "No, brother, I think I need to take my leave now, but I'm sure I will see you soon." He had managed to back up toward a window.

Slade watched, trying to anticipate the bastard's next move. Suddenly, Jill was pushed forward as Mika used her to leverage himself through the window. Jill fell on her hands and knees, rolling out of the way as Jax ran past her. Slade grabbed Jill as they hurried to the window to see Mika hit the ground with surprising grace. He began to touch Warriors who were still outside, changing his appearance. Jax leaped out the window followed by a few more Warriors, trying to keep up with his brother who shifted with ease.

"Okay, that was freaky as hell." Jared frowned, gaining agreement from the other Warriors in the room.

"You okay?" Slade looked at Jill, her eyes searching her again for injury.

"I'm fine." She gave him a small smile.

"I demand you get my husband here, right now!" Alice stood in the middle of the room, surrounded by angry Warriors.

Jill's head snapped toward Alice, then she looked up at Slade who nodded. "I'm in charge," Slade announced to each Warrior. "No one interferes."

Each Warrior spread around the room, making a circle. Jill walked toward Alice who laughed. "Oh, so you think you can take me, breed?" She took a swing at Jill who moved her head slightly as Alice's fist went past her face.

Jill elbowed her in the neck. "There's no thinking about it, bitch." Jill turned, ready for Alice's attack. Alice flew herself toward her. Prepared, Jill thrust kicked her in the stomach, sending her into Jared, Damon and Sid, who pushed her back in the circle.

Alice picked up something off the ground, throwing it at Jill who flinched, giving Alice the opportunity to take her down. Alice got a few good hits on Jill, but Jill swept her foot, rolling so she was on top of Alice. Jill unleashed her rage, but then stopped, climbing off Alice and stood. "Get up!" Jill demanded.

Alice stood, wiping blood from her nose. "You are nothing, breed." Alice took another swing and missed.

"Can't you come up with something different than breed? Be a little more creative because breed is not an insult to me," Jill taunted before punching out, hitting Alice in the jaw. "At least I mixed it up, you stupid slut."

Alice screamed, running at Jill who grabbed her arm and threw her to the ground. Jill reached over and snatched a piece of glass from the broken window, holding it at Alice's throat. "You don't even know how badly I want to slit your throat right now," Jill sneered, pressing the glass deeper. "If these Warriors didn't need their vengeance on you, I would kill you with no remorse." Jill tossed the glass away, then brought her fist back across Alice's head. Using her hand, she pushed up off Alice's face, turned and headed toward Slade.

Slade watched everything and never felt more proud of her. He took her in his arms, his eyes searching every Warrior in the room who was hurting from the day's events.

"Steve would have been damn proud of you." Adam grabbed her

hand, squeezing it.

"So the little dick died, did he?" Alice had clambered to her feet. "I was there you know. I orchestrated the whole thing today. Telling them who to shoot. I could have killed you all." Alice laughed, pointing at each of them like a lunatic.

Slade felt Jill's hand tighten against his waist.

"Poor….what was his name….? Alice's smile was the purest form of evil.

"You are not even worthy to say his name you sick bitch." Jill hissed, not even looking her way.

Alice ignored Jill, but the anger that quickly flashed across her face indicated that she heard every word. "There he was, coming out of the bathroom like a fucking idiot. I did you guys a favor. He wasn't Warrior material. None of the Warriors who died today were Warrior material or they wouldn't have died." Alice looked at them all, her eyes swinging back to Jill. "Look at me, breed. Didn't you hear me? I ordered him to die and he never knew what hit him."

Slade watched as Jill and Adam made eye contact. Everything seemed to go in slow motion as Jill reached for Adam's gun. Slowly, she turned her head to stare directly at Alice.

"He was a Warrior, you bitch!" Jill's voice cracked as she raised the gun, pulled the trigger, hitting Alice in the forehead. Jill didn't watch as she hit the ground. She just turned, shoved Adam's gun in his waiting hand and pressed her face into Slade's chest.

Each Warrior in the room began to chant, one foot stomping with one arm swung across their chest at their heart. Slade looked down, pulling her chin up. "They are honoring you."

Lifting her head, her eyes searched each of theirs. All of them had suffered loss. "No, they are honoring the family we lost today." Jill fully joined along with Adam and Slade, following in on the chant which honored the ones who had fallen at the hands of Alice.

Slade wanting nothing more than to take her in his arms and carrying her away from the madness where she would be safe, but as he watched her join the other Warriors he had never been more proud.

Chapter 25

Jill sat outside the former Halfway House. Sloan had received official orders that the law had been overturned after he sent all the information George Groper had given them. They had also found the Mayor, who was being escorted to jail to await trial on a very long list of charges. Jill watched the happy reunion of families. She also watched others walk off into the night alone, having no one.

Bowing her head, Jill tried her best to keep the tears in, but she couldn't help it. Steve should have been with them. He would have been so excited, running around helping whoever needed help, shouting out jokes to anyone who would listen and laugh. He was such a big part of the changes unfolding; she didn't feel right celebrating.

Feeling a tender touch on her shoulder, Jill looked up into mismatched eyes. "Why are you so sad?" A girl who was plain yet pretty, smiled sadly down at her. Flaming red hair framed her face.

Jill sniffed, wiping her cheek. "I lost a good friend tonight."

"I'm sorry." She sat next to Jill. "Was it because of what you guys did here?"

"Oh, no," Jill reassured her. "It was earlier today, but he did so much to help the shutting down of this place. He should be here."

"Well, I thank you and your friends." She stood to walk away. "I'm really sorry you lost him."

"Do you have anywhere to go?" Jill stopped the girl.

The girl shook her head. "I have no family, but I'll be fine." She waved, turned and walked away.

"You about ready to go?" Slade took her into his arms, holding her tightly. Jill held on and nodded, her eyes not leaving the girl who walked slowly past reuniting families.

"That's the girl who showed me where you were," Slade said, following her line of vision.

"She doesn't have anywhere to go." Jill looked at him. "She has no family."

Kissing her forehead, Slade smiled. "What's her name?" He laughed when her smile beamed across her face.

"I love you," came out of her mouth before she could stop it. Horror filled her stomach with swirling nausea.

His smile faded as he stared back at her horrified expression. Picking her up, he kissed her hard and deep, holding her tightly.

"Come on, guys!" Sid walked past. "Get a room or some shit."

Jared also passed them. "Come on. Jax just got back."

Jill looked at Slade who was looking at her, but not saying a word. Okay, that was telling. She felt like a fool.

"Come on, dammit," Jared called out. "I want to get the hell out of here sometime tonight."

Slade held her hand briefly, following Jared. "I'll be back." He jogged across the street after the girl.

Jill watched as the red-haired girl shook her head, but Slade didn't give up. Finally, the girl nodded and walked beside him across the street toward them. Jill gave her a comforting smile as she moved closer. "I'm Jill." She smiled, hoping to ease the girl's fear.

"I'm Katrina Beach." she smiled shyly.

"Well, I'm glad you decided to come with us, Katrina." Jill touched her arm. "Wait here for a second, okay?" The girl nodded, making her way to sit on the curb.

Jill headed over to where Jax was talking to Slade and the other

Warriors. When Jax saw her coming, he took a step toward her, but stopped when she eyed him warily.

"It's me, Jill," Jax frowned. "I'm sorry that happened to you. I have not seen my brother in a long time."

"Can you do what he does?" Jill asked, still a little weary. "And exactly what and how does he do what he does?"

Jax looked around at everyone and sighed, "In my tribe we had shifters."

"I thought all shifters were extinct," Jared frowned. "I mean I haven't seen one in probably a hundred years."

"There were really shifters?" Jill's eyes widened. "I thought those were just..."

"Stories?" Jared bared his fangs at her, then pointed at hers. "We were stories once, too."

Jill shrugged. "Sorry, it's just weird."

"My mother was a shifter and my father was a Chief." Jax looked at each of them. "And yes, I have the ability also. When me, my sister and brother were turned, we continued to have our shifter ability, but not only can we shift into animal form, we can shift into human form."

"I'm sorry, but how fucking cool is that?" Sid laughed, but then frowned. "Although, if you ever shift to look like me or whatever you do, I will kill you."

"How dangerous is your brother, Jax?" Damon asked, not looking too happy. "And don't you think you should have given us this information when you first came onboard?"

"Very," Jax replied with a sneer. "And I rarely shift. As I said, I haven't seen my brother for many years, but he needs to be found."

"Oh, we'll find the son of a bitch," Slade replied, his stare deadly. "No one threatens mine."

Jill frowned as she glanced up at Slade. She was really confused. Was she okay if he didn't really love her? After all, she said it to him, not meaning to, but there it was. While he kissed her, that wasn't the same as saying it. Actually kissing her didn't mean anything at all. People who didn't love each other kissed all the time. Okay, she was too tired to sort through this.

"Jill." Slade was staring at her. "Are you okay?"

"Yeah," Jill nodded, frowning. "Why?"

"Because I've said your name three times." Slade intense stare made her fidget.

"I'm fine." Jill gave him her best fake smile. "Now, let's go."

"Lola!" George jogged toward her.

Jill smiled at him. "My name's Jill."

He smiled, taking her hand. "Jill," he laughed. "I should have known that wasn't your real name. Anyway, I just wanted to thank you. If you ever need anything, just let me know. I'll make sure you have a direct line to my office."

"So you're going to be Mayor?"

"I'm going to be Mayor," he announced, a large smile spreading across his face. "Thanks to you and your friends."

"I'm really happy for you, George, but I suggest you cancel your membership at a certain club." She grinned at him.

"Done." His face turned bright red.

"And never think she will give you a lap dance again, Mayor or not," Slade growled down at him, taking two hundred dollars out of his wallet and handing it to George. He then patted George on the chest as he grabbed Jill's hand, walking away.

All the way back to the compound, Jill and Katrina talked. She found out that her parents had thrown her out after she had been turned. She had been living on the streets doing odd jobs to make money here and there. Katrina's story was very similar to her own. Even though Katrina was Adam and Steve's age, she seemed older than any of them. She had endured so much without the support Jill had been lucky enough to have. She also told her of some of the things she had undergone in the Halfway House, which made Jill want to kill Alice all over again.

Getting out of the car, Jill waited for Katrina. Slade again took her hand. Jared, Sid, Duncan, Damon and Jax were walking in front of them with Adam and Dillon coming up beside them. As soon as they entered the compound, a flood of sadness washed over her. Glancing at Adam, she knew he felt the same way.

She really needed to go to her room before she lost it. Her gaze caught Sloan giving Slade a huge smile and a nod. Looking up at Slade's happy face made her want to puke. Everyone looked happy, even the women who were all waiting for their Warriors to return. What the hell was wrong with everyone? Steve was dead. Were Jill and Adam the only ones who were heartbroken? Jill dropped Slade's hand like it burned her, tears gathering in her eyes.

"This is bullshit," Adam told her, turning to leave. "I've got to get out of here."

"Hey, where you going?" Sloan yelled at Adam, causing everyone to turn to look. "We've got something–"

"I'm getting the fuck out of here. I lost a great friend today, a best friend, and if you guys want to celebrate, then be my guest." Adam growled, pointing at everyone. "You got a problem with that, then fuck you!"

"Actually, I do have a problem with that, you asshole," a familiar voice came from the game room behind Sloan. "I get shot coming out of the pisser, claw my way back from death's door and you want to leave? Damn straight I have a problem with that, so fuck you."

Jill froze. Her eyes searched the direction Steve's voice came from wondering if she was having a hallucination from the stress and heartbreak of the day, but then he was there, walking out of the game room, his eyes finding hers.

"And you still owe me a true heartfelt thank you for taking that paintball with your name on it." Steve grinned at her, spreading his arms wide. "I'm back, bitches!"

Jill got to him first, throwing herself at him, hugging him tightly. Tears ran freely down her face; too choked up with her emotions, she couldn't speak. Couldn't say a word. Adam hugged them both and they all stood like the biggest pussies ever, hugging each other and crying.

"How?" Jill touched his chest. Pausing, she peered up at him. "Oh, my God."

Steve batted his eyes at her. "Pretty, ain't they?" He nodded toward Slade. "He turned me. Despite being possibly thrown in prison and losing his doctor's license, or whatever in the hell they call that….he turned me."

Sloan stepped in. "I spoke with the Council and received special permission, even though it had already taken place. So Slade is safe from prison time and will continue to be our doctor." Sloan focused on Jill, Adam, Dillon and then Steve. "I just want you to know that you all did me and the other Warriors proud. With the attack against the Warriors and the response of all trainees, the Council has awarded all of you Warrior status, even though the initiation was not completed."

Jill waited for the excitement to hit her, but it didn't really come.

While there was excitement there, she wasn't ecstatic. She wondered what the hell was wrong with her. It was what she wanted most...wasn't it? Her eyes went to Slade who stood watching her. She gave him a small smile, turning her attention back to Sloan.

"And Steve, because of your sacrifice to another trainee, you have also obtained Warrior status even though you were officially out of the test before the trouble started." Sloan gave a rare smile to each of them. "Congratulations. You did us proud today. Unfortunately, the Warrior ceremony will be placed on hold until all the funerals are completed. I expect all of us to attend each funeral and will be letting you know when those are."

"Can we have a much needed drink now?" Sid growled, a tinge of anger in his voice. "And salute our brothers who were lost today."

"I want everyone in my office..." Sloan winked at Jill when the Warriors groaned. "First thing in the morning."

"That's more like it." Jared grinned, heading into the game room. "Drinks are on me."

Lana smiled at her as she passed and Jill stopped her. "Lana, this is Katrina. She needs a place to sleep. Is there any way you can help her out?"

"Of course. I'll take her to Sloan to get his permission." Lana took the girl's hand. "Come on. I'll introduce you to everyone first."

Jill walked away and smiled when she heard Steve flirting with Katrina. They would be a cute couple. She felt bad leaving the girl, but she was not in the mood. Taking two steps, she looked up to find Slade in front of her. He lifted her chin to look into her eyes. Jill really tried to stay strong, but she just couldn't do it. It was all too much. She pulled her chin away, dropping her head. Her shoulders shook uncontrollably as the sobs overtook her control.

Slade didn't say a word as he picked her up, carrying her toward her room. Shutting the door, he sat on her bed and held her. Once her sobs slowed down, he lifted her chin. "A little too much for one day?" He gave her a small smile.

"Why didn't you tell me he was okay?" Jill looked at him confused.

"Because I wasn't sure if it was going to work. We were losing him on the way to the hospital. I took a chance, Jill," Slade sighed. "I've never heard of a half-breed being turned into a full-blood. So far, he seems absolutely fine, but until I came in tonight, I wasn't sure. Sloan stayed here with him. It was a chance, Jill. I didn't want to tell you or anyone else until I was certain."

"I'm glad you took the chance, Slade. Thank you." Jill went to stand, but he stopped her.

"You're welcome. Now why don't you tell me what's wrong?" Slade's voice turned hard. "Look at me, Jill."

"It's been a long, hard day, Slade." Jill glanced toward him, but not at him. "I'm emotionally and physically done."

Jill refused to be one of those women who hinted for the words she longed to hear. Yeah, she wanted to hear them, but only if he was ready to say them…if ever. Her heart hurt, but he didn't need to know that. She wished she had never said the words, but then she wouldn't know exactly how he felt, which was not enough to say the words back to her.

"I'm sorry." She faked a smile. "I'm not very fun tonight." She kissed him on the cheek. Maybe she could love him enough for both of them. She knew he cared and honestly that should be enough.

Standing, he set her on her feet. "Stay here. I'll be right back."

"Where you going?" Jill frowned at the abruptness of his actions.

285

"I have to get something from my room." He opened the door, but paused when he spoke, "I mean it, Jillian. Don't leave."

Jill actually groaned. "Believe me, I'm going nowhere except to bed." She felt tingles of excitement flow over her body at the heat in his eyes at her reply. Damn, that man could turn her on with just a look.

Taking one of his shirts draped on her chair, she smelled it with a sigh. Hurrying into the bathroom, she showered and brushed her teeth. Combing her hair out with her fingers, wearing only his shirt which came to her knees, she froze in her tracks. Slade knelt in the middle of her floor, his head bent to the ground until she walked out, then his head raised.

"I love you, too." Slade's eyes were as intense as his voice. "Will you marry me, Jillian Robin Nichols?" He slowly lifted his hand, a small box in his palm.

"You love me?" Jill's eyes didn't even go to the box, but stayed on his.

"More than anything or anyone I have ever known." Slade frowned when she still didn't answer him or take the ring. "I wanted to wait for a better time to do this, but–"

"This is the perfect time, and yes, Slade, I will marry you." She jumped into his arms, holding him tightly. "I love you so much."

"This is all new to me, Jill. I know there are words that a Warrior is to speak to his mate, but I haven't learned them yet." He pulled her away, handing her the box. "But I will."

"I love you is all I need to hear, Slade." Jill opened the box and gasped. The ring was a beautiful, yet simple slender gold band with a round solitaire diamond. Nothing fancy, just like her. "It's beautiful."

He took it and slipped it on her finger. "On the day of your driving test, I asked your dad permission to ask you, and he gave his blessing."

Jill felt the tears start again. "Thank you." She hugged him with everything she had.

"I want you to have whatever kind of wedding you want." Slade smiled, wiping a tear away from her cheek. "And the sooner the better so everyone knows you're mine."

Kissing his cheek, Jill moved to his mouth, her hands running up his chest and around his neck.

"Don't you want to talk about the wedding?" Slade teased, nipping at the side of her mouth.

"No, not really." She smiled at his teasing.

"Good, because I'm about to get demanding." Slade pulled her up and onto his lap so she straddled him.

"So am I." Jill bit him on the side of the neck, earning her a smack on the ass.

"Watch it, Mrs. Buchanan," Slade growled, but his smile was wide. "I like the sound of that…..Mrs. Buchanan."

Jill groaned her agreement as his hands began to work their magic.

******

Standing outside drinking a beer, Jax gazed at the night sky. He heard the door open behind him. Sloan walked up next to him with his own beer.

"Just got filled in." Sloan took a long draw of his beer. "So how do I know if I'm talking to Jax?"

Jax laughed, though nothing about the situation was funny. "You don't."

"We need to figure this out, Jax," Sloan sighed. "You're a damn good Warrior, but this is..."

"Fucked up," Jax added, looking out into the night.

"Yeah," Sloan nodded. "Definitely fucked up."

The door opened again. "Oh, I'm sorry." Caroline went to go back inside, but Sloan stopped her.

"I'm going in." Sloan waved her over and then glanced back at Jax. "Be in my office first thing so we can figure this out."

Jax nodded, taking another drink.

Caroline stood beside him, her arms wrapped around herself. "Are you okay?"

"No, not really." He turned to glance at her. "Listen, Caroline, I'm sorry about earlier."

"Don't be sorry." Caroline shrugged. "I wanted to help."

Jax sat his beer down, taking off his jacket. Wrapping it around her, he then picked his beer back up.

"Thank you," she smiled. "Do you want to talk?"

"Listen, I really think you need to stay away from me for now." Jax downed the rest of his beer. "It's not safe for anyone with my brother running around."

"But–"

"I'm serious, Caroline." Jax frowned, his eyes darkening. "My brother is dangerous and until I find him, no one associated with me is safe."

"You can't push everyone away, Jax." Caroline's head tilted as she stared up at him. "We can help you, just like you've helped us."

"No," Jax growled, his eyes turning fierce. His gaze ran across her features, her black eye starting to fade, but it didn't take away from her beauty. She was gorgeous with a special heart. Thoughts of maybe one day being with her ran through his mind, but he shoved them away. It wasn't possible with his brother, so there was no use in even thinking it. "You need to stay away from me, Caroline."

"What if I don't want to stay away from you, Jax?" Caroline answered back. "What if I want to take that chance just to be with you?"

Her words hit him hard. Tossing his beer bottle out into the yard, not caring where it landed, he grabbed her and tilted her face up to his. Once again, his eyes searched hers before angling his head as he slowly placed his lips to hers. What he only meant to be a soft kiss turned into much more. Her arms looped around his neck in a tight grip; his arms pulled her flush against his body. Their kiss was one of desperation, of things that were out of their control, but Jax took this one minute, this one kiss that may be the only one he ever received from the beautiful Caroline. The more her body reacted to him, the more he knew he had to pull away, and pull away he did, with much reluctance.

"Stay away from me, Caroline." Jax voice was hoarse with need as he turned and walked away from her.

"I can't do that, Jax." Caroline called out after him. "I don't want to do that."

Her words made it harder for him to walk away. Cursing long and hard, Jax knew kissing her had been a stupid move, because after tasting her, he wanted more and he would never be satisfied until he took more of what her kiss promised. "Fuck!" his deep growled echoed in the night.

****

Caroline stood on the steps watching Jax walk away, her fingers going to her lips. She didn't move until he disappeared. Turning to go back inside, she held his jacket tightly around her, his scent enveloping her senses. Once at the door she turned hoping to see Jax coming back, nothing but inky darkness met her gaze.

Eyes followed her every movement until the door shut tight behind her obviously giving her the feeling of being safe. Shadows played against the porch as a dark figure stepped forward. Quiet laughter echoed in the darkness as the shadows disappeared along with the laughter that held a tinge of madness.

Made in the USA
Middletown, DE
05 August 2022